Other Books & Stories
by Lynn Bohart

Mass Murder

Grave Doubts

Your Worst Nightmare

Something Wicked

Also published in the anthology of short stories:
"Dead On Demand"

INN KEEPING WITH MURDER

An Old Maids of Mercer Island Mystery

♥

By Lynn Bohart

♥♥♥

Cover Art: Mia Yoshihara-Bradshaw

Published by Little Dog Press

ACKNOWLEDGEMENTS

I have so many people to thank for this book. Up front would be my writing group: Lori Church-Pursley, Tim McDaniel, Michael Manzer, and Timera Drake. These guys read the manuscript chapter by chapter over a period of six months, helping to clear up ambiguities, character flaws, and plot points. Thank you to beta readers Kathy Perrin and Chris Spahn, who read it from cover-to-cover and helped with flow, clarification and consistencies. As always, thanks to Liz Stewart, who is an accomplished line editor and is so generous with her time. My deepest thanks go to Detective Peter Erickson from the Mercer Island Police Department, who vetted the book for me, along with prosecutor, Susan Irwin who answered important questions for me.

I am deeply indebted to my friend, Mia Bradshaw, who designed the cover. Mia is a wonderful artist and craftsperson in the Seattle area and shows/sells her work locally. Please check out her website at www.miayoshihara.com.

Disclaimer: This book is a work of fiction and while many of the businesses, locations, and organizations referenced in the book are real, they are used in a way that is purely fictional.

This book is dedicated to my mother, who loved to read. She had a great sense of humor and reminds me just slightly of Julia Applegate.

INN KEEPING WITH MURDER

Because I could not stop for Death,
He kindly stopped for me.
The Carriage held but just ourselves
And Immortality.
~Emily Dickinson~

CHAPTER ONE

It was early morning. An insidious breeze skimmed the lake as she stepped onto the porch of her million-dollar home on Mercer Island. The breeze came unchallenged and alone, bringing with it the smell of lake water and pine and just a pinch of foreboding. As the breeze slithered past the branches and rustled the leaves, it seemed to whisper her name.

Ellen Fairchild.

The sound made her pause. She lingered with her hand on the doorknob, listening, trapped between this world and that, her thoughts filled with shattered dreams. With a sigh, she pulled the door closed, expelling any final doubts from the recesses of her mind.

It was time to go.

The man in the moon smiled down on her from the dark sky above, sending flashes of light to dance across the lake water. All around her, the exclusive neighborhood was quiet, the imposing homes standing silently on guard while their inhabitants slept peacefully inside.

It was 2 a.m.

She stepped off the porch and climbed into the front seat of her new, sky blue Lexus as a headache began to inch its way up the side of her head. She paused a moment to massage her temple before grasping the steering wheel, her perfectly manicured fingernails sinking into the rich leather. The internal message had now become her mantra.

It was time to go.

With a quick flick of her wrist she turned the ignition key and started the engine. Then she put the car in gear and pulled out onto Placer Drive, where she paused to look over at the sprawling St. Claire Inn that took up most of the block on the lakeshore side of the street. The romantic Victorian, with its asymmetrical roofline and wrap-around porch, welcomed guests year-round as the area's most popular bed and breakfast. Her close friend, Julia, owned it. The inn was as familiar to her as her own home.

Certainly, Julia would be asleep at this time of the morning, tucked away in the privacy of her apartment on the ground floor. The normal comings and goings of the staff and guests at the inn would be stilled, leaving only the big grandfather clock in the entryway to mark the passage of time. Ellen would miss the monthly book club meetings there. She would miss the friendly banter and wicked jokes between the women who had become as close as most sisters.

"But I have to go," she whispered.

She exhaled slowly and gave a nod as if to say goodbye to her friend. Then she turned the car toward the east side of the island. As she rolled through the neighborhood, Sybil Moore's bedroom light glared from an upstairs window of her Tudor-style home. Sybil's house was right next to hers, and Ellen glanced up at the window, thinking that perhaps the neighborhood busybody was conjuring up some sort of witch's brew under the full moon. A smile played across her lips despite the blackness of her mood. She wouldn't miss Sybil. She wouldn't miss her annoying accent or the way in which she phrased her vacuous thoughts. But then, of course, she wouldn't actually miss anyone, anymore.

"Goodbye, Silly Sybil," Ellen said with a snicker.

The car moved on.

When it reached the large, modern home on the corner, she slowed to a stop. This house belonged to her best friend, Martha Denton. She peered up the drive to the plate-glass windows and broad decks, picturing Martha comfortably asleep in her big pillow-top bed.

"Goodbye, dear friend," she whispered with a heavy heart. "Please don't be mad. Please try to understand."

But of course Martha wouldn't understand. No one would.

A moment later, she had left her friends and the world she knew behind. By ten minutes past the hour she had circled the island and turned onto Marchand Drive, a two lane road which climbed to Widow's Peak, a small butte that stuck out on the east side of the island, facing the Cascade Mountains. She passed pricey homes nestled amongst tall pines, long driveways with boats and recreational vehicles tucked under expensive awnings, and gated homes invisible from the road. This had been her world for over thirty years, and for thirty years it had been enough. Now, suddenly, it wasn't.

She crested the hill facing I-90 and Bellevue to the east. She knew exactly where she was going. The kids called it, "Deadhead Curve," as a joke. It sat right on the edge of a cliff on the northeast corner of the island. As one teenager told her, "*You have to be a deadhead to drive it at night, especially if you've been drinking.*" At least one person had been killed on the crazy hairpin turn, where there was nothing to stop you from going over the cliff except a flimsy guardrail. Beyond that was a long drop into Crenshaw Bay, filled with rocks and boulders.

Ellen drew the Lexus alongside the last home on this stretch of road and stopped just past the driveway, on the uphill side of the curve. There were only bushes and rocks past this point. Ellen sat quietly for a moment, staring off into the distance, thinking about her husband and her two children, who now lived on the East Coast. A sob caught in her throat. She had sacrificed so much and gotten so little in return. How had she let that happen? There was a time she thought she would own her own business just like Julia, using her creative talents to decorate some of the finer homes in the area. But Ray had disapproved. So instead she puttered away in her garden, volunteered for the homeless shelter, and helped organize fundraising events. Meanwhile, he refused to retire and still spent weeks at a time out-of-town on business; right now he was in Thailand.

It wasn't enough. It had never been enough.

Her fingers sought out the sockets around her eyes as the headache sent shooting pains across her forehead. She was so tired, and the voice echoing in her head droned on and on, egging her on to do this. She brought her foot up to hover over the accelerator.

All she had to do was to press down. That's all she had to do. The car would do the rest. It would be so easy. So painless.

She gazed at the little orange reflector lights embedded into the guardrail at the foot of the hill, warning drivers to beware. That's where the road turned sharply to the right and out of sight. It was only about a quarter of a mile. At full speed, the corner would be impossible to make, even for the Lexus. Beyond the railing, there was nothing except lovely, empty space and the moon, glinting in the distance, teasing her, beckoning to her.

"Do it," the voice said in the recesses of her mind. *"God will greet you with loving arms. Do it now,"* the voice repeated. *"And God will catch you. I am here. It's time to go."*

As tears began to stream down her cheeks, she thought of the girl, Rita, whom she had befriended at the shelter. Rita had been pregnant and all alone, hoping for a better life. But something had gone wrong. She'd had a difficult pregnancy and then suddenly disappeared. Ellen had asked questions, but received no answers. She'd even searched alleyways and street corners throughout Seattle one night, thinking Rita may have returned to the streets. But she'd found nothing.

And that's when the suspicious sounds and lights outside her home began, along with the feeling that she was being watched. Her priest, Father Bentley, had given her something to help her sleep, thinking it was just her nerves. But Ellen had finally realized that help would only come by letting go.

"I'm sorry," she whispered to no one and to everyone. "I'm so sorry."

Her foot finally tipped forward and pressed the accelerator to the floor, making the tires spin in place. Rubber burned, and puffs of smoke evaporated into the early morning air before the car finally jumped forward. Within seconds, she was racing downhill, heading straight for those little reflector lights. By the time she reached the curve, the speedometer had hit 60 MPH. But Ellen never attempted to make the curve; she was aiming for the Moon.

In the flash of an eye, the Lexus crashed through the guardrail and sailed off into the Moon's welcoming embrace, leaving Ellen with only one lingering thought:

"What really happened to Rita?"

CHAPTER TWO

It was a balmy day in the middle of May when the normal rhythms of my life were suddenly and inextricably altered. The sun was out, a rare treat this time of year in the Northwest, encouraging bulbs to sprout and trees to blossom. Sailboats glided gracefully across the lake, and I took the opportunity to work outside in order to lighten my mood after a long, slow winter.

I had already dead-headed the wilted daffodils along the path around the north side of the inn and had made my way to the raised deck in the back, which overlooked the lake. There, I tilled the empty planters that lined the steps and threw the remains of last year's annuals into a compost bin. Next up was removing the covers from all the patio furniture. It wouldn't be long before guests would come to sit lazily in the sun, enjoy a cool drink and watch the nautical world pass by.

I own the St. Claire Inn on Mercer Island, which is thirteen square miles of rocks and trees in the middle of Lake Washington, between Seattle and Bellevue. The inn was originally built in 1945 by John St. Claire, who owned a large shipping company called Pacific Waterways. He lived there with his wife, Elizabeth, and their three children until 1962, when a fire destroyed one whole wing of the house. Mrs. St. Claire, their six-year old daughter, Chloe, and ten-year old son, Fielding, were killed in the fire, along with their dog, Max.

A series of owners brought the house back to its original glory, but none of them stayed for long. In fact, one family moved out abruptly in 1985 after their seventeen-year old daughter threw herself off the faux balcony on the third floor because her father had banished the boy she loved.

Right after that the rumors began.

Someone saw a woman disappear through a closed door. Someone else heard the laughter of children on the second floor. There was the fleeting glimpse of a big black dog. Cups and bowls were said to move unexpectedly in the kitchen. If someone forgot to close a cupboard, it would close by itself. Guests would occasionally feel someone lie down beside them on the bed, or see the face of a young girl in the third floor attic window. And then there was the fleeting smell of smoke.

By the time my husband, Graham, bought the property in 2003, it was just an abandoned shell sitting on a flat stretch of beach on the west side of the island. Graham was a busy state senator then, contemplating a run for governor. He thought that turning the old home into a bed and breakfast would give me something to do, I suppose because he thought all women are themselves left as empty shells once their children are gone. Together we renovated it into a charming gray and white Victorian, with multiple gables and a pentagonal turret. Six months after the renovations were completed Graham asked for a divorce and moved out.

As I drew off the cover to the chaise lounge on that day in May, my cell phone rang. I pulled the phone from my pocket and turned to watch a group of sailboats slip aimlessly across the surface of the lake. I wasn't surprised to hear my neighbor, Martha Denton, on the other end, all a-twitter about something. Martha had a tendency to wind up like a spring when she was stressed, so I tried to slow her down.

"Whoa, Martha. Take a breath. What's that about Ellen?"

"Ellen's been in a terrible accident. Her car went off Marchand Road into the lake sometime early this morning."

I paused, thinking I hadn't heard her correctly.

"Whaaat?"

"A boater found the car early this morning, crumpled on a pile of rocks in Crenshaw Bay," she said, starting to hyperventilate.

I glanced up the coastline as if I might see Ellen's car sticking out of the lake, but of course Crenshaw Bay was on the other side of the island.

"Whaaat?" I repeated.

I was having a hard time wrapping my mind around this terrible news.

"She's at Swedish Medical Center. They took her into emergency surgery," Martha said, beginning to sob. "She's barely alive. They only called me because Ellen carries an emergency contact card with my phone number on it since Ray is out-of-town so much. He's in Thailand. We need to get down there, Julia— they're not sure she's going to make it."

Martha was sucking in enough oxygen to fill a balloon, and my mind finally kicked into gear.

"Yes, of course, we'll go right away. Do you want me to pick you up?"

"Yes..." She was wheezing by now. "I don't think I can drive."

No doubt that was a good call.

"Okay, try to stay calm. I'll be there as soon as I can."

I hung up quickly, afraid she might pass out before I got there. And then my own tears formed. Ellen and I had co-founded our book club together. I'd known her for years. In fact, she lived in a huge home right across the street. Our daughters had gone to the same school, and we'd served on the Library Board together. I couldn't believe what I'd just heard. But I also had trouble shaking the disconnect I felt at such a horrific accident. Maybe if Ellen had been on the freeway or one of the bridges, it would have made more sense. But Marchand Road? Still, it didn't matter. This was an emergency, and I had to get going.

My first thought was to let the rest of the book club members know. I called Doe Bridges. Doe ran her deceased husband's multi-million dollar waste management company, and if anyone could kick the group into gear, she could. I caught her going into a meeting, but she agreed to call the rest of the girls and see who could meet us at the hospital.

Then it was time to tell April. She had been a friend since college and was now my business partner. She was a first-class baker and chef and had relocated her small bakery from downtown Mercer Island to the inn's carriage barn.

I ran across the yard to the old carriage barn, which was left over from the late 1800s, back when a hotel had been built on the island. The hotel had burned down long before John St. Claire had built his home in 1945, but the barn remained. It was a large, rectangular building, which had originally housed not only carriages, but horses, as well. We'd renovated the front portion into April's bakery and added a wall inside to separate the bakery from the back third, where we stored and refinished antiques we sold in the inn. I found April filling a cupcake tin with chocolate batter.

"Ellen Fairchild ran her car off a cliff," I said, breathing hard. "I have to go to the hospital."

I could have sworn April blanched white at the news—not so easy since she's African American.

"I thought something had happened," she said matter-of-factly, before putting the bowl down.

April usually knew important things before I did—in fact, before anyone did.

"I'll hold the fort down here," she said, wiping off her hands. "Where's Libby?"

"She's finishing the rooms, and Crystal is on the front desk."

"Okay," April said, grabbing a towel. "I'll finish this later and go over to the inn. Call me from the hospital. But prepare yourself, Julia." She said this with a grave look.

I knew that look, and it didn't bode well for Ellen. April had never joined the book club; it wasn't her thing. But she knew all the girls almost as well as I did, and I felt my chest tighten at her comment. I just nodded and hurried out.

By the time I picked up Martha, she had pulled herself together, barely. Her tears had washed away what little eye makeup she normally wore, leaving her eyes puffy and smudged, and she was twisting the shoulder straps of her purse into a knot. She was dressed in her signature shirt-waist dress and pastel cardigan sweater, with a string of pearls at her neck. Martha was nothing if not well-groomed. Even her wispy, thinning gray hair was perfectly coiffed. As she got into the car, however, she released a new round of tears and a nonstop string of speculations about the accident.

"I can't believe this," she said, reaching for a tissue. "I just had lunch with Ellen yesterday down at The Ruins. How could this have happened? I mean, she *has* been acting a bit strange lately— maybe that's why she was up on Marchand Drive," she said, taking

14

a breath. "Ellen told me a week or so ago that she couldn't sleep. She was worried about a girl at the shelter who was having a difficult pregnancy. Then, she started talking about hearing things outside her house. She also said that she kept seeing flashing lights in the backyard. I told her to get some Tylenol PM or something, but you know Ellen—she's not one for pills. Anyway, she talked to Father Bentley about it, and he was going to get her one of those subliminal tapes or something. Maybe it didn't help. Maybe she didn't use it. Maybe…"

"Martha!" I interrupted her, thinking that if I didn't stop her babbling, I might just drive off a cliff myself. "Let's keep our fingers crossed. She may pull through this."

"You think so?" She looked at me hopefully, wiping her eyes.

"I'm keeping good thoughts," I said. "You should, too."

"Oh, yes, I will," she said dutifully, twisting her purse straps again.

I felt sorry for the purse; Martha was shortening its lifespan with each punishing twist. But since the purse was a Dooney & Bourke and worth about $400, I thought it could handle it. No pun intended.

"I'm just so stunned." Martha was still rambling. "I can't imagine why Ellen would have been up there. Can you? I mean, Marchand Road doesn't *go* anywhere."

Since she was echoing my own thoughts, I chimed in, careful not to ratchet up her emotions any more than they were.

"I thought of that, too," I said quietly, moderating my tone. "Who do we know up there that she might have gone to see?"

I thought getting her to focus on something specific might help.

"Well, the Abbotts live up there. So does Marilee Brinkley. I suppose Ellen could have been visiting one of them and was just coming home late, although I can't imagine why. She's never gone up there before. Other than the Abbotts and Marilee, the only people up there are…well, you know…the *others*."

Martha said the *others* as if she'd been watching too many reruns of *Lost*. The *others* were merely a rival book club. Did I say rival? What I meant was…well, rival. They called themselves the "*Mercer Island Literary Society*" and turned up their pointed noses at anything written in a genre: mysteries, romances, and thrillers.

On the other hand, our club didn't have a name because we would read pretty much anything suggested by one of our members.

"Then of course Dana Finkle lives up there," Martha said with a sneer.

The very sound of Dana Finkle's name was enough to ruin my entire afternoon—well, perhaps not more than Ellen's accident.

"Who knows?" I said. "Maybe Ellen just couldn't sleep and went for a drive."

Martha glanced at me with an expression that could have curdled milk.

"What?" I said, sneaking a peek in her direction and then returning my eyes to the road.

"When have you *ever* known Ellen to just go for a drive?"

She had me there. Ellen was mostly a home-body. She had very specific things she did, like volunteering, attending the book club, and going to the store. Other than that, she could always be found at home, cleaning or gardening. Spontaneous outings always had to be approved by Ray in advance, which of course meant they weren't spontaneous.

"Okay, you're right," I said.

By the time we made it to the hospital lobby it was after two o'clock. Rudy was already there, pacing back and forth in front of the gift shop.

"I came straight from the golf course," she said.

Not big news there, since she still wore her mauve-colored golf shirt and a visor, with her knobby knees poking out from under a pair of plaid Bermuda shorts. All she was missing were the cleats in her golf shoes.

"Doe is coming from a meeting, and Blair is at her Pilates class," she said in the clipped way she had of speaking.

Just then, Doe appeared, dressed in a striking gray silk suit and carrying the large black leather tote bag that went everywhere with her. Doe is tall and slender, while Rudy is short and compact. Standing next to each other dressed as they were, they looked like something out of a cartoon.

"Sorry I'm late," Doe said. "I was in a union meeting, and I had to find someone to take my place at the bargaining table. Do we know anything, yet?"

"No," Martha said. "We just got here. Can we go up now?"

She was twisting the strap of her purse into a knot again. I placed my hand over hers.

"Take it easy, Martha."

Just then, a woman in the gift shop caught my attention. She was hovering behind the card rack, peering at us through the window.

"Isn't that Dana Finkle?" I said.

Everyone turned around, forcing the woman in the gift shop to quickly turn away.

"Of course it's Dana," Doe said. "How could you not recognize her?"

I grinned with satisfaction. "I just wanted you all to look at her."

Dana Finkle was one of the few people in the world I actually hated. Perhaps hate is too strong a word. Let's just say the very sight of her makes my skin crawl. And that isn't hard to do since she looks like a toad. You see, she is the bane of my existence on the island, challenging everything I do—from having our bakery and antique business as part of the inn, to decisions I support as a member of the Library Board. I can't stand her, which clouded my judgment at the moment, because as I watched her waddle away, I whispered to myself in a tinny voice, "Going so soon? Why, I wouldn't *hear* of it."

"Really, Julia?" Rudy snapped, making me spin around. "You need to stop quoting the *Wizard of Oz* in public. People will think you're an idiot."

"Can we go?" Martha said again, her expression pleading for action.

"Okay. Sorry," I said. "Let's see what room she's in."

We left my nemesis behind and approached the volunteer receptionist, who told us how to find the Intensive Care Unit. Normally, only family members are allowed in the ICU, but before leaving her house, Martha had been able to get hold of Ellen's husband in Thailand. He'd given us permission to visit since neither he nor their children could be there.

After stepping off the elevator, we checked in with the Intensive Care nurse.

"I'm afraid you won't be able to stay long," the young woman said. "She's suffered a lot of internal injuries. We've patched her up the best we can, but..." She stopped short of saying what she thought, and Martha let out a loud sob.

The nurse had us follow her to the last bed on the right, which was shut off by a circular curtain.

"I'll give you just a few minutes," she said quietly.

The nurse left and we were about to step inside the curtain, when Blair came running awkwardly down the hall behind us in three-inch heels. Her bleached blond hair was pulled back into a loose pony tail, and she was still dressed in a pair of tight black Pilates pants. While I tended to dress for comfort, Doe dressed for business, and Rudy dressed for sports, Blair always dressed for attention. So even at age sixty-two, the purple hour-glass tank top she wore showed enough sweaty cleavage to cause a male orderly to hit the wall with a gurney as she passed by.

"Is she going to be okay?" Blair said with restrained urgency.

Rudy put a tanned finger to her lips. "We're just about to see her, but we have to be quiet."

Blair nodded. The five of us slipped inside the curtain and positioned ourselves silently around Ellen's bed. She was lying beneath starched white sheets, with tubes running every which way. I wish I could say she looked peaceful, but she didn't. While her chemically enhanced dark hair lay in soft curls on the pillow around her head, her face looked like it had been beaten with a baseball bat. Her breathing was labored, and a machine monitored her vital signs.

We silently spread out around the bed. My eyes followed a tube that extended from a bag of saline to where it disappeared under her blanket. I reached out and lifted the edge of the sheet, spying the wrinkled green hospital gown that was draped around Ellen's thin figure. Why couldn't hospitals invest in garments that looked less like backless prison-wear and more like actual clothes? Ellen was a snappy dresser, and under normal circumstances wouldn't be caught dead in that thing.

As soon as that thought crossed my mind, I glanced up. Had I said that out loud?

My mind had a tendency to wander, and I'd done it once before when Rudy and I followed the mayor's wife into an outdoor picnic. As I watched her tight little ass sashay its way through the gate, I'd contemplated how she must have air-brushed her jeans onto her

18

butt since there wasn't enough room to sneak a mosquito's wing between the washed denim and her bare skin. She'd turned around wide-eyed and gasped, *"Excuse me?"* and then stomped away. Rudy had suggested that next time I keep my thoughts to myself. Fortunately, this time I had. I gave a sigh of relief.

I returned my focus to Ellen and how she had gotten here in the first place. Ellen didn't drink much, and we all knew she didn't like drugs, even prescription ones. So what else would have prompted her to drive to the top of the island? Marchand Drive would be the perfect place to take your own life if you wanted to, I thought, but....damn! What if Ellen had done this on purpose?

As if she'd heard my thoughts, Ellen's eyes fluttered open. She glanced around the bed and gave us a weak smile, exposing blood-stained teeth. One eye was almost swollen shut, so she struggled to focus on us with her other eye. Finally, her mouth opened, and she mumbled something. We all shuffled in closer in order to hear.

"I'm thorry," I thought I heard her say.

Even though I was standing at the head of the bed, I had to lean in to hear her clearly.

"I...couldn't take it anymore," she said, wheezing and shaking her head ever so slightly. "I wanted my life to mean more. Money can't buy you everything, you know."

She reached out with lightning speed and grabbed my hand, squeezing so tightly that she lifted one of my acrylic nails off its nail bed. I stifled a groan, and Rudy scowled at me from across the bed.

"I let my entire life slip by. Don't let it happen to you," she said with a slur.

Ellen was staring at me when she said this, as if pleading with me. The fire in her eyes—eye—sent a chill rippling down my back.

"Go after your dreams," she said. "All of you!" She swiveled her head to look around the bed at each of us in turn. "Don't settle for the back of the bus. And don't be a bunch of old maids!"

With that, her head dropped back onto the pillow, triggering the bedside alarm.

I extricated my hand from hers just before the hospital personnel appeared through the curtains. They shooed us away, and we retreated down the hallway to a waiting room. We all took

19

seats, and I fought back tears as I contemplated Ellen's final comments. What had she meant by never settling for the back of the bus? I didn't think any of us took a back seat to anyone, and frankly, Ellen had had enough money to buy the bus. So, what did she mean? We certainly weren't a bunch of old maids. All of us had been married, some had children, and everyone now lived purposeful lives.

A nurse appeared in the doorway and spoke in low tones.

"Do any of you know if Mrs. Fairchild ever signed a living will?"

"What's that?" Blair sniffled as she asked this.

"It's also called an advanced healthcare directive. It tells us what to do in case her heart stops, or if she wanted to donate organs."

Blair almost screeched, "She's dead, then?" Her blue eyes flooded with tears, clumping her very thick mascara.

"They're working on her. We'll know soon. I'll keep you posted."

The nurse left and we sat in silence, or nearly silence. Martha and Blair kept sobbing, while I cried silently to myself. It was another several minutes before a young female doctor appeared. Her face was an expressionless mask. I thought she probably had to do this a lot.

"I'm Doctor Ames," she said. "I understand there is no immediate family available. Is that right?"

"That's right," Martha said, standing up. "I'm listed as the emergency contact when her husband is out of town. He's in Thailand, trying to get back."

"Well, then, I'm sorry, but your friend has passed away," the doctor said.

Blair sucked up another sob, and I got up to take Martha's elbow since she looked like she was about to keel over.

"If you'll stop by the nurse's desk and give us his number, we'll find out how he wants to handle things from here. I'm really very sorry for your loss," she said before leaving.

The doctor's departure sparked a new chorus of sniffles, and then Rudy took over, as Rudy was apt to do.

Over the years, I had mentally given all the girls nicknames. In my mind, Doe was the Wiz because she was a tough negotiator and

20

could juggle multiple tasks with ease. Of course, Blair was Catnip, because she'd never met a man she didn't like, or a man who didn't like her. I had never formally given Martha a nickname, although I tended to think of her as the Whiner. But Rudy was the Boss, even though she didn't actually run anything. It was her take-charge attitude, accented by short bristly hair, a sharp chin, small, piercing brown eyes and a snarky attitude. She could have been a drill sergeant in another lifetime.

"Everybody up!" she said with enough emphasis to make us jump.

We all got up and took her cue to grasp hands.

"Dear God," she began. "Please take Ellen into your loving embrace. Bring her peace and let her know that the four of us promise to keep ourselves mentally healthy and alive, just as she wished. Amen."

We each murmured, "Amen."

As we began to unwind our hands, the stern look on Rudy's face stopped us.

"Well?" she said, expecting a response.

We each gave an affirmative nod to Rudy's promise to Ellen. And then, thankfully, we went for a drink.

CHAPTER THREE

We met back at the Mercerwood Shore Club, our favorite place for lunch and libations on the island. Doe and Blair both had boats moored there, and my daughter, Angela, had participated on the swim team back when she was in high school. The clubhouse overlooks an Olympic-sized swimming pool and has a great second-story deck where you can sit in nice weather.

It was almost four o'clock and a little chilly to sit outside, so Rudy selected a table next to the window so we could at least enjoy the view. We ordered our drinks in an uncharacteristically subdued mood, and then waited for Martha, who had run to the restroom to freshen up. She had cried herself out in the car and returned to the table without any makeup at all, but looking slightly more at peace. As she sat down, I noticed that she'd stopped manhandling her purse. After all, it was over; there wasn't any need now for tension or stress. Ellen was gone, and it appeared as if Dooney & Bourke would live to see another day.

As we waited for the drinks, I snuck a glance around the table, wondering what the other girls were thinking. Our book club had met monthly for almost eleven years. During that time, we'd become more than neighbors and fiction lovers; we'd become close friends. We had suffered together through divorces, funerals, illnesses, and family emergencies. We dog sat, house sat, and sometimes even husband sat on the rare occasion when a husband might be sick. While we might differ in faith or politics, or compete on the golf course, we were fiercely loyal as friends.

"I can't believe it," Doe said under her breath. "I just spoke to Ellen yesterday. She was going to help me select some new furniture for the den."

Doe had beautiful dark brown eyes and naturally thick, dark brows and lashes, so she never had to wear makeup. She wiped her eyes and reached into her big black purse to find a tissue.

"I wonder how Ray will take it," I said. "And the kids. I mean, they're all so far away."

"She died alone," Blair said with a sigh.

Martha's round eyes flared momentarily. "Not alone. We were there."

"I suppose," Blair said, tempering her remark. "But it's so sad that her immediate family wasn't there. How long does it take to get back from Thailand, anyway?"

Blair's sarcasm wasn't lost on anyone. Ray wasn't a favorite with the girls in the club, but we'd always been careful not to say anything in front of Ellen.

"Longer than a couple of hours," I replied, feeling the need to defend him. After all, he'd just lost his wife.

"But what did she mean there at the end?" Blair asked with her Botox lips pursed. "All that stuff about being sorry and that she couldn't take it anymore. Take *what* anymore?"

"And that business about 'money can't buy you everything,'" Doe said. "What the heck did that mean?"

Doe had a graduate degree in business and the task of meeting the payroll for 300 employees, so she knew the value of a dollar.

"Let's admit it," Rudy said, getting everyone's attention. "Ellen *was* essentially alone in the world. Her husband ignored her, and her two ungrateful children live out-of-state. She was lucky to see her grandchildren once a year. All Ellen did was travel, shop, and organize fundraisers for the ballet or the homeless shelter. I've never thought she was very happy. I suspect she was just finally letting us know."

Rudy was a no-nonsense kind of gal who had worked for fifteen years as a beat reporter for a big city newspaper, spending two months as one of the few female reporters during the last days of Vietnam. She was a compact 5' 5", with the tenacity of a pit bull and the dental implants to match. She was sixty-eight, the most verbally aggressive of the group, and a woman you didn't want to cross.

"You say that like traveling is a bad thing," Blair said, tossing her head, forcing her pony tail to come loose.

I was resting my hands on the table and had started picking at the fingernail that Ellen had snapped partway off at the hospital.

"And raising money helps organizations who serve the poor," I said. "We all help with the fundraising for different causes."

Just then I inadvertently popped the nail off and flicked it across the table. It landed in Rudy's water glass with a little *clink*.

Everyone stopped.

I stared at Rudy, who merely glanced at the nail floating among her ice cubes and then at me, frowning in the same way my Home Economics teacher used to frown when I couldn't sew a straight line in high school. I mouthed an apology, just as the waitress returned with our drinks. Rudy handed off her tainted water glass without a word.

Once we had all settled back with our alcohol of choice, Rudy asked the waitress for a dictionary. With a raised eyebrow, the young woman glanced down to where Rudy's smart phone sat on the table.

"Wouldn't it be faster to just look up what you want on the net?" she said with contempt.

Rudy tilted her head back to look up at the girl. Her eyes narrowed and the muscles in her jaw clenched. If you looked closely, you could see Rudy's eyes click on the girl's cringe-worthy orange hair (shaved short on one side), and then to the barely visible tattoo of a winged dragon that peeked out from under the black vest of her uniform. Rudy gave a quick snort, prompting the rest of us to sit forward with anticipation.

"Tiffany," she began, reading the girl's nametag. "There are over 171,000 words currently in use in the English language. Did you know that? There are over 47,000 obsolete words, and another 9,500 that are derivatives. Suffice it to say that the list grows daily. I don't expect you to care about words because to you an entire sentence is probably nothing more than LOL or IDK. But to me, the use of a word constitutes the meaning of life. It describes the smell of rain on a summer's day, or the glow of an autumn moon, or dare I say the iridescence of your shockingly brassy hair."

Tiffany started to smile and then stopped, clearly confused as to whether she'd just been insulted or not.

"When I hold a dictionary," Rudy continued, "I can feel all of the things those words bring to life. But...," she reached out and grabbed her phone. "When I hold this...the only thing I feel is its ring tone."

I smiled and glanced at the girl, thinking it was her turn. But clearly, Tiffany wasn't up to the challenge. She stared at Rudy for a brief second and then shrugged.

"Okay," she said. "I'll see what I can find."

She turned on her thick rubber heel and left the lounge.

"Damn, you're good," Doe said with a big smile. "Care to join me at the bargaining table?"

"Bravo," Blair said, in her best cheerleader's voice. "But what's a derivative?"

Rudy shook her head, and we all laughed. Blair wasn't fooling any of us. Even though she played the part of an airhead in real life, she was smart as a whip.

"Look," Rudy said, picking up the conversation again. "When you travel just to get away, it doesn't do anything for your soul. When was the last time you remember Ellen chatting about the culture or historical facts about a specific location? As I recall, over the last couple of years, the only trips she and Ray took were somehow connected to his business."

"Okay, but what's wrong with volunteering for the homeless shelter?" Blair was dipping her little finger into the Lemon Drop in her hand when she asked this. "The homeless need our help."

"Ellen didn't volunteer for the homeless shelter." Rudy made this a declarative statement as if she challenged anyone to deny it. "She mostly sat on the board and made policy decisions. It's not the same thing. What she did filled her time, but not her brain, and certainly not her heart. I think that's what she was trying to say."

"Are you saying that you think Ellen drove off that cliff on purpose?" Doe spoke up, her striking dark eyes pinched with doubt.

Rudy shifted in her seat. "I don't know. But I think her final words could only be construed as meaning she wasn't as happy as we all believed she was."

25

Doe nodded. "She did sound defeated. I've certainly never heard her talk like that before."

"It would make sense," I said, remembering my earlier thought. "I mean, if she did it on purpose. Why else would she have been up there in the middle of the night?"

A pall fell over the group as we sat quietly nursing our drinks. While I thought that all of us had busy, purposeful lives, if Ellen wasn't satisfied with her life, then what could be said about ours? Perhaps we were all in jeopardy. I couldn't imagine driving my little Miata off a cliff, but then I would never have guessed Ellen would either.

I glanced over at Martha, who had started to twist her napkin into a knot.

"You okay, Martha?" I said quietly.

She looked up and nodded, a tear forming. Unlike Doe and Rudy, Martha had never had a career. Caring for her daughter and her husband had consumed the first half of her adult life. With her husband now gone and her daughter married and living in England, her life was filled largely with friends. And Ellen had been the best of the bunch.

"Well, I know Ellen always dreamed of becoming an interior designer," Doe said, staring into her glass of Chardonnay. "She used to talk about it whenever she'd had anything to drink. I think that's why she always volunteered to be decorating chair for all of our events. She was good at it."

Doe sat forward, resting her ample bosom on the table as she was apt to do whenever she wanted to make a point. It was probably the only way she could get the attention of the dozen or so men who shared the board room with her. And even though she was pushing sixty-five, her bosom was a sight to behold.

"Interior design was something she'd wanted to do since she was a girl," she continued. "But she got married and then had children, and her husband wouldn't hear of it. You'll have to admit, that man is a control freak."

"Good ol' traditional Ray," Blair said a little too loudly.

"Ray controlled every aspect of her life," I said quietly. "That alone would have driven me crazy."

"And yet she had all the money in the world," Doe said. "That's what people usually say they want—more money. But in her case, I guess it wasn't enough. She never got to live her dream."

"Exactly!" Rudy slapped the table, making us jump. "Ellen was telling us to forget tradition and not to give up on our dreams, whatever they are."

"Or maybe to create new dreams," I offered, swirling the margarita around in my glass. "New challenges. Don't let life pass us by, that sort of thing."

"But we're too old to start catching up on our dreams, aren't we?" Martha reminded us for the millionth time how set in her ways she was. "I think you'd all agree that we're more than a hair's width past our prime."

There was that whine.

"That's the point, Martha," Rudy stated. "This is exactly the time when we *shouldn't* give up on our dreams, when we should go for it!"

"All the more sweet at our age, don't you think?" Doe winked at Martha.

"But don't you think some of us are actually living our dreams? I mean, look at Julia," she said, gesturing to me. "She runs the nicest inn on Mercer Island. And you, Blair, get to drive any fast car you want."

Blair grinned stupidly. Her first husband had been a NASCAR driver and had introduced her to the adrenaline rush of driving fast cars, actually teaching her how to do it. Now, her current husband owned a string of foreign import car dealerships in the Puget Sound area, giving her access to whatever car she wanted. If anyone had driven off a cliff by mistake, I would have thought it would be Blair.

"You have to admit, Rudy," I said. "Martha is right. As a journalist, you spent your entire career covering some of the most exciting stories around the world."

"Yes…but we all have things we dreamt of as a child," Rudy replied. "What about you, Martha? Didn't you ever have something you always wanted to do, but never got the chance?"

Martha looked like she'd just bit into a lemon. Getting her to go along on this vision quest would require a major change in attitude. At seventy-three, Martha was the oldest amongst us. She had spent the better part of her life as the painted backdrop to a prominent state senator. That's how I met her. We'd sat next to each other at a tea held for the wives of incoming junior Washington state senators some twenty-five years earlier. She was older than me by ten years and already a pro at being the consummate politician's wife since her husband had already been in the state senate for four years. As the wife of a new senator, I watched and learned. Martha knew how to smile with the best of them. And she was better at saying nothing than anyone I knew. I stood next to her in more than one receiving line and listened to her chatter on with each and every guest, realizing later that I couldn't remember one word she'd said. Of course, neither could she. Asking someone like that to share their dreams was like asking them to remember high school algebra. This wouldn't be easy. But with a little encouragement from the rest of us, a mischievous smile slid slowly across her round features.

"Well...I've always wanted to study art," she said shyly.

We all erupted in cheers.

"How about you, Blair?" Rudy said, turning to Blair. "What is it that would make you feel truly alive? And not just driving fast cars."

The alcohol in her Lemon Drop was bringing a good deal of color to Blair's already overly blushed cheeks, and she giggled, flashing her perfectly whitened teeth.

"I've always wanted to be a country western singer." She grinned, and her blue eyes twinkled.

Doe hooted, and I clapped loudly just as the waitress returned with a large dictionary and dropped it with a thud in front of Rudy. Rudy thanked her, gave her a five dollar tip, and opened the book. She whipped out her reading glasses and flipped pages until she found what she wanted. Then, she ran a finger across the page.

"Okay, we don't want the traditional definition of 'old maid.' Wait a minute. This must be what Ellen was referring to." She looked up at us. "Here we go." She began to read from the book. "An old maid is a person who is too much concerned with being proper, modest, or righteous; someone marked by excessive concern for propriety and good form." After a pause, she slammed the book closed and glared at us. "I think Ray turned Ellen into the worst kind of old maid. She was warning us not to follow in her footsteps. Well, I don't plan to."

Rudy grabbed her Gucci purse, threw another five dollar bill on the table and stood up.

"Where are you going?" Blair asked loudly enough to make heads turn.

Rudy stuck out her recently micro-dermabrasioned chin and replied proudly, "To schedule the horseback riding lessons I've wanted to take since I was ten! Anyone care to join me?"

And with that, the Old Maids Club was born.

CHAPTER FOUR

The morning after Ellen died I moved slowly through my regular tasks at the inn and finally tucked myself into the small office behind the registration desk to pay bills. I was staring at an invoice for laundry detergent when a pen that was sitting off to the side began rolling toward me.

"Chloe," I said. "Not now. I'm not in the mood."

The pen stopped. Then it rolled back to where it began.

Everyone who had worked at the inn over the years had described unexplained experiences of one sort or another. Libby, my housekeeper, who lived in one of the upstairs bedrooms, often complained that laundry she'd just folded and stacked on the washer would be toppled over if she left it unattended. Several guests had reported hearing voices, or seeing the image of a woman dressed in a nightgown walking through walls. We believed that to be Elizabeth St. Claire, and I'd seen her do it once or twice myself. Seeing a ghost, any ghost, is a bit frightening. But watching an apparition disappear through a solid wall can turn your stomach. I mean, where do they go? But I forgave Elizabeth the offense, since most of the doors in the building had been moved over the years and she probably didn't know it.

For some reason, the little girl, Chloe, liked to hang around the office and tease me with her ghostly antics. Usually, it delighted and amazed me, but today, I could only think of Ellen, who now lived in Chloe's world—a thought that brought tears to my eyes.

Under the circumstances, I thought maybe I needed to do

something physical. So I decided to take a walk and called the dogs. Mickey and Minnie are my long-haired miniature Dachshunds, which means they each weigh about ten pounds. Mickey is a noble-looking black and tan, while Minnie is a beautiful copper-red. They pretty much follow me wherever I go and were right at my feet. When I clapped my hands and said, "Walkie!" they sprinted for the front door, barking all the way. Outdoor walks provide numerous opportunities to communicate with the outside world, which if you know Dachshunds, is as good as Disneyland to a four-year old.

I decided to walk the neighborhood rather than along the beach, since a stiff breeze had come up. The inn has a circular gravel drive with a parking area for about six cars. I started up the left side of the drive with both dogs pulling on the split leash as if they were a team of miniature horses, kicking up gravel as they went. Once I made it to the sidewalk, I realized that either way I turned I would have to pass right in front of Ellen's house. This made me stop.

I stared sadly at the large two-story Cape Cod-style home, picturing my friend inside busily cleaning a counter or organizing a cupboard. Ellen had been obsessive that way. Although she had a cleaning woman who came once a week, she only allowed the woman to do the heavy stuff. Ellen attended to everything else, and the house was always immaculate —down to the junk drawer.

I know this because I'd helped her move some furniture upstairs once and asked to use the master bathroom. After I washed my hands, I took the liberty of glancing in her vanity. Her vanity was perfectly organized, with little matching plastic trays in each drawer– one for Qtips, one for Band-Aids, and another for tubes of cream. Top drawer blue. Second drawer black. The big bottom drawer also had matching trays for her hair dryer and curling iron, makeup remover, and vibrator. Okay, maybe I saw too much. My point is that while the St. Claire Inn is kept neat and clean on the surface, I tend to just throw things into drawers and let them fend for themselves. Ellen's life, on the other hand, *had* been perfect, down to the little matching trays in her vanity drawers.

As I gazed across the street, I thought how lonely the house looked in the early morning light. Ray hadn't made it home from Thailand, yet. Nor had the adult children arrived from the East

Coast with their families. Soon, the house would be filled with people again, but those little colored trays would sit there in lonely silence. There would be no one to clean them out or rearrange them with such loving care ever again.

I wiped a tear away and was about to turn around and take a walk along the beach, when a white Mercedes pulled up. My neighbor, Sybil Moore, rolled down her window and poked her big head out.

"Julia, I heard about Ellen," she said in her annoying Southern twang. "It's sooooo shocking."

I hated when Sybil drew out words like that. It made me think she had never left the tenth grade.

"Yes, it is," I agreed.

"Martha told me y'all went to the hospital and were with Ellen during her last moments. Y'all were suuuuch good friends."

I didn't know you could draw out the word "such," but leave it to Sybil to find a way.

"I'm just glad we could be with her at the end," I said, feeling tears begin to pool.

When I say that Sybil had a big head, I wasn't kidding. It was out of proportion to the rest of her body. Right now she was tilting her chin to signify sympathy, her goofy up-do hitting the doorframe. I tried not to look at her.

"It must have been hard, though." She tsked when she said this, another of her irritating habits. "I remember I was with my papa when he passed away," she said, gazing off into the distance. "He was hit by lightning, if you can believe it. I was only nine." She sighed. "Just a little thing. We were at an outdoor picnic, and a storm blew in."

You could also always count on Sybil to turn any conversation into one about her.

"I sat right there on the ground with him," she said, shaking her head at the memory. "And I was the only one who heard his last words."

She paused and shifted her eyes to mine, her eyebrows pleading for my response. When I didn't say anything, she leaned that big head forward as if to say, "*Well?*"

"Um…wha…what did he say?" I mumbled, completely bored out of my mind.

She smiled a toothy grin. "He told me how much he loved me and mama. Those words have stayed with me all these years."

Sybil wore big framed glasses and reached under one lens to wipe her eye.

"I hope Ellen said something nice like that. Something Ray can hold on to," she said.

I just stared at her.

Well, no, I thought. In fact, Ellen hadn't even mentioned her family. My brain whirred. That could prove awkward on the off chance Ray might ask, and I wondered how we would handle that once he got home. As my brain re-focused, I noticed that Sybil was still looking at me with expectation. She was obviously waiting to hear the loving words she was so sure Ellen had spoken at the hospital.

Fortunately, my cell phone rang giving me cover, and I put a hand up to say, "*Just a minute.*" Then I reached into my pocket and pulled it out. It was Martha, crying again. I excused myself and turned to retreat down the driveway.

"The police have ruled Ellen's death a suicide," Martha said, erupting in sobs on the phone. "Ray just called me. I can't believe it."

As her grief engulfed her, I heard the Mercedes pull away behind me. I wandered the rest of the way down the drive and plopped down on a stone bench in front of the big porch. Deep down, I had suspected Ellen's death might be suicide, and now the nagging question as to why she had been on Marchand Drive had been answered. When I sensed that Martha's spigot was running dry, I chanced a question.

"How do they know?"

"The skid marks," she blubbered anew.

After several gulps, coughs, and snivels, she finally explained that apparently the skid marks left little doubt that Ellen had accelerated from a complete stop before racing down the hill and ramming through the guardrail.

I dropped my head. I didn't need the dictionary this time to tell me what that meant. It meant there would be a perpetual stigma surrounding Ellen's death. People would whisper in private and speculate on why such a beautiful, wealthy woman would kill herself. They would presume that it was her husband, or her children, or a disease that had caused her to act so irrationally. Her husband would live the rest of his life with a sense of guilt and remorse, and her death would always be shrouded in secrecy when her grandchildren asked, *"What happened to Grandma?"*

"I'm so sorry, Martha," I said with a deep sigh. "I guess we can never know what another person is going through. There must have been something we weren't aware of."

"But she would have told me." Martha cried, her heart broken. "We were best friends. She would have said something."

"Maybe whatever was bothering her was too personal. Maybe it was something sudden, and she didn't have time to say anything. What we need to do now is to celebrate her life," I said with more bravado than I really felt. "We can celebrate her life and all the wonderful things she did for people. She was a great person, Martha. We won't forget that."

I paused, thinking about a time when I'd attended the funeral of a doctor-friend who had injected himself with enough morphine to send him to outer space. People at the service behaved like automatons. No one knew what to say and so just didn't say anything. There were no facial expressions, no laughter, no recounting the man's personal life. I didn't want that for Ellen. She had lived a generous and dignified life and didn't deserve to have people speculate about her emotional stability, relationships, or physical health. Yes, we would plan a wonderful celebration of her life, and then we would honor her in the way we promised—we would live out our dreams.

CHAPTER FIVE

The weekend after Ellen was buried, Rudy called a meeting at the inn to discuss her idea about horseback riding. It was the first of June by then and the inn was full, but all the guests were out for the day. Since the weather was cooperating, I put out a pitcher of lemonade and a plate of cookies in the breakfast room for people when they returned, and then dusted off chairs on the back patio. The planters were filled with colorful annuals, and the bird feeders that dotted the landscape were filled with birdseed, bringing a host of feathered friends to share a snack.

By two-thirty, we were seated in a set of white Adirondack chairs around the outdoor fire pit to enjoy the view and discuss Rudy's idea.

"So, I've been thinking," Rudy began. "It sounds like all of us had dreams growing up that never materialized. As I said, one of mine was horseback riding. I've located a barn that has a covered arena, so we won't even have to get wet. And they offer classes. I'm going to sign up for a six-week course, and I was hoping you guys would join me."

She stopped and waited with her thin lips pursed in expectation. I glanced around the circle to see what other's reactions might be, but everyone seemed suddenly preoccupied. When Rudy had proposed this idea at the club over alcohol, it seemed completely plausible, even if we *were* all over fifty—okay sixty. Now, maybe not so much.

"Horses are big," I said, filling the silence.

Rudy frowned. "Yes, Julia, they are. What's your point?"

"My point is…they're big."

Doe sighed, as she did at the beginning of most sentences.

"I think what she's trying to say is that we could get hurt, Rudy. My niece was thrown from a horse a few years back and ended up in the hospital with a concussion."

Rudy exhaled in exasperation. "I thought when we decided to name ourselves the Old Maids Club it was because we *weren't* going to be old maids." She turned to me. "So you're scared you're going to fall off? No one—I repeat NO ONE—is going to fall off the damn horse!"

And then, of course, she did.

÷

We began our horseback riding lessons two weeks later. My horse was a stocky gelding named, Sugar, but he was anything but sweet. In fact, he was the most stubborn thing I had ever met besides my ex-husband, and not any easier to mount.

But the experience wasn't all bad. I'm a bit accident prone, so the fact that I never fell off was a surprise to everyone, especially Rudy, who slid right out of her saddle at one point and landed face down in the dirt. For someone who prides herself in her athleticism, it was enough to make her blush right through her sprayed-on tan. But I have to hand it to her. She grabbed the reins, put her foot in the stirrup and swung herself back into the saddle. Well, almost. She overshot the swing part and went right over the other side, landing face down in the dirt—again.

In August, we went skydiving with Doe, which apparently triggered my latent fear of heights. I went through the training, geared up, and got on the plane, only to panic when it was my turn to jump. When the instructor reached out a hand to me, my inner hysterical bitch took over, and I yanked my arm away, nearly pulling him off his feet.

He smiled reassuringly. "It's okay. I'm right here. You'll be fine," he said.

I gazed at his plastic smile and thought I saw my short life flash before my eyes—okay, maybe not so short, but it flashed before my eyes nonetheless. Next thing I knew, I was threatening to rip his arms off. When we made it back to base camp, the company owner called me over and informed me that I would never be allowed to come there again.

It was the week before Thanksgiving by the time we could schedule Blair's adventure. She wanted to sing karaoke. I remember Rudy pausing when Blair suggested it.

"Uh…you mean we each have to get up and sing?" she asked.

"Yes," Blair said with a toss of her head. "You made us ride horses, I want to sing."

Rudy's tan was looking a little green around the edges at this point.

"I'm good," I said with confidence. "If I can go skydiving, I can sing karaoke."

Rudy turned to me with a sneer that could have made my mother cry.

"You didn't go skydiving," she said with a snap. "You went up in a plane, something you do every year for vacation, and then you came down again."

"Well, I *meant* to jump out," I said.

"Not exactly the same thing as *actually* jumping," she said.

"What are you afraid of, Rudy?" Blair pinned it.

Rudy puffed out her inadequate chest. "I'm not afraid," she said with earnest. "I just…"

"What?" Blair prodded her.

Rudy stared back at us as we all waited. Finally, she said, "I'll go. It should be fun."

On the first night of karaoke, I reasoned away any fear I had by reminding myself that there was alcohol available, something I noticed Rudy was taking liberal advantage of. By the time it was her turn to go on stage, she turned to Doe, our designated driver.

"Hey Doe," she said with a conspiratorial tone. "Why don't we do it together? I was thinking of doing an Everly Brothers song. Better if there were two of us."

Doe took a moment to consider her idea, shot me a glance and then said, "Okay."

You would have thought the thirty-something crowd that night actually knew who the Everly Brothers were. They all joined in to sing *Hello Mary Lou*. I sat back with a smug look, knowing full well that Rudy had planned that all along.

I received a hearty response to my version of *Killing Me Softly*, probably because by the time I made it on stage I'd exceeded my normal limit of two margaritas and had begun to slur. The line, 'killing me softly with his song' kept coming out as 'killing me softly with his thong.' An awkward visual image to be sure.

Martha's rendition of Cyndi Lauper's *Girls Just Wanna Have Fun* was a big hit. And the surprise of the night was Blair, who really wasn't half bad. As she crooned the lyrics without once looking at the screen, I realized what a good memory she had. But then I remembered that Blair always knew recipes by heart and could recite street addresses and birthdays on cue. Her performance elicited cheers from the mostly male crowd, although I thought more from the sight of her oscillating breasts than her ability to carry a tune.

Around the same time we began horseback riding in June, Martha stopped by the inn one afternoon. I was in the entryway rearranging a pair of antique chairs I was hoping to sell.

"I want to volunteer," she said. "At the shelter where Ellen worked."

"Really?" I said, angling the Queen Anne chair away from the door.

"Yes. Ellen used to talk about the shelter a lot. During the last month or so, she was actually volunteering in the office. She met a number of the women there and talked about how sad they were. It made her feel good to volunteer for an organization that helped them. I'd like to do that, too. Will you do it with me?"

If Rudy was born with a silver tongue, Doe with brains, and Blair with confidence, Martha was born with none of the above. It wasn't that she was scared of life, but she was overly cautious. So, I recognized what a big step this would be for her. I also realized that volunteering sounded good to me, too. She wasn't the only one who had thought about what Ellen had said just before she died. I loved my life, but it was pretty self-centered.

"Sure, I'll volunteer with you," I said, beginning to dust off an old secretary's desk I'd placed in between the chairs. "I'd like to do something useful, too. Are you sure you want to volunteer at the shelter, though? What about someplace like the YWCA or the food bank?"

"No...the shelter," she said steadfastly. She took a deep breath. "I don't think Ellen killed herself."

I stopped and looked up. "Okay…I…uh…what?"

She shrugged her rounded shoulders. "I know what Ellen said at the end, but there wasn't anything really wrong in her life. You all think that she was unhappy because Ray controlled her, but she loved him. And I think she loved her life."

"But the police said… I mean, they said…"

"I know what they said, Julia. I just think they're wrong."

And then Martha farted.

She often did that. But usually it happened when she bent over or laughed too hard. This time it was like the exclamation point at the end of her sentence. Martha seemed oblivious to the indiscretion, so I chose to ignore it.

"But not being able to sleep wouldn't cause Ellen to…you know," I said.

"To drive off a cliff?" She finished my thought with a slight toss of her head. "Yes, I *do* know. So I want to walk in her shoes. Maybe I'll understand then. I think something changed in her life, and I want to know what it was. So, what day do you want to volunteer?"

It took a moment for my brain to shift gears. But finally, I said, "Probably Monday mornings. Those are usually our slowest days since most people check out on Sunday."

"Okay, good. That works for me."

The Good Shepherd Women's Shelter was part of a large regional nonprofit that ran several homeless shelters in the area, and it was affiliated with St. Martin's Catholic Church on Queen Anne Hill in Seattle, where Martha, Doe and I attended services. Our priest, Father Bentley, provided chapel services at the shelter and was on site once a week for private consultations.

Martha and I participated in a half-day of training and then began volunteering three to four hours every Monday morning. I had to admit that after only a few weeks, I stopped complaining about the little inconveniences in my life. These women had it tough.

Martha enjoyed volunteering with the women as much as I did. In fact, when another volunteer left, she began volunteering in the office just as Ellen had done. Volunteering seemed to give her an enormous sense of purpose, so much so that Father Bentley even approached her about joining the board of directors.

And then, the weekend before Thanksgiving, Martha's niece came to visit. Martha brought her along to the shelter to show her niece the good work we were doing. But the Monday *after* Thanksgiving, Martha called to say she wasn't feeling well and wouldn't be going. Then she missed volunteering the first Monday in December, as well as our regular book club meeting. These absences raised questions in my mind, but at the time, I was busy getting the inn ready for the holidays. As a result, I ignored them— something I would later regret.

CHAPTER SIX

It was two weeks before Christmas, and Seattle was in the middle of a cold snap. The meteorologists had even gone so far as to predict snow. The inn was all decked out for the holidays, with an antique sleigh out front draped in garlands and bows, three big Christmas trees inside, and my collection of vintage Santa Clauses scattered throughout the ground floor.

The state Democratic Party had scheduled a reception at the inn on Wednesday evening of that week to honor Senator Joe Pesante, a state Senator from Walla Walls who was in town promoting raising the minimum wage. As a life-long Democrat, I was looking forward to the evening and had even decided to give the senator a gift.

On the Saturday *before* the reception, I'd grabbed a box of my homemade chocolate fudge from behind the reception desk, where we sold it to guests, and wrapped it with my favorite candy cane wrapping paper and a big red bow. Several of the guests happened to stop by as I was doing this, including Sybil, who came in to drop off the animated Santa Claus I'd asked to borrow for the reception.

When I was finished, I left the gift box under the registration desk, thinking I would give it to the senator as he was *leaving* the party the following Wednesday. He was well-known for his sweet tooth, and I suspected he would rip open the box to sample the candy on his way out the door.

But two hours before the caterers were scheduled to arrive that day, the senator's aide called to say that he had been taken ill and couldn't make it. I spent the next forty-five minutes hurriedly calling local dignitaries to cancel.

The girls were set to come for our annual holiday luncheon the next day, Thursday, when we would plan out the next year's reading list for the book club. I moved the gift box from under the front desk to the pantry that morning, thinking I would give it to the senator at the Governor's New Year's Eve party. Then I set about making my award-winning sugarless peach cobbler for the luncheon. It was Blair's birthday, and since she was a diabetic, I was making it in her honor.

By noon, the girls arrived in a chatty, light-hearted mood—even Rudy, who had just gone through her annual colonoscopy the day before. Martha had called to say that she would be late. Everyone was dressed in their best casual holiday attire: Rudy in a crisp denim shirt embroidered with poinsettias, Doe in an elegant red cashmere sweater and green scarf, and Blair in a pair of tight black pants and a glittery stretch blouse designed to accent her best feature—so, not her smile. I had on my favorite Christmas sweater with dogs embroidered all along the bottom wearing antlers.

It was a potluck, so we'd each made a special dish. I'd made the dessert. Doe had brought chicken curry over rice. Rudy had made a fabulous three-bean salad, and Blair had stopped at the store and bought bread.

After lunch, the girls retired to the living room, where I had a roaring fire going. I was just about to get the wine, when Martha showed up. She stopped in the doorway to the living room with her hand resting on the wall and a faraway look on her face. She was dressed as if she were going to wake instead of a holiday luncheon—black shirt-waist dress and a gray cardigan, buttoned wrong.

"Julia," she murmured, "do you have anything sweet? I didn't have lunch."

"Uh…how about something to eat? There's plenty of food left," I said.

"No," she said. "Something sweet."

"Okay. How about a mint? They're on the table."

I started to take her into the dining room, but she waved me away and went in alone. Doe was just coming back from the bathroom and stopped to watch with me as Martha went to the table and grabbed a whole handful of mints and began stuffing them into her mouth. Doe was a disciplined eater who maintained her tall, elegant figure by carefully monitoring everything she ate. She turned to me with a slightly horrified expression.

"Martha," I called to her. "I have peach cobbler for later."

She turned to me with a mint stuck halfway between her teeth.

"That's okay," she said, sucking on the chocolate-covered mint.

I turned to Doe. "I've got a bottle of Chardonnay in the refrigerator. I'll grab it. You grab Martha."

"Okay," she murmured.

While Doe guided Martha into the living room, I headed to the kitchen to get the wine and some glasses. As I passed through the breakfast room, a voice stopped me.

"Mama always said life is like a box of chocolates. You never know what you're gonna get."

I turned to find Captain Ahab, the African Grey Parrot I'd bought at an estate sale a few years back, bouncing around on the perch in the middle of his cage. Ahab had been a spontaneous buy, something I don't usually do. I was at the estate sale to buy an antique Chippendale bar cabinet and came home with him instead. But in my defense, I saw Ahab as a rescue. African Grey Parrots are notoriously good talkers, and this one had a large vocabulary, having lived with an older woman who liked to watch movies on HBO all day. The only person bidding on him was a scraggly-looking kid dressed all in black. I'd overheard him to tell an equally scraggly-looking friend that he was going to bid on Ahab so that he could teach him the lyrics to a song called *I Drink Blood*. Since that was enough to curdle mine, I valiantly stepped in to bid against him. And voila!

I turned away from Ahab and went into the kitchen for the wine. I took everything out to an old marble-topped side table that sat up against the wall. Blair was seated in a tanned leather chair, next to an end table I'd made out of stacking antique suitcases one on top of the other. The girls had been tossing around reading ideas, and Blair was in the process of suggesting a new romance set in Greenland when Martha got up and began to wander around the room.

The living room windows are tall and white-mullioned, while the floor-to-ceiling bookcases are painted barn red to match a

43

variety of red accents. Martha stopped in the corner to finger a collection of old apothecary cans on one of the shelves. Everyone glanced up to watch her for a moment, but Blair continued, and I poured the wine.

As Blair described the book, Martha crossed out of the room. Mickey and Minnie followed close behind as if it were a game. As Martha passed me, I noticed that she was wearing two different colored shoes—a brown one and a navy blue one. I watched her out of the corner of my eye as I finished with the wine. She went down the hall and behind the front desk, where she stooped over and rifled through the shelves. Then she turned and looked through the boxes of fudge and scone mixes for sale on the baker's rack behind the desk. I finally called out to her.

"Martha, do you need some help?"

"What? No," she said, turning abruptly. "You guys just keep talking. I'm not really interested in discussing books today. I need to use the restroom."

She left the front desk and went down the hallway, which wraps around to the back where the public bathroom is. The dogs came back to the living room, and I exchanged a curious glance with the rest of the girls as I passed out the wine and then sat down to take part in the discussion. A few minutes later, we saw Martha cross in front of the living room and go into the dining room, where we could hear the rattle of the drawer pulls in the buffet. I excused myself and joined her.

"Martha, are you looking for something?"

She straightened up with a surprised look, her cashmere cardigan slightly askew.

"No. Of course not. I…I just feel restless, that's all," she said, wringing her hands. "You guys go ahead. I just…want to wander around. If that's okay."

I nodded. "Of course it's okay. How are you feeling?"

"I'm fine," she said, dropping her hands to her side. "Can't a girl be restless?"

"Sure. Sorry," I replied. "Let me know if you need anything."

I returned to a roomful of quizzical looks. But we went on with our conversation, while Martha went into the kitchen. As Rudy made the case for a book set in the New South, we were interrupted occasionally by the sound of cupboards being opened and closed. When Martha came back out to the reception desk, I finally couldn't stand it anymore and interrupted Rudy.

"What is going on with her?" I whispered.

Blair and Rudy got up and peeked around the corner and down the hallway.

"I don't know," Rudy said, shaking her head before coming back in. "I've never seen her so distracted. It's like an alien being has inhabited her body."

"No, I think you're wrong there." Blair turned back with a devilish smile. "I don't think anyone has inhabited that body for a long time."

"Humph." Rudy snorted, settling back into the throw pillows on the sofa. "Just because you're like the Energizer Bunny, ready anytime, anywhere."

Blair laughed. "Hey, sex is good exercise. You play golf, Doe plays tennis, and I…"

"We all know what you do, Blair," I said, cutting her off. "But, let's get back to the book list."

I kept an ear out for Martha as we resumed our book discussion. But just as it was my turn to make a suggestion, my maintenance man, José, appeared through the dining room window to fix a string of holiday lights. He was setting up the ladder on the back deck, wearing a baggy sweatshirt and tight jeans stretched over his very tight…well, you get the picture. As he reached for the lights, his sweatshirt lifted up, revealing his well-toned torso. Suddenly the ladies were ill-prepared to continue their discussion.

So we left the book list behind and arranged ourselves around the dining room table, which offered a better view, anyway. I headed into the kitchen again to get the peach cobbler and met Martha coming out licking her fingers. I frowned, thinking she'd stuck her finger into my cobbler, but it looked intact when I got to the counter. I put a single birthday candle into the center for Blair, grabbed a serving spoon and headed back to the table.

The dining room table stood parallel to the window. Blair and Martha had grabbed seats facing the window, while Doe sat at one end. I was already set up at the other end, leaving Rudy to sit with her back to José. The table was decorated with my favorite poinsettia tablecloth, candy cane trim dishes, and my heirloom sterling silver flatware. A lovely cut glass dish sat in the middle of the table, filled with pine boughs and a thick cinnamon candle.

Martha seemed back to her old self as I lit the candle on the cobbler, and we sang to Blair. When I served up the dessert, Martha even commented on the view, by which I mean, José. She received a good round of chuckles as everyone dug into their dessert. I excused myself to grab the coffee pot and came back just as Blair swallowed a bite of cobbler and made a joke about José hanging his holiday balls. Everyone broke out in laughter. Martha had just landed a second spoonful of the cobbler in her mouth, when I moved in to fill her coffee cup. She suddenly gagged and pitched forward, landing face down in her dessert, splattering a good portion of it onto my crisp linen tablecloth.

I was so startled that I jumped back with a cry of alarm, tripping on Minnie who had followed me around the table. The little dog screeched and scampered off, while I tipped backwards, pouring scalding coffee into Blair's lap. She came straight out of her chair, catching the edge of the table with the large belt buckle accenting her tight black slacks. The table lifted off the floor, sending everything cascading towards Rudy.

I barely grabbed the lit candle from the middle of the holiday arrangement before it slid across the table. Rudy caught the dish, taking the full force of its water in her face and tilting backwards in her chair, smashing into the turn-of-the-century buffet that sat behind her, under the window. Before it was over, I'd lost several of my favorite holiday dishes, a beautiful floral arrangement, a set of demitasse cups and saucers from the buffet, and a perfectly good peach cobbler—not to mention Martha.

CHAPTER SEVEN

Once everything in the room had stopped moving and the shrieks died down, we turned to Martha, now lying motionless on the floor. I pulled out my phone and dialed 911. No-nonsense Rudy hurried around and knelt down to take her pulse. She put up a hand to keep us quiet and then searched around Martha's wrist with her fingertips. She got very quiet to listen for Martha's pulse and then bent down, putting her ear to Martha's lips. With a solemn shake of her head, she gave us the bad news.

Tears sprang to my eyes. I reported the incident to the 911 operator, and then since there wasn't any reason to stay on the phone, they let me go. After I hung up, I called over to the bakery to alert April.

While we waited for the ambulance, Rudy slumped into a chair, picking at the blob of gooey peach cobbler and pine needles that clung to her shirt, while Doe consoled Blair. I just stood and stared at Martha, willing her to stop playing games and get up. But of course, she didn't. As my own tears threatened to reduce me to rubble, I took a deep breath and glanced around the room, forcing myself to take stock of the situation.

The tablecloth had been pulled sideways off the table. There were broken demitasse glasses scattered across the carpet, along with broken dessert dishes, glasses and silverware. And just in front of the buffet table was a congealed puddle of melted red wax from the candle I had let slip from my fingers when Rudy had determined Martha was dead. As my eyes surveyed the damage, a horrified cry escaped my lips.

Mickey and Minnie were licking up the dessert around Martha's face.

"Mickey! Minnie! Get away from there!" I yelled.

"Mickey! Minnie!" I heard an echo from the other room.

It was Ahab. He liked the sound of the dogs' names and would often mimic me when I scolded them.

I shooed the little canines back and quickly called my daytime manager, Crystal, who had just returned to the front desk from the laundry. She got the dogs to follow her to my apartment, her eyes as big as dinner plates as she spied Martha lying on the floor.

The inn sits only a few minutes from downtown Mercer Island, so the ambulance pulled into the drive with its siren blaring before we'd even processed what had just happened. A patrol car followed. This set off Ahab again, who had the uncanny ability to duplicate a range of sound effects. It was normally quite entertaining. Right now, however, having him merrily scream his siren song from the other room was enough to set my teeth on edge.

Minutes later, there was an entire group of emergency personnel parading through the inn. They found Martha's body lying on her side just in front of the table. An EMT knelt down to check her vitals, while another one rolled in a gurney. All any of us could do was stand back and watch.

When Crystal returned, I asked her to run interference with any of the guests who might appear. Meanwhile, the EMTs examined Martha. April arrived just as a young police officer approached me.

"Are you the owner of the inn?"

I nodded, a sob fighting to get out.

"I'm very sorry for your loss, but I need to ask you some questions. What time did this happen?" He whipped out a small notebook.

"About ten to fifteen minutes ago," I said with a tight throat. "We were in the middle of our book club meeting."

"That would make it about two o'clock," the officer said, checking his watch. "Does that sound about right?"

"Yes, that's about right." I was watching the ambulance workers lift Martha onto a stretcher, wishing I could rush over and fix the buttons on her sweater—to let her be seen the way she normally would. "We had just come into the dining room for dessert."

"Is this the dessert?" The young officer was pointing to the squished cobbler on the floor, now disengaged from Martha's face.

"Yes, that's it."

"Did any of the rest of you eat it?"

"We all did."

All the girls nodded in agreement.

"Are any of you feeling ill?"

"No, we're all fine," I said, looking around the room. "Martha had a heart condition. She was on medication. You'll probably find it in her purse."

"Maybe someone could get her purse for us," the officer said, writing something down.

Libby had heard the sirens and had come downstairs with a load of dirty linen in her arms. She stood in the background staring at Martha, her face so pale I thought briefly she was one of the ghosts. Libby was tall and thin, with a long neck and big hands, reminding me of a female Ichabod Crane. I approached her and put a hand on her wrist.

"Libby, can you get Martha's purse from the front closet?"

She nodded silently, turned on her heel and left for the entryway. The EMTs gently covered Martha with a blanket and wheeled her out. We all just stood and stared after them.

"Does she have any next-of-kin that you know of?" the officer asked me.

"Um...just a daughter who lives in England. I'll get her number."

I hurried to the office and retrieved Emily's phone number and gave it to him, along with her purse. He thanked me and followed the rest of the emergency personnel out the door.

After they'd all gone, April met me in the breakfast room and gave me a hug. "You okay, Julia?"

"Yeah," I said without much conviction. "I...just can't believe it."

"Houston, we have a problem," Ahab squawked.

We both turned around and saw Ahab bouncing around in his cage. The sirens and activity had clearly upset him.

"Go ahead, make my day," he squawked, bouncing up and down.

I walked over and talked in a quiet voice to him.

"It's alright, Ahab. It's all over now."

His little beady eyes watched me and then he ruffled his feathers and seemed to settle down. As I stood gazing at him, April squeezed my arm, bringing me back to this life.

"Let me finish up over in the bakery, and then I'll come back and help you clean up," she said.

The girls had retired to the living room, and so I took the opportunity to approach the only guest who had appeared. It was a small elderly gentleman named Mr. Stillwater, all bent over, hovering uncertainly behind Crystal at the foot of the stairs. He was in town for a funeral and had been quite specific on the subject of funerals when he'd arrived. He hated them, fearing his own demise now that he was an octogenarian. I explained to him what had happened, adding that it was probably a heart attack that had taken Martha. It couldn't have been encouraging under the circumstances, but he pushed his glasses up his nose, expressed his condolences and hobbled back to his room.

José had also come inside when he'd heard the sirens, and I asked him to help Libby begin cleaning up. I found Rudy, Blair and Doe sitting and staring silently at the floor in the living room. Well, what could one say after all of that?

I joined them by slumping onto an ottoman.

"I feel drained," Doe muttered under her breath. "We've lost two friends in less than a year."

"People come and go so quickly around here," I said quietly, staring into the fireplace.

"Julia!" Rudy warned.

I looked up. "Sorry."

Rudy didn't like it when I quoted the *Wizard of Oz*. But sometimes it just seemed to fit so perfectly.

"You don't think they're connected, do you? Like some weird curse or something?" Blair said with her eyes wide. She was sitting on the sofa, her hands shredding a tissue in her lap.

"No, Blair," Rudy said. "Let's acknowledge Martha's death for what it was—an odd coincidence."

"Let's face it," Rudy began, drumming her fingers on the arm of the leather chair. "Martha was in her early seventies and suffered from things like high blood pressure and arthritis. And she had open heart surgery a few years ago."

"But she maintained a rigid diet and exercise program," Blair said, countering Rudy's assessment. "She looked completely healthy when she got here today."

"She may have looked fine," I said. "But I think we can all agree that she wasn't acting like herself. Did you notice she was wearing two different colored shoes? Maybe something was wrong." I took a deep sigh. "She said something really strange to me a couple of weeks ago."

They all stopped sniffling and looked up at me with frozen expressions.

"She came by to talk about finally selling me that big drop-leaf table. You know I've wanted it forever. She said she was thinking of re-doing her den and didn't think she'd keep the table." I paused, picturing Martha in my mind that day. "On her way out the door, she stopped and asked me if I thought taking something that wasn't yours was a sin if it was for the greater good. Then she asked me about the last time I went to confession."

"What did you say?" Doe said with the hint of a smile on her lips.

"That I haven't been to confession in years," I said, returning the smile. "I told Martha that the last time I went to confession was when Graham got remarried, and I'd thought seriously about puncturing the tires on Kitty's car."

The girls chuckled.

"Martha laughed at that, too," I said, remembering. "When I asked her why she wanted to know, she just kind of blew me off."

"You think she needed to confess something?" Doe asked.

"I don't know."

"I can't imagine Martha taking something that wasn't hers," Blair said. "I wonder what she meant."

I shrugged. "That's all she said."

"Well, I guess we'll never know," Doe said, getting up. "Will you call Emily, Julia?"

Emily was Martha's daughter, who lived in London.

"Yes," I said, sighing. "There really isn't any other immediate family, I suppose." I stood up as the rest of them got ready to leave. "Are you guys up for planning another memorial service?"

They looked at me with blank expressions.

"Of course," Rudy finally replied.

"Yes," Doe said. "Tell Emily we'll do whatever she wants us to do."

The girls gathered their purses and coats and promised to come over Saturday morning to begin plans for the service. Then they each gave me a hug. Doe was the last to go. As we stood on the big veranda, watching Rudy pull up the drive in her vintage BMW, Doe put an arm around my shoulder.

"It's not your fault, Julia. It was just Martha's time. We'll all get there soon enough."

She gave my shoulders a squeeze and then descended the steps and climbed into her big Mercedes, leaving me to wonder why Martha's time had come so suddenly, and just when she happened to be eating my peach cobbler.

CHAPTER EIGHT

Once everyone had left, Libby, José and I began to clean up the dining room, allowing Crystal to return to the front desk. Since every moment of inaction threatened to reduce me to tears, the work acted as a diversion. April finished up whatever she was doing in the bakery and joined us. It was a good thing, too, because Libby was moving as if her feet were encased in cement. I finally asked her if she was feeling ill.

"No," she said, "I'm fine. I just feel badly, that's all. Mrs. Denton was very nice."

"Yes, she was," I said, a quick tear forming.

Libby's sentiments surprised me. She had come to work for me two years earlier after having lost all of her savings when the market crashed. As a retired obstetrics nurse, she was a disciplined worker, with one good-for-nothing son who had a gambling problem and lived in Las Vegas, of all places. I realized that while Libby was more comfortable living her life in the background, she was still affected by the comings and goings of the people around her. It made me resolve to find ways to include her more often in conversations and special events at the inn.

"Martha thought very highly of you," I said, patting her wrist. "She made special mention of that time you helped her get that gravy spot out of her jacket."

You would have thought I'd just told her that her own mother had died. Her hand flew to her mouth, and she ran from the room. I was left standing with my mouth open as if I'd just missed my cue on stage. April looked over at me, her hazel eyes dancing.

"You have such a nice way with people, you know that?"

"Very funny. But now it's just the three of us," I said, nodding toward José.

"No problem," she said. "José, can you help me move this?"

She pointed to another buffet she wanted to move up against the window, and José stepped in to help. While she did that, I pulled a beautiful antique Santa from a box and placed it in the center of the table to replace the missing candle arrangement. Then I turned to José.

"Can you bring over that small blanket chest from the storeroom?" I said. "I'll find some Christmas linens to drape out of the drawers, and we'll put it in the corner."

"Sure," he said. "What do you want me to do with the damaged buffet?"

"Take it to the warehouse. Mr. Garth can work on it when he gets back from vacation. By the way," I said, stopping him. "I bought a table last week from…from…Martha." As soon as I said her name, a sob caught in my throat and I had to pause. I placed my hand on my chest and counted to five. "Anyway," I said with difficulty, "I had arranged that you would pick it up tomorrow so that Mr. Garth could get started on it before he leaves. But now…well, I'm going to call Martha's daughter tonight to find out what she'd like to do about the memorial service. I'll ask her about picking up the table."

"I'm sorry about your friend," José said with a solemn nod. "She seemed like a nice lady."

He rolled the buffet out on a dolly as an elderly woman approached us from the entryway, walking with a cane. It was one of our single guests–a Mrs. Devonshire, another octogenarian.

"Hello, Mrs. Devonshire. Can I help you?"

"I was just wondering what happened," she said tentatively, leaning on her cane. "I was napping earlier and thought I heard sirens."

"A friend was here for the book club, and…well…we think she had a heart attack."

I stopped because I wasn't sure what else to say. Mrs. Devonshire's eyes grew wide.

"Oh, I'm so sorry," she said with feeling. "Will she be okay?"

"No, I'm afraid not," I replied, my throat tightening again. "She was in her seventies, and was taking heart medication, so…"

She began nodding, as if this was a subject she was all too familiar with. "Well, I'm very sorry for you. It's hard to lose our friends as we get older."

She patted my arm as if we shared this in common. I inwardly cringed as she left and glanced into the mirror that hung on the wall opposite me. What stared back was a healthy-looking woman who was sixty-three, with short, auburn hair, good cheek bones, brown eyes and a heart-shaped mouth. Not bad. At 5'2", Graham used to call me, "pretty and petite." But as I contemplated the beginning folds of skin at my neck, I thought that maybe I needed to have one of those lifts advertised on TV.

I turned to find April grinning at me. We're only three months apart in age.

"What are you smiling at?"

"You," she said. "Don't worry. We both have a long way to go before we're in Mrs. Devonshire's age bracket."

It was late afternoon by the time we finished and guests began returning from their daytime outings. I decided to inform them about Martha as they returned, so they wouldn't hear it from either Mr. Stillwater or Mrs. Devonshire. Martha's daughter, Emily, called just after six o'clock.

"Oh, Emily," I said. "I'm so sorry. I was going to call you later. I thought you'd be asleep."

"I can't sleep. I'm just devastated," she said, choking back sobs. "I don't understand how this could have happened."

"We're all in shock," I said. "If it's any consolation, she was laughing at a joke…she was enjoying herself."

I knew that was weak, but I didn't know what else to say. I just hoped Emily wouldn't ask me to tell her the joke.

"I just talked to her last weekend," Emily said, breaking down in sobs. "She said she'd just been to the doctor and got a good report. She didn't complain about anything, except that she was thinking of quitting the shelter."

"What?" I suddenly became alert. "I didn't know that."

"I thought she loved it there," Emily said, sniffling. "But she said it wasn't what she thought it would be."

She got very quiet for a moment, and then she said, "By the way, Julia, I told the police I wanted to have an autopsy done.

They weren't going to do one. They said for people her age and with her health problems, there was no reason."

"So why did you ask for one?"

"Because she wanted it."

"What do you mean?" My heart began to race as I realized something about this conversation was very wrong.

"I don't know," Emily said, sniffling. "But I think she knew she was going to die. She told me last weekend that if anything happened to her within the next few weeks I should make sure they do an autopsy immediately." This revelation ratcheted up her emotions and she began to gulp air. "Why, Julia? Why would she ask for such a thing?"

These last words came out in a screech as she broke down in tears again. I felt the adrenaline flowing through my own body as I strained to understand Martha's last request.

"I…I don't know, Emily," I said, having trouble breathing.

"I just feel…" Emily tried to continue but stopped. "I just feel that if I'd been there…"

"You couldn't have done anything, Emily," I said, quickly. "None of us could. There wasn't even time to say goodbye."

She sighed on the other end of the phone, trying to control her emotions. "I agreed to pay for the autopsy, and I'm paying extra to have them do it right away. It's what she wanted. We have a flight into SeaTac at 8:30 Sunday night. I'll stop over at the inn on Monday. I know you volunteer in the morning, so I'll come by in the afternoon."

"Emily, one more thing," I said, stopping her. "This may not be the right time, so you tell me if it isn't. But I bought your mother's drop-leaf table last week and was supposed to pick it up tomorrow. It's paid for and I have a receipt. Mr. Garth is all set up to begin refinishing it before he goes on vacation. Would it be okay if I had José pick it up?"

"Of course," she said. "Mom told me she was going to let you have it. That was my grandma's table, you know. I'd love to see it restored to its original beauty. Will you keep it or sell it?"

I cringed, realizing that I hadn't really decided. I kept very few of the things I acquired, since selling the antiques was a business. But before I realized it, I was saying, "Of course, I'm keeping it. I have the perfect place in my apartment."

I swear I felt my nose growing.

"I'm glad," she said with relief.

"Do you want us to wait until you get here to plan a memorial service?"

"No," she said quietly. "You ladies were her best friends. I know whatever you plan will be exactly what she would have wanted. In fact, when you pick up the table, you might want to pull out some of the family photos. She kept them in a box I made when I was in Girl Scouts."

This brought on a new round of tears, and I felt a sob catch in my chest.

"I think that's a great idea. Blair is really creative. I bet she'd be willing to put together a video. How about if I reserve the church for Wednesday afternoon? That way, you'll have some time to be involved in the planning when you get here."

"That sounds good," she said. "Thank you, Julia. I know this has to be hard on you, too. I'll talk to you Monday."

After we hung up, April joined me in the main kitchen for a light supper. I told her about Martha telling Emily to ask for an autopsy. April's eyes opened wide.

"That's weird. What do you suppose she meant?"

"I have no idea. But now I'm wondering if it's somehow connected to how she was acting today. You should have seen her, April. She couldn't sit still."

April shrugged. "Well, I suppose we'll find out more after the autopsy. But how horrible for Emily. It's tough enough to lose your mother, but it's a lot worse if you think there's something suspicious going on."

April was my greatest comfort. We'd met in an English class at the University of Washington when we were both freshmen. Halfway through the class, April had warned me one day that the professor was going to give us a pop quiz. It was just one of those things she seemed to always know. We'd been friends ever since. Having her with me as I struggled to process Martha's death was like being wrapped in a warm quilt; it didn't make the pain go away, but it helped me through it.

By 7:30, she gave me a hug and headed out to the carriage house to close up and head home. As I watched her hurry across the back drive, I silently prayed that when the time came, I would go before April. She was the best friend I had in the world. I'd lost my mother recently and now two close friends. Losing April was something I didn't think I could survive.

CHAPTER NINE

As much as I love the inn, my apartment is where I feel most at home. I have purposely filled it with the things that mean the most to me: working antique clocks, colorful Tiffany lamps, old steamer chests, woven area rugs, assorted whimsical tea pots, and my *Wizard of Oz* collectibles scattered around to make me smile.

By the time I retired to my apartment that night it was almost eight o'clock. My back ached and my energy level had bottomed out. I made a cup of hot cocoa and collapsed into my favorite overstuffed arm chair in front of the gas fireplace with a dog on each side. An original framed *Wizard of Oz* movie poster of Dorothy, the Tin Man, the Scarecrow and the Lion hung above the fireplace. I tried to relax, but I was more than a little curious as to what had happened to Martha, not just her death, but her life in general. Something had changed over the past couple of weeks. She had missed two days at the shelter and one of our book club meetings. I had noticed it. But life had gotten in the way, and I hadn't stopped to question why my friend was retreating.

I felt a pang of guilt when I realized that I'd overlooked Martha, perhaps when she'd needed me most. And now I wondered if her question about going to confession had been her inadequate way of reaching out for help. Then there were her comments to Emily about quitting the shelter and asking for an autopsy. What in the world could all of that mean?

No sooner had those questions arisen in my mind than my cell phone rang. I was surprised to hear my ex-husband's voice on the other end.

"You okay?" he said. "I heard about Martha."

"God, do you have your minions and spies everywhere?"

"No, of course not," Graham said. "But when someone dies in the home of my ex-wife, people tend to tell me about it. I'm sorry to hear about Martha. She was a good friend to you."

"Yes, she was," I said, tears threatening again.

"Do they know yet how she died?"

"I thought maybe you were calling to tell me."

"No," he said, that deep resonant voice still able to make my heart flutter. "I just…I just wanted to make sure you were okay. I figured Ellen's death was hard on you, and now this."

I sighed. "And my mother."

"And your mother, yes."

My mother had been a force in my life. Not always a good force, but a force nonetheless. Having been a smoker for many years, emphysema had finally confined her to a wheelchair, and she'd come to live with me. And although we'd shared a challenging relationship while she was alive—meaning that she criticized every decision I made while I mostly ignored her—I missed her.

"Too much death," I said, taking off my reading glasses to rub my eyes.

"You have had your share. How are *you* feeling?"

I perked up at that. "I'm fine."

I'd had a lump removed from my left breast over the summer. Fortunately, it had been benign. But Graham's mother had died from breast cancer, so he was hyper-sensitive about it. "Thanks for asking, though." I felt warmth rise to my face at the thought that Graham actually cared enough to ask.

"Well, keep me informed…on everything," he said. "You have my number."

"Yes. Thanks, Graham. Say hello to Kitty."

I heard him chuckle on the other end of the phone as he said, "I will."

We hung up and I relaxed back into the chair, stroking Mickey's head and thinking about Graham and Kitty. I'd met Graham just after college when I became involved in state Democratic politics. He was an up-and-coming attorney in a Seattle law firm and already planning his foray into politics. He

60

was handsome, intelligent, and charming. How could I resist?

We'd married and moved to Mercer Island. When it became clear after several years that I wasn't going to get pregnant, we adopted a baby girl from China. Angela was twenty-six now and had followed in her father's footsteps, landing a job in the King County Prosecuting Attorney's office in Seattle.

Once Graham became a state senator, he spent most of his time in Olympia. One day, out of the blue, he bought me the old St. Claire home to create, "…the business of your dreams." It was just a huge, empty, dilapidated building that required extensive work. Once we'd turned it into the elaborate building it was today, he asked for a divorce and then quickly agreed to give me the inn as part of the divorce settlement. I suspected it was meant as a consolation prize of sorts. A few years later, he switched parties and won the election as a Republican, moving into the Governor's mansion in Olympia, sans me.

Kitty, his thirty-something wife, was cute, blond, and looked spectacular in a pencil skirt and three-inch heels. While that may sound odd coming from the ex-wife, I can't deny what's true. While I was at peace with the divorce, the thought of him in bed with that perfect size 0 was enough to make me contemplate lap-band surgery, even if I was only fifteen pounds overweight. After all, it wasn't the sex that I missed. It was the size 0, which I hadn't seen since, well, ever.

As much as I hated to admit it, Kitty was the right wife for Graham at this point in his career. I had no doubt he had higher aspirations than governor of a Western state. He had his eye on a cabinet position in the White House, perhaps the White House itself. Well, good luck with that, I thought. I had no desire to live in Washington D.C.

As I got up to reheat my remaining hot chocolate, a cold spot near the sink stopped me. I glanced around. Cold spots were common at the inn. If you've never experienced one, it's like walking past an open refrigerator door. A group of paranormal investigators had spent two days at the inn early in the year and had explained that a cold spot usually meant a ghost was near. I thought this cold spot might be Elizabeth.

Elizabeth had appeared to me several times in my apartment, and even freaked me out by appearing next to me in the car on one occasion. So she could move around. Her image was never distinct, but rather a kind of milky haze that was always accompanied by the scent of Rose water. I felt she was somewhat protective of me. The time she appeared in the car, she spun the wheel only moments before I would have hit a deer. Another time, she left a message written in the steam on my bathroom mirror warning me about faulty wiring in a kitchen outlet that could have caused a fire.

Encountering one of the ghosts never ceased to elevate my heart rate. But it seemed that I was alone now, so I turned and put my mug into the microwave. I watched the cup turn round and round, allowing my mind to wander back to what Doe had said about the deaths of two of our friends in less than a year.

Ellen's suicide in May had bothered me enough that a few days after her funeral I had driven up to the spot where she'd flown off the cliff. I sat there in my own car trying to picture my friend sitting in hers just before she gunned the engine and left this world behind. What could she have been thinking? Martha had never been convinced that Ellen was depressed enough to kill herself. And yet, as I looked at the skid marks that day, the evidence didn't lie.

And now Martha had fallen face first into her dessert, dying in a way that could only be thought of as a bad joke. I assumed the coroner would discover it had been her heart. But as I took out my hot chocolate and leaned against the counter to take a sip, I realized that Martha hadn't grabbed her chest. Nor had she seemed in any kind of pain. It appeared as if she'd choked on something and then pitched forward. This realization began to explain the need for an autopsy, and I was suddenly glad her daughter had asked for it.

I finished my drink, got into my pajamas and climbed into bed, kicking Mickey, who had burrowed to the foot of the bed. Dachshunds were bred to go underground to hunt badgers and are well-known for their near obsession for burrowing under things. Mickey would often scuttle all the way to my feet, while Minnie usually snuggled under a soft throw I kept on top of the bed. I could see Minnie's little copper nose poking out from under the throw and reached out and gave it a rub.

I was just about to grab a book, when I was startled by the faint jingle of a song. My ears perked up. I hadn't heard that song for over a year. It was *Rock Around the Clock,* the ringtone version played on my mother's cell phone.

I climbed out of bed and hurried into the front room, trying to remember where I'd put my mother's phone after she died. I followed the sounds and finally found the gaudy, pink device buried in a drawer. As soon as I picked it up, the ringing stopped. Frustrated, I clicked the button that would show me who had called, but the screen was dead. I snapped it shut and dropped it back into the drawer, surprised the battery had worked at all. When I felt a hand on my shoulder, I spun around with a gasp. The smell of roses flooded my nostrils.

The faint, misty image of a woman floated behind me, the kitchen counter behind her visible through the haze. Elizabeth was dressed as I always saw her, in a white nightgown, with her long, dark braid draped over one shoulder. Right now her blurred and faintly transparent features were drawn into a grief-stricken mask, and she held her hand over her heart.

"What?" I said, my heart thumping. "Are you worried about Martha?"

She nodded, the hazy outline of her face distorted, her dark eyes bulging and creepy.

"Yes, Martha was a good woman," I said. "It was her heart, I think."

Elizabeth shook her head vehemently, sending out renewed bursts of rose scent. She then put her hand to her transparent throat and squeezed, lolling her tongue as if she were being strangled. You can imagine my reaction. Well, maybe you can't. After all, you probably have never had the pleasure of talking with a ghost, especially one that was attempting to strangle itself. It made me queasy.

"What do you mean?" I asked, hoping she would stop.

Just then, Mickey lunged at the sliding glass door and barked at something outside.

"Mickey!" I snapped at him.

And then Elizabeth was gone.

Damn!

I glanced around again, but her image had disappeared, along with her signature perfume. It was if she'd never been there at all.

I stomped over to the door and closed the curtain, all the while chastising Mickey. He let the curtain fall over his back, while he kept his long snout pressed up against the window, staring intently at some unknown monster in the dark.

CHAPTER TEN

It was Friday morning, the day after Martha died, when I woke to a light dusting of snow. The white crystals sat lightly on pine branches and layered the backyard like a fine mist of powdered sugar. I let the dogs out, watching them leave little footprints everywhere they padded. Mickey ran immediately to the gate, sniffing along the bottom.

"C'mon, Mickey. Let's get going."

When they'd finished, I went back to the bedroom and threw on a turtleneck and jeans and my favorite sterling silver hoop earrings.

"Okay, let's get you guys fed," I said, leading them to the kitchen.

While Minnie waited patiently for her food, Mickey liked to spin in circles. Why, I don't know. Every dog has a personality, and this was part of his.

As I got ready to place his bowl on the floor, I commanded, "Mickey, stop!"

He stopped abruptly, listing to one side, a bit dizzy.

After feeding the dogs, I closed up the apartment and the three of us headed for the main kitchen. As we moved through the breakfast room, I uncovered Ahab's cage and greeted him.

"Good morning, Ahab."

"Good morning, Sunshine," he replied, dancing back and forth on his perch.

I filled his food tray and then joined April in the kitchen as she was finishing up a batch of cinnamon rolls for breakfast.

We designed our kitchen for warmth and efficiency. It would be considered cottage style, with white cabinetry, black marble countertops, a large center island with a farmhouse sink and white bead board on three sides. Barn red fabric accent lights hang over the center island, while a small butcher block table and four wooden chairs sit off to one side under a Victorian chandelier. The whole room is accented with red and white checked curtains and a small red and blue floral wall paper. An old fireplace sits at the far end of the room, now only used for ambience. Above it hangs white-washed wooden letters that spell out, "Good Eats." All in all, the kitchen could be the centerfold of *House and Garden Magazine.* Add the smell of cinnamon and sugar on that particular morning, and when I entered, I felt like I had just walked into heaven.

The dogs bustled in, their nails clicking on the hardwood floor. April looked down and said, "Hello, wieners." They greeted her and then hurried over to a cupboard in the corner where I kept a box of toys. I pulled out a couple of squeaker toys and left them to fight over them while I joined April at the center island.

"Need help?"

April smiled at me. She was the most efficient person I know, and cinnamon rolls were one of her specialties. From what I could see, she had everything under control. But I needed something to do to keep me from thinking about Martha.

"Why don't you beat a bunch of eggs for a frittata?" she said.

I grabbed a carton of eggs and a bowl and started cracking, while the dogs chased each other around the kitchen, stealing and re-stealing each other's toys. Their repetitive growls served as background noise to our conversation.

"It wasn't your fault, you know," April said over her shoulder.

It's spooky how she could always read my mind.

"I know," I said. "But first my mother, then Ellen, and now Martha. They say death comes in threes…I hope that means we're done for a while."

"I think the rule of threes only applies to famous people," she laughed. "Not everyday people like you and me."

She flashed her brilliant smile at me, making her hazel eyes dance. She'd told me once that those hazel eyes had come from her great, great granddaddy who had been a Civil War soldier. Since she'd never told me anything else about him, I suspected it might be a tall tale. Still, hazel eyes against her black skin and black hair was a stunning combination.

"Well, who knows?" I said reflectively, as I whipped eggs and milk into a frothy lather, "I just know I'm tired of going to unexpected funerals."

"Your mother was ninety-three and confined to a wheelchair. I don't think she falls into the unexpected category."

"Maybe. But the women in our family are known for their longevity. My grandmother toppled over on her way to get a second piece of cake at her ninety-eighth birthday party. I plan to beat her by at least two years."

April chuckled as Minnie barked in the background. I glanced over as she lunged for the nasty-looking skunk held firmly in Mickey's mouth.

"Good for you," April said. "I plan to slide gracefully to the other side when I'm ready, and then spend my days in heaven eating whatever I want and never gaining a pound."

I laughed, but in truth, I was the one who carried the extra weight on my small frame. April was taller than me by three inches and merely round where she needed to be.

"Wait a minute," I said, lifting my eyes to hers. "I don't want you dying before me. You'll come back to haunt me for sure."

"No, I won't," she said, shaking her head.

Her hair was braided into corn rows, accented with beads that rattled whenever she shook her head.

"I have no desire to become one of those spirits that can't seem to get on with their heavenly life. When I'm gone, I'm gone."

Her comment made me think of Elizabeth's appearance the night before, but I decided not to say anything.

"We'll see," I said skeptically.

Breakfast was available for the guests between 7:30 and 9:30 each morning. We currently had six adults (two couples and two singles) and two young children staying with us. Another guest had left early that morning. When April and I brought in the chafing dish, the Pedersons were already there with their five-year old son and two-year old daughter. The kids were talking to Ahab. He was always a hit with the guests, especially the children. I helped April finish setting out the cinnamon rolls, coffee, and juice. Then I wandered over to the dining room with a cup of coffee and a cinnamon roll to be alone.

As I looked at the room, it looked as if nothing had ever happened the day before. It was as if Martha's death had been erased. It made me sad to think we would never watch her face twist into stubborn confusion, or hear her whine again about something she didn't want to do. While she was alive, those traits had driven me crazy at times. That's why I privately thought of her as the Whiner, a name I'd never shared with her, of course. But now, I realized those traits had only added depth to a very kind and generous woman, who may have never really had a chance to discover who she was.

I reflected on my fondness for applying nicknames to my friends. Perhaps it was because for most of my life, my mother had called *me* by a nickname. It was something I equated with affection, even if the nickname wasn't so flattering, like the Whiner. Of course there were the outliers, like the one I used for Dana Finkle, my nemesis, whose nickname I couldn't express in polite company.

Once the sun was up, I forced myself to get busy. I called the church to reserve the chapel and meeting room for a Wednesday afternoon service and reception. I also called the shelter to let them know what happened to Martha and texted back and forth with the girls to set up a meeting for Saturday morning.

It was quarter to nine when Matt Samson, the Program Director from the shelter, called.

"Julia," he said, "I heard about Martha. I'm so sorry. We'll really miss her."

My throat swelled so that it felt as if I'd swallowed something large that wouldn't pass.

"Yes," I said. "We're devastated."

"Well, I'm calling because we're short a volunteer this morning. I was hoping you could come in, but I'd completely understand if you can't."

I allowed my eyes to linger on a picture that sat on my desk of the book club from the year before. It included both Ellen and Martha. What would they want me to do? I breathed in, filling my lungs in an effort to revive my spirit. It didn't work.

"I'll come in," I said. "I think Martha would want me to."

"Thanks, Julia. We've got a couple of new kids, including a

little boy who doesn't speak English. I already spoke to Rosa and she said she could help."

"That would be great," I said. "I'll be there in about forty minutes."

My decision to go to the shelter gave me a sense of purpose and helped lift my spirits, if only briefly. It was almost nine-thirty when I made it to the shelter in Ballard. The shelter was located in a converted auto parts store and housed only women and children. Its twenty-five rooms were almost always full. The numbers of children varied, ranging from infants to sixteen years of age, but never any boys over the age of twelve. The school-aged children attended school during the week, but there were always a few toddlers and infants to look after, and that was usually my job.

I checked in with Matt. He was a good-natured young man with a master's degree in social work. As the only man on the premises, he also provided the only male role model for the kids.

"Good morning," he greeted me. "Thanks so much for coming in."

"Well, I thought this would give me something positive to do."

My heart started to race as I thought about Martha again. I had to keep my emotions in check. I hoped that being out among other people would help.

"I understand," Matt said. "The kids will be happy to see you. The new little boy is named Julio. He's four and cries a lot, and we have twin five-year old girls, Sierra and Samantha. They're already in the children's room with Emma. I think Rosa is in her bedroom."

Rosa was one of the homeless women who had been found living on the streets several months earlier. She was eight and a half months pregnant and spoke only Spanish, and so would often help with the Spanish-speaking children. A few of the other women were from the Ukraine. Since the shelter's executive director, Faye Kramer, spoke both Spanish and Ukrainian, I figured social services sent those cases to her.

I put my purse in a locker just outside the office and went to Rosa's room and knocked. No one answered, so I started for the playroom, thinking she might already be with the children. As I turned a corner, I passed the chapel, a small room set aside for private contemplation. It wasn't much bigger than a small bedroom, but had a water feature that helped make it quiet and peaceful. As I passed, I heard the muffled sound of someone crying. Tears weren't a stranger in the shelter, where all the women were down on their luck. But this sounded different—more desperate, more frightened.

I took a chance and quietly pushed the door open and found Rosa sitting with her back to me. She was rocking back and forth, sobbing uncontrollably and muttering to herself. I came up behind her and was about to place a hand on her shoulder when I heard what she was saying.

"No tome a mi bebé. No tome a mi bebé. Please, please, you can't take my baby girl," she sobbed, saying the last phrase in English.

When my hand landed on her shoulder, she jumped up and spun around as if I'd dropped an electric wire on her.

"No. Please don't take my baby!" she cried out. "Don't…!"

"Rosa. Rosa," I said, holding my hands up in a gesture of peace. "No one is going to take your baby. It's just me…Julia."

She started gulping air and wiping her eyes.

"Come and sit down," I said, directing her back to the chair. "Please, no one is going to hurt you."

She hesitated and then returned to the bench and sat down, her hands shaking as she placed them on her enormous belly. I sat down next to her and kept a reassuring hand on her back. She used a sleeve to wipe her nose, and I got up and grabbed the box of Kleenex that was kept on the front table.

"Here, Rosa," I said, handing it to her.

She took it gratefully and pulled out a handful. "Gracias," she said.

That's when it hit me. A minute earlier, she'd been speaking English.

"Rosa, you can speak English," I said, somewhat astonished.

Again, she pulled away from me as if I was going to hit her.

"No, no, Miss Julia. Please, don't tell anyone." She began to cry desperately again. "Please," she pleaded. "No one knows. Please. They're going to take my baby." She crumpled into the seat sobbing again.

I quickly put my arm around her shoulders and pulled her to me.

"Shush, I won't say anything, Rosa. I'm your friend. Why are you so frightened? Who do you think is going to take your baby?"

Her entire body was shaking now, and I realized that whatever her fear, it was real. I had to wait patiently for the sobbing to subside before she could speak.

"I heard them talking...outside. I was in...washing my...uh..." she gestured to her legs.

"Your pants? You were in the laundry."

"Si. They whisper outside. I hear through...uh...hole in the wall."

"You mean the vent? Near the dryer?"

"Si. Si," she said quietly, sniffling and wiping her nose. "No one knows I speak English. My father teach me when I was little. I hear many things. But I no say anything because I have no one. But now I hear my name, and I..." She stopped and started to cry again. "Please Miss Julia," she said, tears streaming down her face. "Help me."

Rosa probably wasn't more than nineteen or twenty. She had dark eyes, long dark hair, high cheek bones, and a long, slender neck. She was very pretty, but I often found her with a troubled look on her face. In my ignorance, I'd always chalked it up to being homeless, figuring that would put a frown on anyone's face. But perhaps I'd been wrong. If she was hiding something, it had to make her anxious. As she rocked back and forth, seemingly inconsolable, I tried to quiet her again.

"Rosa, who are the people you're talking about? Who did you hear outside the laundry?"

"The woman who bring me here," she sobbed. "I thought she is my friend."

"You mean the person who brought you to the shelter?"

She shook her head. "No. From Venezuela. I live in a small town there. Very poor. I met a girl at...hmmm...the doc-tor office. I was very scared. I was pregnant; I have no family now...no money. She said she know people who help girls like me...bring them to America to have babies and start new life. But she say they no take girls who speak English. So, I lie. But now...I..." She stopped, unable to go on.

Just then the door swung open and Faye Kramer, the Executive Director, stepped in. We both jumped up and turned to face her.

"Ms. Applegate," she said sternly. Then, seeing Rosa, she stopped. "Oh, I'm sorry, is something wrong?"

Faye was in her late thirties, tall and thin, with hard edges everywhere. She and I got along fine, but I thought she was in the wrong job. While Matt seemed to truly care about the women who stayed at the shelter, Faye sometimes reminded me of Nurse Ratchet.

"Um…no, I think Rosa's hormones are just a little out of whack." I felt my nose grow again as I lied. I ushered Rosa toward the door. "I was just trying to give her some comfort, but she doesn't understand what I'm trying to say. Maybe you could explain to her that she should just go back to her room and lie down. I can handle the kids today."

"Um…sure," Faye said, looking from me to Rosa.

She turned to Rosa and said something to her in Spanish. Rosa nodded and hurried from the room. Faye turned to me.

"Did something happen?" Faye asked.

"No…uh, like I said, I just found her crying. I used to do that when I was pregnant. Just cried for no reason. Your hormones are just completely screwed up. It's like you're on an emotional roller coaster."

Faye crinkled her eyebrows. "I thought you adopted your daughter."

I paused for a moment in reflection. I wasn't very good at lying.

"I had a miscarriage," I said. "A long time ago."

"I'm sorry," she said, without much emotion. "My sister lost a baby. She's never gotten over it."

"No," I said, faltering. "You don't."

"Well, thank you for coming in. Now you'd better get going—the children are waiting."

"Of course, I'll go right now."

I continued down the hall, feeling the adrenaline thrum though my veins. Lying wasn't really in my nature. I was more inclined to say exactly what I thought minus the social filters. But I was halfway down the hall before I realized that Faye hadn't said a word about Martha's death. Typical.

When I got to the room, three toddlers were sitting quietly at a low table, coloring. Emma, one of the staff members, was watching them. When I came in, she nodded and left. I spent the next hour and a half entertaining the twin girls and Julio, the four-year old boy, who had no idea what I said to him. But as long as he had crayons and a truck to play with, he seemed happy enough.

By eleven-thirty, it was time for lunch, and after that, the children would take a nap. I walked them to the kitchen, where Emma had peanut butter and jelly sandwiches waiting. They sat at small tables to eat their meal and then she took them off for nap time. At this point in the day, I sometimes helped with laundry or cleaning up in the kitchen before I left at twelve or twelve-thirty. I decided to check out the laundry, since Rosa had mentioned it. It was at the back of the building, off to one side.

No one was in there, but I found a couple of bags of dirty linen, so I went ahead and threw them into the big washing machine and got it started. Then I glanced around to make sure I was still alone, before leaning around the dryer to where the dryer hose was attached to a vent. Above the dryer hose was a louvered vent, and I assumed it was through this that Rosa had overheard the conversation. As I stood there, the sound of a car pulling into the parking lot outside came through loud and clear, and I thought that if someone stopped right next to the vent, it probably wouldn't be too difficult to hear what they had to say.

I left the laundry and stopped in to see Rosa before heading home to tell her I'd be back on Monday. She was resting quietly, but clearly still nervous. Since she was several weeks from her delivery date, I assured her that she would be safe until then, and that over the weekend, I would come up with some ideas to help her.

I returned to the inn with mixed feelings. On the one hand, by going to the shelter, I had been successful in replacing the immediacy of Martha's death with something positive. On the other hand, I was worried now about Rosa and had no idea whether her fears were credible. I also didn't know how I could help.

I had to step in and help change sheets and clean rooms, since Libby wasn't feeling well. After that, I paid some bills and began returning phone calls. Then Sybil showed up.

"How'r you doin', Julia?" she said in her usual twang. "I've been thinking about you aawl day."

She was leaning over the reception counter, peering into the office at me. I was sitting in an old swivel desk chair and rolled back and turned to her.

"I'm fine. I was going to stop by later, anyway. I have to go over to Martha's to pick up a table she sold me. I thought I had a key to her house, but I can't find it. Do you still have one?"

She reached into the pocket of her wide-leg pants and pulled out an enormous ring of keys.

"Here you go," she said, quickly pressing a button and releasing a single key. "This is the key to Martha's back door. You'll have to jiggle it a little. I'll need it back tomorrow, though. I'm taking care of her fish."

She laid the key on the desk and I got up to get it.

"I also have to find a box of pictures Emily wants me to get for the service. Any idea where I'd find that?"

"In the extra bedroom," she said without a second thought. "There's a box of pictures in the bookcase. By the way, Julia, you look awfully tired. If those circles under your eyes get any deeper, you'll have to…"

The front door knob clicked loudly behind her, and the door swung open, making us both look around to the empty space. No one was there. She snapped her big head back to me.

"I have to go!" she said. She turned and skidded past the open door as if it might reach out and grab her.

I went to close the door, feeling a cold spot hover around my knees.

"Thank you, Chloe," I said with a smile. "Now, go outside and play."

The cold spot evaporated, and I closed the door.

The rest of the day passed uneventfully, and guests began returning from their outings around three o'clock. I put out the pitcher of lemonade and some cookies and grabbed a handful, realizing that I'd forgotten to eat lunch.

José stopped in a few minutes before five o'clock and asked what time I wanted to go pick up the table. My eyes burned and my back ached, so I pleaded for some extra time. We agreed on six-thirty, allowing me to join April in the main kitchen for dinner.

At six-forty, José and I backed up to Martha's garage in the van. Since it was December, it was already dark, leaving her driveway illuminated only by the streetlight. Her house was a large two-story contemporary home that looked out over the inn to the lake beyond. José opened the back of the van and lowered the lift, while I slipped through the side gate to the back door. José found me there a few minutes later, still jiggling the key as Sybil had instructed. The back door light was out, making it difficult to even find the key hole.

"Let me try, Ms. Applegate."

José must have the eyes of a cat, because with a quick flick of the wrist, he had the door open. The two of us stepped inside and I closed the door. I turned on the lights, releasing a wave of nostalgia as I pictured Martha moving from the stainless steel countertop, to the double-wide stainless steel refrigerator. This had been her domain.

We moved into the den, where a giant aquarium bubbled against one wall, and the gate-leg table sat against another wall with its flaps down. The table was covered with a burgundy silk tablecloth that draped to the floor. The hand-blown glass bowls that usually sat on top had been set aside, and a sob caught in my throat at the thought that Martha had been getting the table ready for me.

I threw off the tablecloth, releasing a momentary whiff of men's cologne. I thought it was José and turned, thinking he was behind me. But he was on the other side of the big room, opening the garage door. He quickly joined me, and we each grabbed an end and moved the table into the garage. I stopped and turned on the garage light, illuminating Martha's red Volvo, sitting there all alone. A momentary sadness enveloped me. I shook it off and punched the button to open the garage door so that we could carry out to the van and put it onto the lift.

"Listen, I have to go back in and find a box of pictures for her memorial service," I said. "I'll be right back."

I returned to the den, feeling Martha in every color choice, book selection, and piece of artwork. She *had* been very artistic. Although her personal style had been understated, her home was filled with bold colors and modern sculptures—a strange juxtaposition to her introverted personality.

I crossed through the kitchen and into the darkened hallway, which led to the back bedroom. The faint aroma of men's cologne again made the hairs on the back of my neck stand on end. Then a noise made me stop at the open bedroom door and listen. I was just turning to look back up the hallway, when someone flew out of the bedroom across the hall and slammed into me, shoving me into the darkened room. I cried out as I toppled over a chair, hit my elbow on something hard, and landed on one knee at the end of the bed. The door banged shut behind me. Disoriented, I pushed myself up and stumbled back through the dark to the door, my banged-up body parts on fire.

My right hand searched the wall to find the light switch, and I flicked it on. With trembling fingers, I tried the door and found it unlocked. I yanked it open. No one was there. I hurried into the hallway and back into the kitchen, my heart racing. José came in from the garage, took one look at me and stopped.

"What's the matter?" he said.

"I…someone…someone attacked me."

My eyes drifted towards the kitchen door, which now stood wide open.

The sound of a car engine had José spinning around and sprinting back through the garage and down the driveway. I followed him as quickly as I could and got to the back of the van just as he came trudging back up the hill, his dark features set in a grim expression.

"Who was it?" I asked, my heart thumping.

"I don't know. Are you all right?" His face was creased with concern.

"Yes, but whoever it was pushed me into the study and closed the door," I said, rubbing my elbow. "What do you think they were doing here?"

He gave me a grave look, the moonlight glinting off the gold cross around his neck. "Maybe people know the house is empty."

My eyes grew wide. "You mean someone was here to steal something?"

He shrugged, stuffing his hands into his leather jacket. "Maybe. There's plenty of stuff to steal," he said, glancing up at the big home. Then he turned to me with caution in his eyes. "This place is like a big invitation. There were a couple of cars parked at the curb when we got here. A sweet vintage mustang. A Toyota Camry. And a black Hummer. The Hummer's gone."

José knew his cars. He and a group of friends restored old cars and showed them on the weekends.

"Why don't you stay here? I'll lock up," he said.

"No, I'll go with you," I said, glancing around nervously. "I still have to get the box of pictures."

As we returned to the house, I pondered how much José might know about things like break-ins. He was in his mid-twenties and was taking night classes at one of the local community colleges to become a computer graphics designer. His artwork was very good. So good that I'd asked him to re-do our website. But I suspected that he'd had a hard life.

From what little I knew his mother had died from an overdose of heroin when he was only thirteen, forcing him to live with an abusive uncle. It was one of the reasons I suspected he kept in such good shape. He was only about five-foot eight, but hard as a rock and with a black belt in some kind of martial arts.

José had said once that growing up on the streets of L.A. had taught him a lot. I'd been too embarrassed at the time to ask him what that meant. Had he been in a gang? Or been a car thief? Truth was, I just didn't know. But the tattoo on his upper arm told me that at one time he may have belonged to a gang. He didn't belong to one now, I was sure of it. But he needed to be able to protect himself, especially since he was gay, a fact I hadn't yet shared with any of the girls. After all, they'd be heartbroken. But the girls would be far more forgiving than former gang members if they ever found out.

He accompanied me to the bedroom, where I found the box of pictures right where Sybil had said they would be.

"Now what?" I said to him.

He looked at me a bit skeptically, but then said, "You call the police."

CHAPTER ELEVEN

By the next morning, my elbow was black and blue and my knee smarted, but otherwise, I felt fine. The police had come to Martha's home and taken our report, but weren't encouraging about finding the intruder. So I chalked it up to bad timing and tried to forget about it—at least for the moment.

It was Saturday, and April wouldn't be into work until just before noon because she was visiting her husband, Stewart, in a Bellevue dementia care facility. And Mr. Garth was due to arrive around lunch time to begin refinishing Martha's table.

The girls weren't scheduled to arrive until ten o'clock, so I recruited José to help me switch out a few of the antique pieces of furniture that hadn't sold—an antique apothecary chest was replaced with a turn-of-the-century baker's cabinet, a cherry tea table with a Chinese painted drop-leaf table, and a Queen Anne chair for a Victorian wicker rocker. Then I took the time to change out vintage linens, antique spice cans, and glassware displayed on an old kitchen hutch that sat in the breakfast room—all accented with delicate silk roses that sat in various tea cups. Coming to the St. Claire Inn was never the same experience twice—just the way I liked it.

Blair and Rudy arrived at ten o'clock to discuss the memorial service, but Doe had called to say that she would be late because she was stuck in an emergency union meeting at work. It was all over the news that the drivers in her waste management company were close to a strike over health benefits.

Before we settled down to discuss the memorial service, I had to fill Blair and Rudy in on events. I repeated what Emily had told me about the autopsy and then dropped the bomb about the intruder at Martha's home the night before. You would have thought I'd just announced aliens had landed. Both Blair and Rudy came out of their seats.

"What?" Rudy said.

"Are you okay?" Blair ran over to me.

I was still standing, giving Blair the opportunity to take me by the arm and plant me in the newly appointed Queen Anne chair as if I was a stroke victim.

"I'm fine," I said. "I wasn't hurt. He just scared the hell out of me."

"Did you call the police?" Rudy asked.

"Yes. But they didn't have much to say. It could be someone who broke into Martha's home, knowing that it's empty now."

"Doesn't matter," Rudy said. "That's awful. I'm glad José was with you."

"Me, too," I said. "But now I'm worried about why Martha thought it would be necessary to order an autopsy if something happened to her. Don't you find that strange?"

"Maybe she didn't trust the care she was getting at the clinic," Blair said, sitting back down. "Wasn't she seeing a new doctor?"

Rudy leaned back and crossed one leg over the other. "Or maybe she just knew it was her time. My aunt was like that. She actually went and picked out a coffin a week before she had an aneurism and died."

"I don't know," I said. "It seems more ominous to me."

"Maybe that's just your mystery-reader mind talking," Blair said, smiling. "I'll bet they'll just find it was her heart."

"By the way," Rudy spoke up. "I'll be happy to write the obituary."

"Thanks," I said, glad to change the subject. "Don't forget to include her years on the church council."

"And when she won that gardening contest," Blair said to Rudy.

"Has anyone thought about music for the reception?" Rudy asked. "I was thinking we could ask little Jenny Rayburn to play her harp. Martha was pretty close to their family, wasn't she?"

"Yes, she was," I said, feeling my energy rise. "That's a great idea. Blair, any chance you'd be willing to take the pictures and get that neighbor kid to help you put together a short video?"

"Sure," she said in an uncharacteristically quiet voice. "I hope there are pictures from the Mardi Gras dinner last year. Martha absolutely loved that feathered mask she wore."

The doorbell interrupted us, and I left the girls to find three men standing on the front porch. One was dressed in a suit and tie, about my age, with thick gray hair, and tall enough that I had to crane my neck up to look into his wide-set, brown eyes.

"I'm Detective Franks," he said, looking down at me. "I'm with the Mercer Island Police Department."

Two police officers in uniform stood behind him. I invited them in, feeling a flutter of disquiet in my chest. I led them past a curious Crystal into the living room and introduced the other women.

"Mrs. Applegate," Detective Franks began, "you probably know that Mrs. Denton's daughter asked for an autopsy. In fact, she paid to have it done right away. We just got the results back and the coroner has determined that she didn't die from a heart attack." He stopped and looked around the room as if to gauge our response. "I'm sorry to say that your friend was poisoned."

He fixed a steady gaze in my direction; I felt suddenly faint.

"Poisoned?" I exhaled, feeling behind me for a chair. "How in the world was she poisoned?"

He took my arm and guided me into the nearest chair.

"She ingested a large dose of arsenic."

"My peach cobbler?" I asked with a hand to my chest. "That was the last thing she ate."

"The coroner couldn't tell the origin," Detective Franks said. "There were a number of things found in her stomach, including your peach cobbler. But there was also chocolate and a few other things."

"The chocolate mints?" I said in surprise.

"I don't know," he replied. "But however she got the arsenic, the coroner says she had to have ingested a good dose of it just before she died. Can you tell me what time she arrived here on Thursday?"

I glanced at Rudy and Blair before answering. They both looked like they'd been turned to stone. I wasn't even sure Blair was breathing.

"Well, we had just finished lunch," I said, struggling to remember. "And we had sat down to discuss our book list. So, I'd say around one-thirty."

I nodded to the other women for confirmation. Rudy finally spoke up.

"I...think that's about right," she said, her facial muscles coming back to life. "Martha was behaving oddly, though. She didn't seem ill. I mean, she wasn't frothing at the mouth or anything."

I thought that was an unfortunate image to create under the circumstances, but Detective Franks seemed to ignore it.

"What do you mean she was behaving oddly?"

"She was distracted," Blair said, "and kept wandering around opening drawers and cupboards as if she were looking for something. We all commented on it."

"Yes, Detective," I said. "It seemed almost as if there was something else on her mind. But she didn't seem ill in the slightest. She wasn't out of breath or sweating. I even asked her if she was feeling okay, and she said yes. She just took a bite of the cobbler and suddenly..." I stopped, unable to verbalize her death. The detective just nodded.

"I see," he said. "That doesn't sound like what the coroner described. He felt certain that she swallowed a large dose of the poison only moments before she died. Is there any chance she found it in one of the drawers she was looking through?"

"I don't think so. To my knowledge we don't have anything like that in the inn."

My gaze swept across the room as I spoke, stopping when I noticed that the cut glass candy dish on the coffee table in front of Rudy had begun to move. We were all used to this at the inn, and I suspected it was Chloe again. I shot a glance back to Detective Franks, but he was reaching into his pocket for something and didn't notice. So I flashed a warning look at Rudy and nodded toward the dish. She followed my lead and reached out and grabbed it.

"Well," Detective Franks continued, pulling a piece of paper from his inside pocket. "This may just be an accident, but we have a search warrant to see if we can find out where the arsenic came from."

He produced the requisite piece of paper, which I didn't even bother to read.

"Please, go ahead," I said with a wave of my hand, glancing back to the table.

Rudy was still holding the dish tightly in her hand, a false look of complacency on her face.

"Can you tell me which rooms she went into?"

"Yes," I said, turning back to the detective. "Um…the kitchen and the dining room." I pointed to the other rooms.

"And she went several times to the reception desk," Rudy added, gesturing with her free hand.

"That's right," I agreed with a burst of enthusiasm.

Detective Franks gave me a curious look, apologized for the inconvenience, and then he and the other officers fanned out to look for arsenic.

"Oh, my God!" Blair exclaimed, leaning forward to peer after them. "This is like right out of CSI."

"Don't be absurd! There's got to be a perfectly simple explanation," Rudy said. Then she looked at me. "And tell Chloe that now is not the time to play games." She returned the dish to the center of the table and let it go.

Doe appeared at the doorway dressed in a black pantsuit and carrying her black leather bag big enough to hold a microwave. For some reason, Doe always looked like she was an attorney on her way to court, carrying enough business folders and paper to sink a battle ship.

"A perfectly simple explanation for what?" she asked, looking behind her at the officer going through the reception desk. "What's going on? And why are the police here again?"

We explained about the arsenic. Doe collapsed onto the piano bench, dropping the bag to the floor with a loud thud. I sensed by her reaction that even the union bosses didn't have that effect on her.

"Where the heck would Martha get arsenic?"

"Not only that," Blair said, "but did you know that Julia was attacked last night?"

Doe turned to me, her dark eyebrows arched high.

"What?"

I explained again about being attacked at Martha's the night before. Then I finished with, "Martha also told Emily last weekend that if something were to happen to her within the next couple of weeks, to order an autopsy."

"Oh, my God," Doe exhaled softly.

"And now they've found poison in Martha's system," Rudy said.

"Oh my God," Doe said again. "What's going on?"

A banging cupboard rendered us silent as we listened to the officers searching through the kitchen. I couldn't help but contemplate what the guests might think if one of them were to come back suddenly and find a police car in the driveway. I contemplated going to get Libby or April, but it wasn't long before I heard one of officers say, "Detective, take a look at this."

We all stood up and moved like a chain gang into the breakfast room. Rudy put a reassuring hand on my shoulder. Detective Franks reappeared through the swinging kitchen door, surprised to find us all standing there. He was holding something that made my heart stop.

"Mrs. Applegate, we found this. You don't suppose this could be where Mrs. Denton got the chocolate, do you?"

In one hand, he held the gift box I had wrapped for Senator Pesante the weekend before. The wrapping and bow had been torn part way off, and the top of the box was gone.

"Go ahead, make my day," Ahab squawked from the corner.

Detective Franks turned in Ahab's direction and then back to me. I glanced inside the box and felt sick to my stomach. Three chunks of fudge were missing, along with half of the fourth piece.

"That shouldn't be open," I said, gesturing to the box. "It was a gift for Senator Pesante. There was a reception scheduled here in his honor on Wednesday evening. I was going to give it to him then, but he cancelled and I never had the chance."

He looked at me suspiciously. "And you didn't open it later?"

"No. I was going to give it to him at the Governor's New Year's Eve party instead."

"What about the fudge?" he asked.

"I have probably ten more boxes behind the desk. We sell it." I pointed to the reception desk.

"But someone had to have opened it." He looked around the

83

room.

"It wasn't any of us," Rudy said.

Blair and Doe shook their heads and murmured their denials.

"So, you don't know who opened the box?"

He had a deep, melodic voice, which for some reason made me blush. *Stop it!* I thought. Focus on the issue at hand.

"No. I swear," I said, turning away to avoid his gaze.

"I swear on my mother's life," Ahab said in the background.

We all ignored him.

"What about Libby?" Rudy asked.

"No," I shook my head. "She knew it was for the Senator. I can't imagine who opened it, other than…" I turned back to the detective. "When I went in to get the peach cobbler that day, I almost bumped into Martha coming out of the kitchen licking her fingers. I thought she'd just stuck her finger into Doe's curry or my cobbler."

Detective Franks was watching me closely, his very sexy eyes squinted in thought.

"This was in the pantry. Why would she have been in there?"

"I don't know." I felt the blush deepen as I realized that I could have somehow been responsible for Martha's death.

"We told you," Rudy said, stepping forward. "Martha couldn't seem to sit still. She kept moving around, opening drawers and looking through the baker's rack."

"That's right, Detective," Doe said. "She wouldn't even sit with us as we discussed our book list. And I saw her come out of the kitchen, just like Julia said."

"Was she eating fudge?"

We all looked at each other, but frankly, we were stumped.

"I don't know," I said. "She was late that day and said she'd missed lunch and wanted something sweet. So, I gave her some mints. Later, I thought she'd poked her finger into something in the kitchen. I didn't really pay that much attention, and the girls… well, the girls weren't really paying *any* attention to her by that time."

"Why is that?" he said.

Rudy and Doe shifted uncomfortably, clearly not willing to admit to how José had held their attention. Blair, on the other hand, stepped forward.

"Oh, for heaven's sake, we were preoccupied watching Julia's maintenance man put up Christmas lights." She flung her hair back as if she dared anyone to comment. "We may be over fifty, but we're not dead."

"Frankly, my dear, I don't' give a damn!" Ahab murmured in the background.

All three officers smiled, whether at Ahab or Blair I wasn't sure, but then quickly tried to hide their amusement. Detective Franks turned to me with a lingering glint of humor in his eyes. As the humor faded, he said, "If this fudge was poisoned and was meant for Senator Pesante, it changes things. I think you'll need to come down to the police station to answer some questions."

A ringing in my ears made me lean into him as if I hadn't heard what he'd said. "Excuse me?"

"It'll be okay, Julia." Rudy took my arm again. "Let's get your purse."

Rudy started to steer me out of the room, but Detective Franks stopped her.

"Actually, you'll all need to come to the station. I take it you were all here at the time your friend died?"

Everyone nodded, although reluctantly.

"Well, you may be able to provide important information." He turned to the other officers. "Officers Barnes and Stimson can take two of you," he said. "Mrs. Applegate and one other can come with me. I'll send a couple of officers out to speak to your staff as well," he said. "We should also take the rest of the fudge with us...just in case."

My throat tightened at the thought that we were under suspicion.

"Okay," I squeaked. "If you think that's necessary. I'll let everyone know to stick around."

I pulled out my cell phone to call April at the care center, and then called Crystal over from the front desk where she was huddled in the corner watching us like a scared rabbit. She helped the officers gather up the rest of the fudge and helped them put everything into a box. I didn't help. I couldn't. I just stood there in stunned silence, like a toy whose battery had died. Libby clumped down the stairs a few minutes later. She hadn't fixed her hair and looked paler than normal, but I told her to stick around, and to let

José know to stay available for the police later that afternoon.

I'm not sure how to describe my feelings about being driven away from my home in a police car. I suppose I should have been humiliated. I knew that not only were the closest neighbors already on their phones reporting the gossip, but Mrs. Devonshire had returned and was standing on the front porch as we departed, leaning on her cane, her eyes narrowed in consternation. But I was more concerned with the fact that Martha might have been poisoned by something found in my pantry. Since I knew I hadn't supplied the poison myself, it meant that someone else had tampered with it. And that thought made my blood run cold.

CHAPTER TWELVE

The room they took me to at the Mercer Island Police Department was nothing more than an empty conference room with a blackboard, a couple of dented file cabinets, and a water cooler that dripped constantly. Rudy, Doe and Blair were taken...I don't know...somewhere else. I sat alone for a good twenty minutes listening to that annoying drip, drip, drip before the door finally opened and Detective Franks entered carrying a file folder. He was followed by my daughter, whom I'd called before leaving the inn. Detective Franks looked at me uncomfortably, as if apologizing for the inconvenience.

"Don't say a word, Mom," Angela said with a raised hand.

Angela was dressed in a severe-looking black suit, with a white, crew-necked blouse. She called it her uniform. Her long coal-black hair was pulled back into a pony tail, and she had on the pearl stud earrings I'd given her for her birthday. All-in-all, not a bad look if you needed to sign a contract or plan a funeral.

She took the chair next to me and threw a legal pad on the table as she sat down. Detective Franks sat across from me with a manila folder held loosely in his hands. He snuck a glance or two at me and then shifted his eyes back to the table. My muscles tightened, and I turned to Angela for comfort. But those dark eyes of hers seemed to peer out from a face cast in stone. She'd told me more than once that the women who worked in the criminal justice system had to prove they could compete with the men. However, I thought a little smile would go a long way in breaking the ice with Detective Franks.

"Thanks for coming, Sweetheart," I murmured. "I didn't know if I'd need an attorney."

"I'm not here as your attorney, Mom," she stated flatly. "I'm a prosecutor. I'm just sitting in to make sure you don't hang yourself."

That smarted. But I suppose I'd earned it over the years. I'd once gone to court to argue a parking ticket only to openly admit that I had, in fact, parked illegally—but just for a moment. The judge wasn't sympathetic. And when Angela was in the third grade, I inadvertently told her entire class that Santa Claus had been created merely as an advertising ploy back in the 1930s. Children left the room in tears, and the teacher asked me to leave. Angela had a long memory.

As the three of us sat fidgeting, waiting for what I didn't know, the door opened and a tall drink of water walked in.

The newcomer was probably in his early thirties and over six feet of chiseled masculinity that moved with the kind of fluid grace saved for athletes. His eyes were blue and he wore his brown hair short and a little spikey at the top. And damn if he didn't have a squared-off, dimpled chin, covered in the five o'clock shadow so popular nowadays. The moment he entered the room the energy noticeably changed, and I felt my temperature rise. I swallowed, more anxious now than ever. Who *was* this guy?

"Mrs. Applegate," he said, extending his hand. "I'm Detective Sergeant Abrams."

I shook his hand, and then he pulled out the chair to sit down, resting his forearms on the table. The rolled-up sleeves of his white shirt revealed a tattoo on the underside of his right arm of a five-pointed star with the word RANGER stenciled across it.

"Nice to meet you." I exhaled slowly to control my breathing.

"This is Angela Applegate," Detective Franks said, nodding toward my daughter. "She's with the prosecuting attorney's office. She's also Mrs. Applegate's daughter."

Detective Abrams shifted his gaze to Angela. "I know the counselor," he said, his blue eyes dancing.

I turned abruptly to Angela who had dropped her gaze to her notepad. My mouth fell open a notch, as I became acutely aware of the heat rising off her body.

"Nice to see you again, Detective," she said to the table. "I didn't realize you had left the Seattle PD."

I glanced back over at the two detectives. Detective Franks was really quite nice-looking. But sitting next to Detective Abrams, who exuded a kind of celebrity sex appeal, he could have been an accountant with a bunch of pens stuck in his pocket protector. I studied my daughter a moment, and then glanced back to Detective Abrams, who was now smiling to himself.

"I've been here about five months," he said. "Better clientele." He shifted his gaze to me. "Well, let's begin."

I swallowed a hard ball of spit.

"Mrs. Applegate," he began, "We understand Senator Pesante was scheduled to attend a reception at the inn this week."

"That's right."

"How well do you know the senator?"

My mind really does have a tendency to wander, so I had to force myself to leave the intrigue with my daughter behind and focus my attention on the situation at hand.

"Um...not well at all, really," I said, sneaking a glance at Detective Franks. "He's one of the newer state senators. I've only met him once or twice. I was asked to host the reception by the chairman of the state Democratic party."

"The senator was in town to promote raising the minimum wage," Detective Abrams said.

"That was my understanding."

"That isn't too popular with the business community, I take it." He studied me closely.

"That's probably why he's on the road promoting it," I said with a shrug.

My answer was accented with a little more sarcasm than I intended. Detective Abrams narrowed those blue eyes in response.

"Mrs. Applegate," Detective Franks cut in. "Are you aware that Senator Pesante is planning to challenge your husband for the governor's seat in the next primary election?"

I switched my attention to the nice-looking Detective Franks.

"Ex-husband," I said. "Yes, I'd heard that through some of my Democratic friends. If you're implying that I would try to poison someone just because they planned to run against my ex-husband, then there would be any number of people dead already."

"Correction," Angela said. "It's only a rumor at this point that Senator Pesante will run for governor. And, Mom, cool it with the sarcasm," she whispered to me.

Detective Abrams' blue eyes shifted to Angela. "We're not in court, counselor." He affirmed this quietly, his gaze resting on her a moment longer than necessary.

"I recognize that, Detective," she said, stiffening. "But I don't want my mother to admit to actually knowing something that isn't a fact."

He nodded towards Detective Franks. "Let's allow Detective Franks to continue."

His patronizing tone made Angela clench her jaw.

Detective Franks picked up again. "So, Mrs. Applegate, you would have no reason to harm the senator?"

"Of course not."

"But you said that if you wanted to kill someone who might challenge your husband in a political race…"

"Ex-husband," I said again.

"Ex-husband… then several people would be dead already. I see here that you had a run-in with the former state attorney general three years ago, just after he won the Republican primary to run against your husband."

"I didn't have a 'run-in' with Attorney General Williams," I countered. "I ran into him—literally—with my car."

I stopped, realizing how incriminating that sounded.

"My mother was cleared of any charges in that case," Angela said. "It was an accident and all part of the public record."

"Your mother drove her car *into* the attorney general," Detective Abrams snapped.

"There's a simple explanation," I said, gaining the floor again in my defense. "I had just gotten my Miata and had only driven it a few times. He was standing right in front of my car down at the Capitol building, talking to Representative Olsen. I thought I'd put the car in reverse, when actually it was still in drive. And, yes, I may have driven into him, but he survived with only a few scrapes and bruises."

I said this as if *not* putting him in a wheel chair was a solid defense.

"So, you weren't taking your anger out on him?" Detective Franks said, prodding me.

"For heaven's sake, no." I dismissed his question with a wave of my hand. "I like John. He's a good man, but he didn't have a chance in hell of winning against my husband. Everyone knew that."

"Are you saying you'd only go after someone who might have a chance of beating your husband? Like Senator Pesante?"

Detective Frank's gaze bored into me, as if he was hoping to break my will. Suddenly, those beautiful brown eyes didn't look so nice anymore.

"Of course not." I turned to Angela for help. "Isn't that leading the witness, or something?"

Angela shook her head in exasperation. "No, Mom, you're not in court." She turned to Detective Franks. "Detective," she said to him in her most belittling tone. "You know you're only fishing. Let's get on with trying to find out some real information."

I glanced at Detective Abrams who couldn't hide a quick smile as he got up to get a glass of water. He was enjoying this. I was beginning to question my initial thoughts about him, too. He returned to his seat with a paper cup filled with water.

"I believe there was another incident at a dinner party with the mayor of Mercer Island. Something having to do with a burrito?" he said, unable to hide a smile as he raised the cup to take a drink.

Again with the smile. This guy should never play poker. I leaned forward this time.

"I was trying to make a point," I said. "And threw the burrito…"

"By mistake!" Angela chimed in.

"Really?" Detective Abrams said. "How does one throw a burrito at someone by mistake?"

I sat back, my adrenaline pumping.

"We were at a library meeting arguing about tearing down the old library," I said, containing my anger. "He was *for* it. I was *against* it. That was an historical building and meant a lot to people here. You haven't been here long enough to know that, I suppose. The menu that night was Mexican food, and I was holding a burrito wrapped in tin foil, like this…"

I have spent my entire life wishing I could turn back the clock on certain moments. Like when I offered to show a bunch of elementary school girls how to make pot stickers and set off the school's fire alarm with my electric wok, forcing everyone to leave the building. I was about to do it again. I picked up Detective Abram's pen.

"I was trying to make an important point to the Mayor and gestured at him with the burrito like this..."

I snapped the pen at Detective Abrams, just like I had with the burrito. And just like the burrito, the pen flew out of its casing and hit him in the face, just under his left eye. Angela's hand went to her mouth. Detective Franks flinched to the side. And there was a long moment of silence as Detective Abrams reached up to touch the spot where the pen had nicked him.

"I'm so sorry," I said, starting to get up. "I...I really am sort of accident prone."

"Mother, shut up!" Angela pushed me back into my seat. "Just put your hands in your lap."

She said this as if she were talking to a four-year old.

I put the rest of the pen down and put my hands in my lap as she instructed. I thought perhaps this wasn't going as well as it could.

"Detective, where are you going with this?" Angela asked, clearly enjoying his discomfort.

"I thought it was obvious," Detective Abrams replied, rubbing his cheek where a red spot had appeared. "Your mother has a reputation for accosting people. Especially those she disagrees with."

"I don't accost people!"

"Really?" he said with raised eyebrows.

"Mrs. Applegate, you have a lawsuit filed against you by a...a Mrs. Dana Finkle," Detective Franks said, referring to the file.

"She's a putz!"

"Mother!" Angela warned.

"Well, she is."

"It says here that you purposely threw a cup of scalding hot tea at her, giving her second-degree burns."

"No. I tripped and spilled the tea all over her very broad back," I said. "It was hard to miss under the circumstances, but I didn't throw anything."

92

"Mother, be careful."

"Look, she owns an antique store downtown and can't stand the fact that I not only own the St. Claire Inn, but I have a thriving antique business on top of it."

"So?" Detective Abrams said.

"You must know by now that there are pretty strict zoning laws here, and I had to get special permission to have both the bakery and the antique business on my property. Anyway, Dana Finkle doesn't like it and keeps going to the City Council asking them to rescind my permit. Then, of course, there's the fact that my peach cobbler beat her sour cream rhubarb pie at the Summer Celebration last year."

"So, explain the hot tea," Detective Franks said, getting back into the conversation.

"I had just been to Starbuck's and Dana stopped me on my way out. She began arguing with me about computer access at the library—I'm on the library board. It was last summer, and I was wearing flats. I had stepped in some bubble gum on the sidewalk, and when she turned to walk away, I took a step and came right out of my shoe. It threw me off balance and the tea went flying. That's it. I apologized, but she just couldn't pass up the opportunity to get back at me and filed a lawsuit."

Both the detectives stared at me expressionless.

Count to three.

"Okay…well then, back to Senator Pesante," Detective Franks said with a slight shake of his head. "Mrs. Applegate, do you know anyone who would want to harm Senator Pesante?"

"No."

"Anyone have a grudge against Mrs. Denton?" Detective Abrams asked.

"Martha? No." Switching suddenly to Martha had taken me by surprise. "She was one of the sweetest, most… unassuming people I know." My heart was thumping, and I began to pick up speed. "Martha was an introvert. Half the time you would forget she was even in the room. Why would someone want to kill someone you could so easily forget?" I inhaled. "Um…that didn't come out right."

"Mom, just slow down." Angela put a reassuring hand on my arm.

I leaned into Detective Abrams, now feeling desperate to defend my friend.

"Martha was a wonderful woman, Detective," I said, tears coming to my eyes. "She was kind and generous, and never asked for attention. No, I can't imagine anyone wanting to kill her."

"How did *you* get along with Mrs. Denton?"

It was Detective Franks this time, changing the subject.

"We were good friends."

"You never argued?"

I had to think about that. "No. Actually, we never did."

"Did she ever say anything that made you suspicious or concerned in any way?" he said.

I paused now, wondering if I should mention Martha's comment about going to confession. Detective Abrams was watching me closely.

"What?" he said.

"It may not be important, but a couple of weeks ago Martha asked me if taking something that wasn't yours was a sin if it was for the greater good. I don't know what she was talking about, but then she asked me if I'd been to confession lately."

Detective Abrams exchanged a look with Angela.

"I wondered at the time if she was thinking of going to see Father Bentley. That's our priest. But for the life of me, I couldn't figure out why. To my knowledge, Martha didn't lie, or cheat, and I certainly can't picture her stealing anything. So I don't know why she asked."

Detective Franks took a note. "We'll talk with Father Bentley. So you don't know of anyone who might have had a problem with her? A neighbor, perhaps?"

I shook my head vehemently. "No. I'm telling you…Martha didn't have enemies. But you know it was Martha who instructed her daughter to order that autopsy."

Both detectives looked up at me.

"What?" Detective Abrams asked.

I told him what Emily had said about ordering an autopsy. When I'd finished, Detective Abrams looked thoughtful. In fact, he was chewing on the end of the broken pen.

"We'll talk with her daughter again," he said with a nod.

"Look, unless you're going to charge my mother with something," Angela said, "I think she's told you all she knows."

She started to get up. Detective Franks stood as well. Detective Abrams stayed where he was.

"Your mother isn't under suspicion, Ms. Applegate," he said, looking up at her. "We're just trying to get to the facts."

"Just the facts, ma'am. Is that it?" Angela eyes flashed. "Call me when you have some real information."

This time, Detective Abrams got up, towering over everyone else in the room.

"I'll do that. I still have your number," he said to Angela.

Well, that raised all sorts of alarms in my head. But he wasn't finished.

"And don't go out of town, Mrs. Applegate," he said, turning to me. "We may need to speak with you again. And please... do me a favor," he said with a lift to his eyebrows. "Remind me never to go skeet shooting with you."

÷

A frigid breeze met us when we left the building, and it looked like it could snow again at any moment. I pulled up the collar of my coat and then placed a gloved hand on Angela's arm as she started for her car.

"Just a minute, young lady."

"I've got to get back, Mom. Can I drop you at the inn?"

"Not so fast."

"What is it?" she said, drawing open her purse to look for something.

I have always known when Angela isn't telling the truth. She averts her eyes and busies herself with something else. When she was little, she would begin looking for toys. As she searched through her purse, I suddenly knew the truth.

"Oh my God! You're dating him!"

Angela blanched. "No," she said firmly. "We are *not* dating."

"Okay, you slept with him. So you can stop looking through your purse."

"No..." she said, hesitating when she found her lip gloss. "We're...look...after we finished that case last summer...you know, the young woman that was found out by Green Lake with her stomach ripped open... anyway, we'd spent so much time working together to build a case against the suspect, that when he was found dead we decided to have dinner together at my place to commiserate, and... well, one thing led to another, and..." She shrugged. "It was an accident," she said sheepishly.

"Angela, I've been to your apartment. Your bed doesn't sit anywhere near the kitchen, so it would be hard to have that sort of an *accident* before, during, or after dinner."

"Look," she said, forgetting the lip gloss. "I only saw him that one time. He'd been divorced for a year or so, but he was still really angry towards his ex-wife. I suspect that's why he took a job over here. I think he needed to get away. Anyway, he's an arrogant pig sometimes." She grimaced to emphasize her opinion. "And, then, there's Phil."

"Oh, for heaven's sake, get rid of Phil!"

Her eyes grew wide. Phil was her on-again, off-again boyfriend who really *was* an accountant.

"I can't just get rid of Phil."

"Sure you can. We get rid of all sorts of things in life we don't need anymore," I said. "Black and white TVs and single slice toasters! We just take them to Goodwill when we're done with them."

I didn't like Phil much. He was as boring as...well, an accountant with a pocket protector.

"I am *not* taking Phil to the Goodwill. And I don't need you telling me who to date. Now, do you need a ride home?"

I stuck out my lower lip. "No. I'll go back in and wait for the others."

When I suddenly remembered why we were there, I crumpled onto a bench like a deflated balloon.

"God, I can't believe this is happening, Angie. Who would want to kill Martha?"

Her face softened and she sat down next to me and put her hand on my arm. "It's going to be okay, Mom. We're going to figure this out."

A tear welled in my eye. "But they think I did it, Angela."

"No...well, yes they might think that right now. But you didn't, and we'll find out who did. Detective Abrams is very good, whatever I might think of him."

She tried to give me a reassuring smile, but came up short.

"I've really got to go, Mom. Can you get home okay?"

I pulled out my cell phone. "Yes, I'll call José to pick us up in the van when the others are done. You go along. And thanks, Honey."

She gave me a kiss on the cheek and hurried off. I went back inside and waited for the others. An hour later, José was dropping us off at the St. Claire's front door.

CHAPTER THIRTEEN

All the girls all left for afternoon appointments when we got back, promising to return that evening. A few guests were milling about, and they asked about the police cars that morning. By the time I was done explaining things, I was tired and starving. April had arrived and was out in the bakery, but I needed time to refuel before I filled her in on the day's events.

I had just heated up a polish sausage in the microwave and gotten out a bagel bun, when Sybil's voice cut through the silence.

"Yoo, hoo, Julia!"

She waltzed into the kitchen wearing a sweatshirt embroidered with the head of a moose, wearing a big red nose and holiday lights caught in its antlers. As the swinging kitchen door opened, Ahab mimicked her from the breakfast room, "Yoo, hoo, Julia!"

"Stupid bird," she said, glancing back at him with a frown. As the door closed, she said, "Anyway, what was that all about earlier? You simply muuust tell me. I wanted to come over this morning, but I was expecting the pest control people. And now I see that the police have been here, again. What in the wuuurld is goin' on?"

Since we all considered Sybil to be the biggest native pest to the island, it was all I could do to refrain from making a snide comment regarding the pest control company's inability to do its job.

"Slow down, Sybil," I said, putting my hand up like a crossing guard. "I've got to get something to eat. Do you want anything?"

I turned and opened the big double-door refrigerator to get some butter.

"Maybe just some coffee. I'll help myself."

She grabbed one of our wide-mouthed mugs and stepped back into the breakfast room where we kept a pot of coffee brewing all day. Meanwhile, I put butter on the bagel bun and got a pickle. Sybil was fifty-something and didn't work. While we were friendly, I didn't consider her a friend. She was just too much of an opinionated chatterbox. And after the day I'd had, I just wanted some peace and quiet.

As she returned with the coffee, Ahab sniped in his best Wicked Witch of the West imitation, "Going so soon? I wouldn't hear of it."

Sybil's lip curled into a snarl as the door closed, nearly bumping her from behind.

"Just ignore him," I said.

I removed the sausage from the microwave and sat at the table under the window to assemble my sandwich. Sybil sat across from me, cradling the hot mug of coffee between her overly large hands.

"Well," she began, "it must have been truly awful the other day, what with Martha dropping dead right in your own dining room."

I shot her a severe look.

"I'm sorry, Julia. That was insensitive. What I meant was that…well, it must have been hard. We all loved Martha. She was such a dear. Do you know what happened, yet? Did they say it was her heart? She was sooo good about eating right and taking her medication. I saw her out walking almost every day and…"

"It wasn't her heart," I said.

I took a deep breath, wondering how much I should say. On second thought, it didn't matter. Sybil was the neighborhood busybody and would find out anyway. I often thought she had every house bugged within a four mile radius.

"She was poisoned."

Sybil has very round, blue eyes and right then they looked like large marbles stuck into her head.

"Poisoned? How could that be? Oh my God!" She threw a hand to her chest, momentarily covering the moose's eyes. "How in the world could she be poisoned? People don't just get poisoned. I mean, you never hear of people getting poisoned. How could something like that happen?"

I sighed, knowing I couldn't avoid this. "They say it was arsenic, and they think she may have gotten it from my chocolate fudge."

There I said it. Sybil inhaled deeply enough to suck up the universe.

"Oh my God, I just mailed that box I bought from you to my mother!"

"Don't panic," I said. "They haven't even tested it, yet. But Martha ate some just before she died. Just tell your mother not to eat any before we know for sure," I said, fingering my sandwich.

The sausage kept sliding back and forth in the bun, making me press down to keep it in place.

"That's why we were with the police," I said, lifting the sandwich to my mouth. "They wanted to know what we knew, which wasn't very much."

I opened my mouth wide and bit down hard, anticipating a great burst of sausage flavor. Instead, the sausage flew out of the bun and across the table to hit the moose right between the eyes. It then fell into Sybil's coffee mug with a splash.

For a moment, even Sybil was speechless. She glanced down at her sweatshirt, which now oozed sausage grease and butter, and then used a finger to wipe a blob off the moose's big red nose.

"Oh my God, I'm so sorry," I sputtered. "I must have used too much butter." I put down the now empty bun.

I got up and grabbed some paper towels. I handed one to her and began to wipe up the spilled coffee. I eyed the sausage and scooped it up, tossing it into the trash. I was about to offer to get Sybil another cup of coffee, when one of the cupboard doors silently swung open. I deftly moved around the table and shut it and then removed the mug and put it into the sink. Now was not the time for Elizabeth or one of her dead children to play games.

"Let me get you another cup of coffee," I said, starting out of the room.

"No! I'm fine," Sybil said with restraint, wiping her hands on a paper towel. She stood up. "I just wanted to know how you were, Julia. I worry about you. You run this business all by yourself."

She often dismissed April as if she didn't exist. When I stiffened at her comment and opened my mouth to reply, she quickly corrected herself.

"Let's just say that you carry the bulk of the load. Anyway, maybe it's all too much. Maybe there was a mistake," she said, tossing the paper towel into the trash. "I saw on one of those CSI programs that just about everyone has some form of arsenic at home. Not me, mind you. But I suppose it's not such a stretch that either Martha picked it up somewhere around here," she said, waving her hands around the room as if arsenic might be sitting out in the open, "or you inadvertently used it in your fudge recipe."

"I did not use it in my fudge recipe," I said, bristling. "The police think that someone may have poisoned the fudge *after* it was put into the box, you know, the one I was going to give to Senator Pesante."

She stopped, her eyes growing huge again. "It was meant for Senator Pesante? I've told you before that politicians are not honest people, Julia."

I started to protest, but she held up a hand.

"I know, Julia, I always exclude Graham when I say that. But that's why people are always trying to kill politicians."

"No," I said, stopping her. "No, they're not, Sybil. Where do you get stuff like that? People aren't running around trying to kill politicians all the time. And we don't know yet if Senator Pesante was even the target. We don't really know what happened."

She shook her head. "Mark my words, Julia. It will have something to do with that Senator Pesante. And if it did, then our poor Martha was killed by mistake."

As I was about to respond, the cupboard door behind Sybil swung open and then slammed shut making us both jump. The moment was saved when April appeared through the back door.

"You're back," she said, coming in with a couple of loaves of bread in her hands. "Everything okay?" She noticed the surprised look on Sybil's face. "What's up?"

Sybil had turned towards the cupboards and began backing out of the kitchen. She was often the butt of ghostly humor at the inn, although why, I never knew. I thought that perhaps Elizabeth didn't like Sybil's banter any better than we did and would use whatever she had in her spiritual arsenal to hasten her departure. It usually worked.

"I'd better get going," Sybil said with a slight tremor to her voice. "And believe you me, I'm going straight home to call my mother," she said.

Slam! The cupboard did it again, forcing Sybil to turn and flee.

As she flew through the kitchen door, leaving it swinging behind her, Ahab squawked, "What we've got here is a failure to communicate...communicate...communicate."

"God, I hate that woman," April said after we heard the front door slam.

"She's not so bad," I said, chuckling. "I think most of the time Sybil's just lonely. Her husband pays no attention to her and has never said more than four words at a time in my presence."

"Maybe that's because he can't get more than four words into the conversation when Sybil is around," she said. "She *does* like to talk."

"Yes, and apparently she goes through people's drawers."

April raised her eyebrows. "Really? I thought we were always just being catty when we said things like that."

"Nope. Yesterday, she told me exactly where to the find box of pictures I needed for Martha's service."

"No kidding. Maybe she's been in here rifling through your drawers and that's why
Elizabeth doesn't like her," April said, smiling.

"I don't think our ghostly kids like her, either. Chloe sent her scrambling yesterday by opening the front door for her. You should have seen Sybil sidestep it to get out," I said, laughing as I returned to the refrigerator for another sausage.

"When you think about it," April said, leaning against the counter, "our ghosts are the perfect pest control. They're free, non-toxic, and safe around pets. Now, if only we could bottle and sell them."

I looked up and around me. "Hear that, Elizabeth. That was a compliment."

April laughed and turned to put the loaves of bread into the bread box.

"By the way, the Pedersons checked out. Libby still isn't feeling well, so Crystal and I turned the room. It's ready to go."

"Thanks," I said, throwing a second sausage into the microwave.

April looked over at me. "How did it go downtown?"

"Not great. Did they question you, too?"

"Yes, two officers were here when I got here," she said, leaning against the counter. "It wasn't pleasant, but I survived. Although I thought both Crystal and Libby were going to wilt under the scrutiny. How about you?"

"I survived, too, barely. But I want this to be over."

"Why don't you lie down after you finish eating? Crystal said she can stay late today, and I'll be in here making coffee cake for tomorrow's breakfast."

"Maybe," I said. "But the girls are coming back over this evening."

The microwave beeped, and I removed the sausage and returned to my seat. April came and sat down across from me.

"How was Stewart?"

She sighed and clasped her hands together on the table in front of her. "Today was a bad day," she said.

Her whole demeanor changed as the muscles around her mouth tensed, and her gaze dropped to the table.

"I took him some cinnamon rolls," she continued. "You know, they're his favorite. But he wouldn't even let me into the room. He got very confrontational and actually pushed me out."

A tear welled in her eye, and I reached out and grabbed her hand.

"I'm sorry, dear. You don't deserve that."

"He doesn't know any better," she said, shaking her head. "But he didn't even recognize me this morning. Erin was hoping he could be home for Christmas, but they don't think I'll be able to take him out at all anymore. They say it's just too risky. So, it looks like he's there for good."

April's daughter Erin lives in Bellingham, near enough to the Canadian border that she couldn't be much help. I didn't know much about the nether world of dementia, other than to know how hard it was on both of them when Stewart didn't recognize them. Besides that, it was costing April an arm and a leg to keep him in the swankiest care facility in Bellevue.

She reached into her jacket and pulled out a tissue to wipe her nose. As she did, a piece of paper fluttered to the table. I reached out for it, but April snatched it away.

"Sorry about that," she said, stuffing it back into her pocket.

Her abruptness took me by surprise and for a brief moment, I thought she was hiding something from me. But perhaps she was just feeling the strain of the past two days. After all, she may have felt under suspicion as well.

"Will you keep the house?" I asked quietly.

"For now," she said with a nod. "It keeps me close to him."

"You can always come and stay here, you know."

"I can still afford to stay in Bellevue," she said with a sour look.

"I know. I'd just love to have you closer to me, that's all."

"Well, let's see how it goes," she said, softening. "How are *you* doing? I mean, really?"

I allowed my hands to drop to the plate, momentarily forgetting the sandwich and the rumbling in my stomach.

"I can't stop thinking about Martha, and the fact that it may have been my fudge that killed her. But it couldn't have been a mistake. I mean, what would I mistake as arsenic? Sugar? Even if I had, we've used the leftover bag of sugar to fill the sugar containers on the breakfast tables. And no one has gotten sick or died. So I don't think it was my cooking, which means that someone must have poisoned the fudge intentionally."

"I never thought it was your fault, Julia. You're far too good a cook."

"Yes, but that would mean the poison would have had to have been injected into the box somehow, because the box was heat wrapped in plastic. And that means it really was murder."

I had trouble wrapping my head around that word.

"I know," she said quietly. "All of this is hard to believe. But give it some time. It will sort itself out."

I glanced at her, my expression hopeful. "What do you know?"

She smiled, her hazel eyes finally coming to life. "You know you give me much more credit than I deserve. It's not like I have a direct line to the other side. I don't actually *see* anything. I just get impressions, and I don't know anything about Martha's death."

"But you knew about it before I called over to the bakery the other day."

104

It hadn't even fazed me that when I'd called April to let her know about Martha that afternoon, she had merely said, *"I know. I'll be right over."*

"I only knew something had happened," she said. "Although it did feel as if someone had passed over."

"But maybe you have a sense of where this is all going."

She shrugged. "No. Other than it's not over."

"What do you mean?"

She took a deep breath and shook her head. "I'm not sure. But I think there is more hardship ahead. And some surprises," she said, pinching her lips.

"I don't want any more surprises."

She reached out and wrapped her hand around mine. "Don't worry, Julia. I also have a deep feeling that everything is going to be okay...with this anyway," she said with a sigh.

"What do you mean...with this?"

"Nothing," she said with a quick shake of her head, withdrawing her hand.

My cell phone rang. It was Angela.

"Hello, Honey," I said.

"Hi, Mom. I meant to ask you if you could watch Lucy for a few days. I'm having my hardwood floors refinished."

"Sure. Bring her over. The puppies will love it." Lucy was her enormous black and white Great Dane.

"Okay. It'll be tomorrow afternoon."

"Sounds good," I said.

"How are you doing, by the way?" she asked.

"I'm okay. April is here with me, and I'm just getting ready for a late lunch."

"Okay, I'll see you tomorrow. Thanks."

We hung up.

"That was Angela," I said to April. "I get to babysit Lucy."

April smiled. "Aw, a grandchild in the house."

"Very funny. But you won't be laughing when you're tripping over the little dogs and then slamming into the big one."

I lifted my sandwich again and pushed the sausage back into the bun, remembering the look on Sybil's face when the last sausage hit her in the chest. I stopped and glanced up at April.

"You might want to move."

CHAPTER FOURTEEN

I took April up on her suggestion and went to my apartment after eating to lie down for a few minutes. The girls were scheduled to arrive at six o'clock, when I thought I'd order a couple of pizzas. I stretched out on my bed, but I couldn't sleep. My mind was filled with questions. Finally, I got up and went to the computer to Google information about arsenic. I wanted to know how fast it worked and learned that apparently it worked quickly if you swallowed enough of it. Where the heck had Martha gotten arsenic if not from the fudge? She couldn't have eaten it before she arrived that afternoon, because it was a good forty minutes or so before she died. And she'd shown no signs of being ill beforehand.

In the end, I couldn't avoid concluding that the poison had to have been in the fudge—my fudge—and the guilt was nauseating. I'd once sent an entire dinner party home early with food poisoning because I'd used a tainted can of tuna. Had I somehow done something far worse this time?

I left the computer determined to find a way to relax. I grabbed my book and snuggled into my big chair with a puppy tucked in on each side of me, trying valiantly to lose myself in my mystery again. But thoughts of Martha's death and the person who had attacked me at her house kept invading the storyline. I finally closed the book and dropped my head back against the chair, gazing into the fireplace.

Martha had been my friend. She had died in my home, eating something I had made. It was too close for comfort. I had to do something. Until now I'd gone along with the Old Maids Club idea, joining in on the girls' singular adventures. But I hadn't had a chance yet to express my own. To be honest, I hadn't really known what to do. I already had everything I wanted. Up until now I thought that if I had a hidden desire, it probably wasn't much more important than finding the quintessential early American spittoon. And that wouldn't motivate anyone to join me.

But suddenly I realized there was something I wanted to do. In fact, there was something I needed to do. And I was ready to spring it on the group that night.

÷

As the big grandfather clock in the entryway chimed six, its rich tones rolling through the building like distant thunder, the girls began arriving as if on cue. The night was cold, bringing them out of their cars and through the front door in crisp, quick movements. Everyone was dressed accordingly - gloves, sweaters, and wool pants. As I surveyed Blair's long, belted sweater draped over slim black slacks and a pair of black riding boots, I lamented over my lifetime disappointment at being only 5' 2" and unable to pull off long skirts, leggings, or boots. I was comfortable in my stretch jeans, cable knit sweater and penny loafers, but still....

The fire drew everyone into the living room where I'd set out some light hors d'oeuvres and wine. As everyone settled in, I announced a change in plans.

"I thought maybe we could go down to the Mercerwood for dinner," I said. "Frankly, I could use a change of scenery."

I inadvertently glanced toward the dining room where Martha had died. My unspoken reference to that moment in time prompted everyone to agree.

"But let's have a glass of wine first and warm up," I said.

We used the time to exchange stories about our ordeal at the police station that morning. The enormity of Martha's death had flat-lined any enthusiasm for friendly banter, but Doe had brought the most recent issue of the *Mercer Island Reporter,* and she settled back to skim the headlines with a glass of Merlot. As she flipped through the pages, she suddenly sat up straight.

"Oh," she cooed. "It looks as if the fire department has decided to raise money by doing a calendar. Roger Wilson's son will pose for June." She looked up grinning. "Sign me up for June."

This news lifted everyone's spirits. Wilson owned the local gym, and his son, Skip, had worked there as a personal trainer until recently hired by the fire department. In all that time, Roger had never really needed to advertise for the gym, at least not for female members. I assumed June would be a popular month. Too bad it only had thirty days.

Doe kept flipping pages and then stopped again.

"Uh, oh!" she warned. "Here's a headline that won't make you happy. *Finkle Files Paperwork to Run for Mayor.*" She closed the paper. "You can't let her do that, Julia. You have to run against her."

"Dana Finkle?" Blair exclaimed. "Dana Finkle is an idiot. She can't be mayor."

"Oh, yes she can," Rudy said, grabbing a cracker. "She sits on the City Council. Why can't she be mayor?"

"And she's no idiot," I said to Blair.

"No, she's a crafty witch," Rudy said, layering a piece of cheese onto her cracker. "That woman would sell more than her soul to the devil if she thought it would get her what she wanted."

"Julia," Doe began, looking at me over her reading glasses.

I fiddled with the doily on the side table next to me, trying to ignore her.

"Julia! You have to run against her," Doe said.

"Why do I have to do it?" I was whining, but I couldn't help it. I'd thought about running for mayor, but had no desire to run against Dana Finkle "There are plenty of other people who could run against her and win," I said.

"Even I know that's not true," Blair said with a roll of her eyes.

She put her wine glass down next to a white octagonal bird house that sat on a stack of books and reached for a cracker.

"C'mon, Julia," Doe said, putting the paper down. "You're a member of the Library Board and you're a business owner."

"And your husband just happens to be Governor of the state," Blair added.

"Ex-husband," I said.

"Doesn't matter," she said. "You've legally slept with the most powerful man in the state of Washington. You have more intimate political knowledge than anyone else on this island."

"Yeah, you're a minor celebrity, you know," Rudy said, swallowing. "And fortunately, Graham is popular."

I sighed. "I don't know. I can't imagine surviving four years with Dana Finkle as mayor, but…"

"But what?" Blair said. "We'll help."

"Look," I started to object. "I have the inn, my antique business, my volunteering. Where would I find the time?"

"You're not going to run the city, silly," Doe said with a smirk. "The City Manager does that. You show up at events and smile a lot."

"You know you'd win," Blair said with confidence. "Most people can't stand Dana."

She emphasized her comment by popping the cracker in her mouth.

"But what about the lawsuit she filed against me? That can't look good."

"It's probably why she filed it," Rudy said, now munching on a bruschetta. "She probably figured it would keep you out of the race."

"The lawsuit is a joke," Blair said with a toss of her head. "Ignore it."

"I agree," Doe said. "And if she goes forward with it, it will make her look like a fool."

"But don't say anything yet," Rudy cautioned, holding up a finger. "The deadline for filing isn't until January. Let her think she's got this thing wrapped up. Then we'll file and blow her away."

"What do you mean, *we*?" I said.

They glanced at each other and then back at me.

"Well, you didn't think you'd be in this alone, did you? We're a team," Rudy said with a smile.

"And we're going to beat her ass," Blair said with a flair.

"This could be your adventure," Doe suggested. "We haven't done yours, yet. How about it?"

"No," I said, my heart rate picking up. "There's something else I want to do."

"What?" Doe asked, reaching for her wine. "What could be better than beating Dana Finkle?"

Everyone was staring at me and a prickly blush crept up my neck as I glanced from face to face.

"Wait a minute," Rudy held up her hand to stop me before I could say anything. "I hope it has nothing to do with baking or antique hunting."

"No, it's not hunting for antiques," I said with a petulant tone. "It's much more important than that."

I paused again, nervously tapping my fingers on my leg.

"Okay, here's the deal," I said, getting everyone's attention. "I want to solve Martha's murder."

I said it quickly and then held my breath.

Blair's mouth dropped open, while Rudy's and Doe's features froze in place. It felt like those stop-action cameras, where suddenly everyone is caught in mid-motion.

Count to three.

"You've got to be kidding!" Doe suddenly exclaimed, her face reanimating.

"First of all, no one has said conclusively that it *was* murder," Rudy said. "But even if it was, do you think just because you read mysteries, you could actually solve one?"

Her derisive tone stopped me.

"I don't know, but I have to try."

They continued to stare at me with dubious expressions.

"Look, I'm probably the prime suspect," I said. "I could be arrested at any moment. If that happens, I'm out of time."

"But you can hire a lawyer or a private investigator. Or just get Angela moving. That's what they get paid to do," Rudy said, throwing up her hands and looking to the others for support.

"I'm with Julia on this one," a familiar voice said, rising above the rest.

April stood at the doorway with her feet apart and her hands stuffed into her apron. I felt a flood of relief at her entrance. Doe sat back, while Rudy leaned onto the arm of the sofa.

"You do realize," Rudy began, directing her comment to April, "that none of us knows the first thing about sleuthing or solving a murder?"

"I know," April replied. "But it's not rocket science. And we have resources we can call upon that the police don't have." She looked at me. "For instance, what about that guy you know who teaches a class in becoming a private investigator at the community college?"

I cringed. "Noooo... not him. Remember, he tried to get me to go out with him. He's just too weird. He actually carries rubber gloves in his pocket wherever he goes, just in case."

"Ewww," Blair said, wrinkling her nose.

"Seems to me, you can't be too picky right now," April said, looking at me over her glasses.

"This could also be dangerous," Doe said.

As a CEO, Doe only made decisions after careful consideration, and she was reminding us to be careful. She looked back and forth between us.

"No matter who the target was, if this really was murder, then someone out there is a killer. We can't forget that."

"I doubt anyone has forgotten that," April said to her. She came into the room and sat on the piano bench. "But life is short, and I for one don't really like having it yank me around. Remember that I was also questioned by the police. And they weren't too polite about it, seeing as I do most of the cooking around here. I would assume that anyone working here is as much a suspect as Julia."

My fear had been validated. April felt as if she was under the heavy weight of suspicion. I wondered then about Libby, José, and Crystal.

"She's right, you know," I said. "Technically, we're all under suspicion right now."

"So, how would we go about this?" Rudy asked, her skepticism waning. "I mean, what could we do that the police can't?"

I could tell that Rudy was coming around. She would go along with this if we could tell her how it could logically be done.

"Wait a minute," Blair said, holding up a hand. "Before we get knee-deep into crime-solving, I'm hungry. If we're going to dinner, let's go. We can talk about it there." She eyed April. "And you're coming with us," she said. "Minus the apron, of course."

April grimaced momentarily. "Uh...I have a ton of stuff to do here," she said, starting to rise.

"No way," Blair said. "This is my treat and everyone is going."

"No, Blair," I said, standing. "It was my idea to…"

"Forget it, Julia," she stopped me as she stood up. "I want to hear how we're going to solve Martha's murder, and I'm willing to pay for it. So, let's go."

Everyone laughed, even April, and headed for the door.

The restaurant was nearly full, but a large table got up to leave just as we arrived. We were seated near the kitchen and quickly ordered drinks and dinner. While we waited for the food and beverage, I leaned forward to get the girls' attention.

"Look," I said, "I thought about this all last night. The police are focused primarily on Martha, and yet I wrapped that box of fudge for the senator."

Doe was absentmindedly folding and refolding a cocktail napkin. "And you're positive the box hadn't been opened?"

"No. I moved it from under the reception desk and put it in the pantry the morning of our book club luncheon."

"Julia," April suddenly said, "it just dawned on me that whoever put the poison into the fudge would have had to get it past the heat wrapping."

"I know. I've thought of that," I said.

"Whoever poisoned the fudge could have taken a box from behind the reception counter," Doe said. "And then switched it with the one Julia wrapped."

I was picturing the opened box in Detective Franks' hand as Doe said this. The pattern of the wrapping paper flashed in my mind.

"Oh my God!" I blurted.

The waitress arrived with our drinks, stalling the conversation. Once we'd each received our order and had a chance to take a sip, Blair leaned in to me. "What is it?" she said. "What did you remember?"

I shook my head as I stirred my margarita. "I'm such an idiot. I was so shocked when Detective Franks held out the opened box of fudge that I didn't notice the wrapping paper. I wrapped that box in green wrapping paper with tiny candy canes on it. That's our theme this year—candy canes. Several of the fake packages under that big tree in the living room are wrapped in that paper. But it just dawned on me that when Detective Franks brought out the gift box, there were no candy canes on the wrapping paper. I'm sure of it. I think it was wrapped in a Santa Claus paper. Same basic colors, but a different pattern. Don't you remember?" I looked around the table. "I don't think I even have any Santa Claus paper this year. And besides that," I added, "where was the shrink wrap? I didn't see it."

"You should let the police know," Doe said, her eyes wide. "Have them check the paper."

"But wait a minute," Blair said, stopping mid-sentence. "If the box Detective Franks brought out of the pantry had a different wrapping paper on it…"

"Then someone really did tamper with it," Rudy said, finishing her sentence.

I could almost feel the adrenaline flowing around the table. Everyone took the opportunity to sip their drinks.

"Okay, but let's think this through," Rudy said, bringing our focus back. "Someone either tampered with the gift box and then rewrapped it, or…"

"Or, what?" Doe asked, her voice reflecting her anxiety.

"Or, like Doe suggested, perhaps someone who already had a box of Julia's fudge, poisoned it, wrapped it, and then brought it back and switched it for Julia's."

"Wow," Blair said. "That's good, Rudy."

A pall fell over the group as we just stared at each other.

"But that would mean it could be any of us," Doe said. "I have a couple of boxes at home."

"I do, too," Rudy said with a shrug.

"Even I've taken a few boxes to give away as presents," Blair said.

"Who else?" April asked me.

"Oh, for heaven's sake, April, I've given boxes to dozens of people, especially at this time of year," I said.

"Anyone recently?" she asked, not willing to give up.

I contemplated her question. "Well, Sybil bought one just before Thanksgiving for her mother. Angela took one home with her just last week. And come to think of it, I gave one to the Executive Director of the State Democratic Committee when he came to look at the inn in advance of the reception."

"Don't you sell them to the guests, too?" Doe asked.

"I sold one just yesterday to the Pedersons and two boxes to Ms. Jenkins when she checked in on Saturday," April said. "But anyone could have taken one. We keep several boxes on that shelf behind the reception desk. Hell, the caterers or florists could have taken one. Besides, if someone switched boxes, they could have taken one six months ago and only decided to use it now. I mean, the fudge wouldn't have been very good anymore, but they were poisoning it anyway, so why care?"

I ran my fingers through my hair. This was going to be impossible.

"The question is, who had the opportunity to switch the boxes," Blair said.

"Well, I wrapped the box last Saturday, and it sat under the reception desk until Thursday morning," I said. "I never checked on it again. Frankly, almost anyone could have quietly exchanged one for the other. I would never have noticed."

"Okay," Rudy said, "I think you should call Detective Franks tomorrow and tell him about the wrapping paper and the shrink wrap. Maybe that will at least take some of the pressure off of you for a while."

I shrugged. "If they believe me."

The same waitress appeared again with a cart filled with five plates of steaming food. She placed the proper plate in front of each woman and then stood back.

"Is there anything else?" she said with an efficient smile.

"No, we're good," April replied. "Thanks."

Each of us took a moment to survey our order and negotiate an initial bite or two. As we began to eat, Rudy spoke up again.

"You know, I doubt anyone would have had the time or the guts to tamper with the box right there at the inn," she said. "There are too many other ways to get the fudge, inject the poison somewhere else and then just exchange it for the one you wrapped."

"One question that bothers me," Doe began, holding her fork mid-air. "I know we're saying the senator was the target, but why did Martha go into your pantry and open the gift box in the first place?"

"Especially without asking," Blair said, cutting off a piece of fish. "If Martha was anything, she was polite. I'm sure she would have asked first if she wanted to open something like that. I can't even picture her sticking her finger into the curry without asking."

"I've thought about that, too," I said, toying with the chicken parmesan in front of me. "But regardless, if the target was Senator Pesante, then Martha was killed by mistake."

"But that's where I was going," Doe said. "If someone meant to kill Senator Pesante, their plan blew up the moment he cancelled the reception. Did you have another opportunity to give the box to him?"

"No." I shook my head. "At least not now. I was going to give it to him on New Year's Eve at the Governor's Ball. What are you thinking?"

She looked around the table with a grave expression, just as a group of young women passed our table, talking loudly. Doe waited until they were out of earshot.

"Think about it," she said. "What if you had decided to give it to someone else? They could have been killed instead. But it was Martha who opened it."

"And Martha was killed by mistake," Rudy said with a roll of her eyes. "I think we've got that part, Doe."

"No, that's not what I mean," Doe said, leaning forward. "Listen. We'd all agree that it seemed like Martha was looking for something that day. What if she was looking for that fudge?"

Even though the restaurant was full of people, it seemed as if the air in the room had stopped moving. We all stopped and stared at Doe. When no one responded, she prodded us.

"Martha could have gone for any other box of fudge in the inn if all she wanted was something sweet. But she went into the pantry, ripped open that gift box and opened *that* particular box of fudge. Why?"

"So you think that for some reason Martha was actually looking for that particular box," I said, breathlessly.

"Let's face it—we can't explain any of her behavior that day," Doe said with a shrug of her shoulders.

Doe returned to her dinner, while April finally spoke up.

"But if we follow your logic," she said, resting her elbows on the table, "then that would make Martha the target and *not* Senator Pesante?"

We were quiet for a moment, the weight of that statement rendering us silent.

"But why would anyone want to hurt Martha?" Blair shook her head, tears in her eyes.

"We don't know the answer to that any more than we know why she was behaving so strangely," Doe cautioned. "I just think it's a scenario we shouldn't rule out."

Rudy's tanned hands had encircled her glass of white wine, and she was staring into it as if it might reveal a clue. "So," she began, "our two theories are, one—Senator Pesante was the target and Martha got the poisoned box by mistake. Or two - someone poisoned the fudge *after* the reception was canceled, *knowing* that Martha would find it and open it."

She looked up asking for confirmation, just as a waiter used a lighter to enflame a dish of cherries jubilee next to us.

"Yes," Doe finally agreed. "Which makes the outlier in all of this... what made Martha open that particular box of fudge?"

"Boy, how are we ever going to figure that out?" Blair said, dangling her little finger as she raised her Lemon Drop to her lips.

"Look," Rudy said, "Since we don't know which scenario it is, we'll have to work on two different tracks. Just in case."

"I think you're right," I said. "First, we need to eliminate Senator Pesante as the logical target." I turned to Blair. "So Blair, if this was political it might have been a Republican effort to get rid of Pesante. Isn't Mr. Billings pretty close to that guy who does the financial bundling for the Congressional Republican Committee?"

Even though Blair's husband's name was Jacob Babcock, for reasons Blair had never explained, she always referred to him as "Mr. Billings." It had to be some sort of nickname, but none of us had ever had the guts to ask. Blair nodded mutely to my question.

"Think you can find out what they might know about Pesante's enemies? Especially any that have to do with the minimum wage bill he was here to promote?"

"You mean like a detective?" she said, her eyes taking on an inner glow.

"Yes, Blair, like a detective," Rudy said patiently. "But you can't be obvious about it."

"Okay, sure."

Her response was too quick to be convincing.

"No, really, Blair," Doe said. "You have to be subtle. Can you do that?"

"Subtle" was probably not in Blair's vocabulary. In fact, my secret nickname for her had always been "Catnip." She was what a friend of mine once referred to as a "man's woman," meaning that she loved men—every shape, every size, every age—and they loved her. And when she was around them, she assumed a persona of someone only slightly brighter than Marilyn Monroe, but just as alluring. She had been married to four of the richest men in the state. What's more, they all still loved her *and* got along with each other. When Blair had gotten pneumonia the year before and ended up in the emergency room, her three ex-husbands had all converged on the hospital to wait with Mr. Billings. It was an odd support system, but it worked.

Blair frowned as if she wasn't sure she could deliver on the expectation. Then she brightened up again, putting down her drink.

"Yeah, I can do it. I mean, let's face it, after four marriages, I know how to keep a secret or two."

She winked a blue eye playfully, revealing a more devious side to her than I'd ever seen.

"That's good, Blair," I said. "Thanks."

"I still have some pretty good contacts with the press in Olympia," Rudy said.

"Don't forget Elliott," Doe said.

Elliot was Rudy's ex-husband and owner of a chain of local newspapers throughout the state. Although they'd been married forever, he'd up and left only a year before, stating that he needed to find out who he was. Seriously? At sixty-eight, he needed to find out who he was. A little late for that, I thought.

Rudy's mouth turned into a frown. "I never forget Elliot. I'll talk to him if I have to."

I was smiling. They were really going to do this. I turned to Doe.

"Doe, didn't you say that one of your drivers was dating Martha's housekeeper, Carlita?"

She raised her eyebrows. "Philippe Gravas, that's right." Her eyes were literally sparkling at the idea. "That's a good one, Julia. I'll see what I can find out."

117

"What about you and April?" Blair asked. "What will you guys work on?"

I looked over at my dear friend who was listening quietly, while she cut off a piece of steak.

"We'll work on finding out how someone could have poisoned the fudge. We'll have to see if we can recreate the last couple of days—who was here, who wasn't—and map out every minute we can. It won't be complete, but maybe we can identify time gaps when someone could have taken the box from the reception desk unnoticed."

"You'll have to figure out who has keys to the inn," Doe said with a raised eyebrow.

"Uh... I have a key," Blair said sheepishly. "Remember when I needed to run back to the inn to get your punch bowl the day we were holding that reception at the ballet? I never gave it back."

"But didn't you say your purse was stolen last week?" Doe said.

Blair blanched and threw her hand to her mouth, her long red fingernails nearly slicing open her nose. "Oh my God, that's right." She turned to me. "Your key was in that purse. I'd forgotten about that. I'm so sorry, Julia."

An awkward silence settled over the table as we contemplated the fact that at least one key was completely unaccounted for. A tinkling sound made us all look up to the windows overlooking the pool. It had begun to rain, and a breeze was throwing sleet against the glass.

"Looks like you've got your work cut out for you, Julia," Doe said quietly. "Think you're up for it?"

I shrugged.

"I don't think I have a choice."

CHAPTER FIFTEEN

By 8:15 p.m., I was back at the inn and everyone but April had left. I put Ahab to bed, while April went out to close up the bakery, saying she'd meet me in my apartment later to get a head start on our investigation.

I made a cup of hot chocolate and snuggled into my big chair with a quilted throw over my lap. The dogs were stretched out on their pillow in front of the fireplace. I began making a list of everyone who had keys to the inn and anyone I could remember giving a box of fudge within the last six weeks. I had half of the lists finished when the phone rang. Not my landline and not my cell phone, but my mother's cell phone again.

Even at ninety-three, my mother had loved technology and social networking. She'd mastered the Internet, Facebook, and Twitter, and was never without her cell phone, which she used daily to text Angela, me, or members of her bridge club. I hadn't thought about that phone since she died; now it had rung twice in two days, even though the phone's battery should have been long dead.

I got up and went to the drawer again, this time with a little trepidation. I reached out and touched the phone, pulling my fingers back for a minute from its cold exterior. The ringtone continued, and I finally answered it. The voice on the other end almost brought me to my knees.

"Julia!" my mother barked in her usual commanding voice. "What's going on?"

I could actually feel the blood drain from my face, and a glance in the mirror on the wall confirmed that my jaw had sagged open.

"I...uh...Mother?!"

"Of course it's your mother. Who else would be calling you on my cell phone?"

I glanced at the phone in my hand. It was covered with a God-awful pink, sparkly "Hello Kitty" jacket more appropriate for a fourteen-year old girl. My mother had loved it, but I felt like an idiot standing there talking on it—especially to a dead person.

"Did you hear me? I need to know what's going on. I think you may be in danger."

"Hunh?" I pulled myself back to the moment. "Uh...I..."

"Really, Julia, is that all you can say? You sound like you've had your tongue cut out."

The phrase "rooted to the spot" suddenly made perfect sense to me. I seemed incapable of movement of any kind. I'm not sure I was even breathing. This person sounded exactly like my mother, who had a voice that would be hard to duplicate. Even though she'd quit smoking when she was in her seventies, after twenty years of that stuff tearing up her lungs, her voice was raspy enough to strip paint.

"Julia?" the voice asked again. "Are you there?"

A crackling sound, like static, echoed on the line and then was gone.

"Um...yes," I squeaked. "I'm here. But where are you?"

"Where do you think I am? I'm dead."

My feet finally moved, and I stumbled backwards to fall into my chair. My heart was thumping wildly and there was a ringing in my ears. Mickey and Minnie perked their heads up from their bed.

"Who is this...really? I mean, this is not very funny, you know. My mother died over a year ago. Why are you pretending to be her?"

Martha's death popped into my head. Did this call have something to do with that? Was there some mad person out there who had killed Martha and now wanted to torment me?

"Don't be an idiot, Julia. This is your mother. Who in their right mind would pretend to be me?"

She had me there. Indeed—who would?

"Alright, tell me something only my mother would know. Something from my childhood."

I was trying desperately to remain calm. I'd grown up in Illinois, so no one locally would know anything about my childhood. There was a loud sigh on the other end.

"You were thirteen years old when you first started your period, and you happened to be in your history class. When you got up to leave, the boy behind you, a boy you had a crush on, burst out laughing because the back of your white skirt had a big red blotch on it. Good enough?"

Oh my God! No one knew that story except my mother. I don't think she'd ever even told my father, and I had never told Graham or any of my friends. Even now, my face burned with humiliation.

"Stop blushing," the voice on the other end said as if she could see me. "Let's move on. We have to talk and there's not much time."

Even though the inn was filled with ghosts, I found it absolutely unnerving that I might be talking to my deceased mother. Even Elizabeth didn't actually talk to me.

"Okay, listen, I'm not in danger," I said breathlessly. "Martha died—here in the inn. She was poisoned."

"Poisoned? Who would want to poison Martha?"

"We don't know. We're trying to figure that out."

"What do you mean, *we*?"

There was a crackling sound again.

"The girls and me," I said, waiting for the crackling to stop. "We're going to try to solve the mystery."

"What?!" she croaked. "Julia, you have no idea how to do that. You read a lot of mystery novels, and you can usually figure out who the murderer is before the end of the book, I'll give you that. But this is different. This is real life."

Muffled voices whispered in the background, making me look around. Then I realized the voices were in the background on the phone.

"Um… she was poisoned with something from my pantry," I said, a chill rippling down my back. "And I may be arrested for the crime."

"*You* poisoned her?" the other voice said. "Oh, Julia, you've done some dumb things in your life, but …"

"No," I said with a sigh. "I didn't poison her. Someone else did. What are those other voices? Mom, are there other people there with you?"

Oh my God, I was talking to this person as if she really was my dead mother. I'll admit most people would be skeptical that the inn was haunted, or that our resident ghost left messages for me sketched into the steam on my bathroom mirror. But having a ghost call you on a cell phone? Well, even I had trouble with that.

"No," the voice said. "No one's here."

"But I hear other voices on the line," I said.

"Maybe it's a party line," she replied.

I groaned. "Really, Mom? A party line?!"

"I was trying to make a joke— for heaven's sake," the voice replied with a snort.

"For heaven's sake? Another joke, Mom?"

"Never mind," she snapped. "Your sense of humor always was a little stunted. Okay, if you're intent on doing this, then you'll need my help," the voice continued.

"What can you do for me? You're dead," I said.

"You're kidding me, right? I can see things you can't. Not everything, but I get impressions."

"Then just tell me who did it. That would save me a lot of trouble."

There was a loud sign on the other end of the line—wherever that was.

"I can't. Since I'm connected to you by birth, I'm around you all of the time and my impressions about you are stronger than they are about other people."

That was unsettling news.

"What do you mean you're around me all the time?"

"Okay, not all the time. Often. I'm around you often. But I'm kind of new at this. I'm still learning how it all works."

"Was that you who called me last night?"

"Yes. I was able to get the phone to ring, but I couldn't make the connection."

Story of my life, I thought.

The buzzing in my ears had stopped, although the whispering continued. It gave me the creeps.

"All right, tell me," I said. "What should I do first?"

I thought this might be the question that would finally stump whoever this was and reveal them for what they were—a fraud.

"Call that philandering ex-husband of yours and let him know what's going on before he hears it from someone else," the woman said. "He's a prick, but he can help in case you get into trouble. You know him. He likes to be the big savior, but if he thinks you've ignored him, he's likely to leave you to your own devices—especially if he thinks you've embarrassed him. Don't forget that time you decided to run for the school board and didn't tell him first."

All of a sudden, it hit me. I mean—it really hit me.

"Oh my God, you really are my mother!"

And then...

"And you're calling me on your cell phone!?"

My mother chuckled on the other end. "Did you think I'd appear to you in a dream or something?"

I considered her question. Given the spirits who inhabited the inn, I actually had thought that she might appear to me at some point. But I'd never thought I'd be talking to her again as if she'd never died. The display window on the phone said, "Out of area" again, making me laugh out loud.

"What are you laughing at?" she demanded. "I haven't made a joke."

"The phone says you're calling from out of the area. Wherever you are, you're about as far out of the area as you can get."

"I'll have to admit that's funny. Now if you're done acting like an idiot, let's continue."

If this wasn't my mom, then whoever it was had her snarky personality down to a T.

"Okay, I think you're right about talking to Graham," I said, still smiling. "But then what?"

"Then look closely at the people around you. That's why I called in the first place. There are some bad vibes nearby."

"That's it? That's all you've got?"

"I told you, I get impressions. Just like April. Only in reverse. The impression I get is that someone close to you is not who they seem to be. That is all."

The line went dead. No pun intended.

"What do you mean, that is all? Mom? Hello?"

There was silence on the other end. Even the whispers were gone. I shook the phone and put it back to my ear. Nothing.

"Damn!" I muttered. I didn't even have a chance to tell her I missed her or ask about Martha. A sob bubbled up in my chest and I took a deep, cleansing breath, wondering at my own sanity. Had I really just talked to my mother? I leaned back in the chair, my heart racing. God, what a strange life I led. But whether that had been my dead mother or just my inner demons, the advice was good and I intended to follow it.

I immediately grabbed my own cell phone and dialed the governor's mansion in Olympia. Graham knew about Martha's death, but he may not have been told about the fudge and potential scandal that would erupt if I was arrested.

Second wife, Kitty, answered the phone.

"Um…just a minute, I'll get him," she said in a lazy monotone.

A minute later, he answered the phone. After apologizing for the late hour, I told him briefly what I knew about the fudge.

"I already know, Julia," he said. "You forget that the Prosecuting Attorney used to work for me. He called me right away. I was going to call you in the morning."

"Do you think that Senator Pesante could have been the target?"

If anyone knew the politics involved, it would be Graham.

"I don't know anyone who would want to kill him, if that's what you mean. He's a bit of a lightning rod and is certainly not well-liked in Republican circles, but we typically don't kill off the opposition."

"Yes, but there are a lot of fringe people who don't like the fact he's trying to raise the minimum wage," I said.

"But killing him wouldn't stop that effort," he replied in a rather patronizing tone. "If anything, it would garner support. The President and every other Democrat in this Washington and the *other* Washington wants the minimum wage raised. Personally, I doubt Pesante was the target. At least not for political reasons. You just need to sit back and relax, Julia."

I sighed, knowing he was probably right.

"But thanks for giving me the heads up, anyway," he said more gently. "I'll let you know if I hear of anything at this end."

I thanked him and we hung up.

Our divorce had been amicable, despite my jealousy of Kitty. I suppose no one is immune to the loss of prestige to a younger woman. But Graham and I had been lucky, because we'd had a good marriage. It had just run its course. We had kept up appearances for several years, mostly for Angela's sake, but once she was out of college and on her own, there wasn't any point. Now we maintained a distant yet comfortable relationship, something my mother could never understand. She thought I should have been bereft when Graham left. Instead, I had almost welcomed it. But as I contemplated the pain of losing Martha and the fear of an impending murder investigation, I silently wished I had someone like Graham by my side.

CHAPTER SIXTEEN

It was almost 9:30 p.m. when April knocked on my apartment door, holding a plate with a large raspberry crème cupcake on it. No wonder I had trouble losing weight, I thought grimly.

"I come bearing gifts," she said, smiling.

"Thanks. You think I need to beef up in case I go to the big house?"

She placed a hand on my shoulder. "You're not going anywhere, Julia. We're going to figure this out."

"Well," I said, eyeing the dessert. "I didn't have dessert at the restaurant, so I suppose I could use a sugar fix. Do you want some tea?"

"Sure. And I'll share this with you."

I went to the kitchen and grabbed two forks and one of my favorite small porcelain plates. We brought everything to the mahogany pedestal table on the other side of the kitchen counter and sat down. While April cut the big cupcake in half, I went and got my list.

"Okay," I said, coming back. "I've made a list of everyone who has a key to the inn and their contact information. I added the caterers and florists. And I got about halfway through a list of people I've given fudge to."

"I talked to Erin, and she still has a key," April added quickly. I had given April's daughter a key the summer before while her condo was being remodeled.

"Wow, I'd completely forgotten that. I should get that back from her."

I updated the list again.

"I also talked to Libby and Angela," I said. "Libby swears that her key is with her all the time. You know, she wears them around her neck on a lanyard. I also called Angela. She keeps hers on her main key chain, which she keeps in her purse. And she keeps that in a locked drawer in her office."

"And here's mine," April said, pulling it out of her pocket. The key to the inn was bright blue. "I never label my keys, so there's no way anyone would know this is the key to the inn," she said, holding it up. "It could be a key to anything. They'd have to stand there and try all of these keys, and there are a lot of them," she cringed.

I laughed. "Yes, there are. I've always wondered why you carry so many on one key chain. What are they for, anyway?"

"The inn, the bakery." She started peeling them off. "My car, the guest house, the church, the van, your apartment… my home," she said with a sigh.

Her mood had suddenly changed as she stared at the key to her home.

"Okay, I've got it," I said. "You okay?"

She perked up. "Sure. I always wear pants with a big pocket. Or, I use my fanny pack. I never leave them lying around."

"Okay, then… check," I said, putting a check next to April's name. "You're off the hook, and so are Angela and Libby."

April was savoring a bit of cupcake, the pink frosting sliding off her lip. She rolled her eyes in delight.

"This is wonderful, if I do say so myself!"

"It's new, isn't it? You don't usually have these," I said, taking a bite. My taste buds exploded in sweet raspberry.

"I've been trying some new recipes," she said.

"Well, I think you should definitely add it to the dessert case."

"Maybe I will," she said, swallowing a second big bite.

"Okay, back to priorities," I said, licking my fingers.

"If you want, I'll talk to Crystal and José," April offered. "I don't think they would ever do anything on purpose, but you never know who might have wheedled their way into their confidence or asked to borrow their key for some reason. We'll have to check out José's boyfriend, too."

"That's true," I agreed, swallowing a last bite of cupcake.

"By the way, I mentioned it to Mr. Garth," she said. "He said he doesn't have a key to the inn, anymore. Just the carriage house. He says he gave it back to you when your mother moved in."

My eyebrows shot up. "That's right. He never used it much, anyway. Come to think of it, that's the key I gave to Blair. Okay, so we can remove him from the list, and of course we don't know where Blair's key is. So, let's talk about the florists and Gwen."

Gwen was our caterer of choice for all events at the inn, since we didn't do catering ourselves. I explained to April that Gwen had actually stopped by to discuss the food for the reception *before* I'd even wrapped the box. And then the event was cancelled, so she hadn't come back to the inn to set up.

"And the florists were here for such a short time," I said, "They brought the arrangements in while I was standing right there and put them where I wanted them. I don't know how they would have even seen the box since it was under the reception desk."

"Okay," April nodded, swallowing a last bite. "By the way, who selected the box of fudge you wrapped?"

"I did. Why?"

"I was just wondering if anyone had handed one to you. You know, as if they had just pulled it off the shelf, but in fact had pulled it out of their purse or something."

"I see. No." I shook my head, thinking back to that day. "I grabbed one off the shelf from behind the reception desk. Although, come to think of it, the Jenkins woman saw me do it. You know, she's the one who checked in that day. I was chatting with her about the reception, and she asked about the fudge and who I was wrapping it for. Then she bought two boxes for herself. But several other people saw me wrapping it, too."

"Maybe that's something you should mention to that nice-looking Detective Franks."

She smiled at me, and I looked at her in surprise.

"He's not so nice-looking," I said, feeling myself blush.

April just narrowed those hazel eyes at me.

"Right. And I'm your fairy godmother."

"Okay, he's not bad looking," I said. "But so what? Right now he thinks I'm a killer."

She chuckled. "I doubt it. But just the same, let him know about Ms. Jenkins and anyone else who saw you wrap the box."

"I will," I said.

"Okay," April said. She picked up the empty plate and started for the kitchen. On her way back, she happened to glance at the Hello Kitty phone next to my chair. "Why is your mother's phone out?"

She scooped it up, and I tensed.

"Uh… I was just going through a drawer and found it."

"There are a lot of nonprofits that collect these, you know? They can make money off them. You could give it to one of them."

"No," I said quickly, grabbing it out of her hand. "I'm going to keep it."

She paused, staring at me.

"Okay, what's going on?"

"What do you mean?" I asked.

"You know what I mean," she said. "You're exuding enough nervous energy to power a mini-mall. Something has happened. Something having to do with your mother, apparently."

I took a deep breath, wondering if I should tell her the truth. I busied myself with brushing imaginary crumbs off the table into my hand, giving myself time to think. The thought of admitting that my mother was calling me on her cell phone made me dizzy, but if anyone would believe me, it would be April. As I got up and pretended to throw the crumbs into the trash, she interrupted my thoughts.

"Yes, you should tell me the truth."

I spun around. "You know how spooky that is, don't you? How do you do that anyway? You've never told me.

"Don't change the subject. What's up?"

She narrowed her eyes, scrutinizing me, and then tilted her head as she seemed to listen to some inner voice. Then her eyes grew wide.

"Oh, my God, you've been talking to your mother!"

My heart almost jumped into my throat. "Okay, I give up," I said, slumping into the chair again. "Between you and my mother, I'll never have any secrets again."

April began to laugh. "Well, at least now you'll understand a little bit of what I go through. So, tell me, what happened?"

I related the activity on my mother's phone and what she'd said. April didn't seem surprised at all, other than the fact that my mother had chosen to contact me on her cell phone. She thought that was pretty creative.

"How do you feel about it?" she asked me.

"What?"

"Having your mother…your dead mother…contact you."

"Well… it's really weird and kind of creepy, if in fact it really was her. But if it was her, it's kind of nice, too. I mean, how many people actually talk to someone they loved after they've died…or, for that matter, *anyone* after they've died?"

"Consider yourself lucky," April said. "Maybe now you'll finally get *rid* of her."

I gasped. "What do you mean?"

She laughed. "I mean get rid of her ashes, along with all the dead dogs and cats you have out in the garage."

All my friends teased me about the fact that I had stored the ashes of two of my past dogs and one cat in the garage, along with my mother. Truth be told, my mother had always wanted to be buried in Illinois next to her sister; I just hadn't had the time to take her ashes back there, yet. And I had always planned on planting a special garden just for the animals. But I hadn't done that yet, either.

"Do you think that's why she's still here, because I have her ashes?"

"No. But if we're talking about weird and creepy, having her ashes in the garage is all that."

"She'd think it was funny, you know," I said with a smile. "She'd throw back her head and let out that cackle of hers."

Suddenly, there was a catch in my throat as I heard my mother's throaty laugh in my mind. April picked up on it immediately and changed the subject.

"Well, at least you're only hearing from one individual. It's more difficult when you hear from many."

I quickly wiped a tear away. "Is that what it's like for you?"

April paused a moment and then seemed to make a decision. "That's a conversation for another time," she said, standing up.

She'd only shared bits and pieces of her gift with me over the years. Instead, I usually just watched from a distance as she seemed to know things that no one else knew. Sometimes it only surprised me, but many times it freaked me out. At least now that

I'd had my own experience, I had someone who understood what I was going through.

"Don't fight it," she said. "Your mom will have your best interests at heart. And who knows, she might be able to help." She looked at her watch. "I've got to get going. I won't see you until Monday, but I'll call José and Crystal tomorrow. You ought to talk to Sybil."

"Lucky me," I said with a sneer.

CHAPTER SEVENTEEN

It was early Sunday morning when I climbed out of bed, my body protesting loudly. Life was weighing me down and I felt it in my bones.

I got dressed and then decided to charge my mother's phone, just in case. I plugged it in and was about to make breakfast when my landline rang.

"Julia, you need to get over to the barn!"

It was April.

"What do you mean? What's happened?"

"Someone's broken into the warehouse."

She was breathing hard and her voice was shaking.

"It's… it's awful."

"I'll call the police and be right there," I said.

I hung up and stopped, staring at the wall. How could this be happening? I took a deep breath and quickly called 911 to report the incident. Then I threw on a coat and ran out the door and around the north end of the inn, up the garden steps, and across the drive to the old carriage barn.

I used the side door to come directly into the antique storeroom. What I found stopped me in my tracks. The room was 1,000 square feet, with a cement floor and a row of horse stalls we'd left in place on the far wall to store small things like collectibles, antique utensils and old hand tools, all waiting to be displayed inside the inn at some point. The hay loft above was used to store extra lumber and rods. The major portion of the room was used for furniture, which we stored in rows, some stacked on top of one another.

Every table in the room had been tipped over, and any that had drawers in them had been pulled out and tossed aside. Dining room tables, writing tables, side tables, even library tables. In addition, two large bookcases along the left wall that held antique books had been swept clean, leaving fragile, decades-old books piled on the floor, many of them with their spines broken.

It took me a good minute to finally move from the doorway into the room. April sat in a straight-back chair and looked up when I stepped inside.

"Julia," she said, starting to rise. "I'm so sorry."

I stopped, because I was speechless. I swallowed and then said, "The police will be here in a minute. Why don't you go call José and then wait out front for them?"

She left me to wander around by myself, my breath catching every few feet as I came upon another dismal scene. Beautiful pieces had been marred, cracked, or broken. Others, like turn-of-the-century beds or flour mills had been left alone. I weaved my way up and down the aisles, mentally calculating the damage. When I made my way back to where we actually refinished furniture, what I found stopped me. I wondered if April had even been back this far.

Across the room, the office door had been broken open and the small enclosure trashed. Papers were strewn across the floor. The drawers from the small desk had been pulled out and emptied. The shelf above the desk had also been swept clean. But before I could even get to the office, I stopped to survey Martha's table, which Mr. Garth had begun to work on only the day before. There wasn't much left. It had been a beautiful ebony-stained drop-leaf table with two leaves that could be raised for extra seating. But it wasn't beautiful anymore. It had been smashed to pieces. Not merely turned over or broken like the other tables. It had been utterly demolished.

Before I could move, I felt someone at my shoulder and turned to find April.

"Who would do this?" she said.

She leaned over and lifted up the pink inventory slip that had been taped to the table. It was marked with the date, Martha's name and address, and the price I paid for it. We attached them to all the furniture until we had them logged in for inventory purposes. April held it in her hand. Then she lifted her eyes to the office across the room.

"What's going on, Julia? What's this all about?"

"I don't know." I reached out and took the inventory slip from her hand and looked down at it. "But, I'm beginning to get an idea."

José appeared behind us with Detective Franks. José glanced around nervously, shifting his weight as if I might accuse him of something. Detective Franks was dressed more casually in jeans and a Seahawks jacket. After all, it was Sunday. But he'd gotten there so quickly, I wondered if he lived close by. A single uniformed police officer stood to the side.

"What happened?" Detective Franks asked, surveying the scene.

"April found it this way when she came in this morning."

"Do you think this was the same person at the house the other night, Ms. Applegate?"
José asked. "The one who attacked you?"

Detective Franks threw a suspicious look at José.

"And where were you during all of this?"

José looked up at him. "I went out with friends last night," he said a bit defensively.

"You were gone all evening?"

"Yes," he said, glancing at me.

"And you didn't see anything suspicious before you left?" Detective Franks asked.

José shook his head, his dark eyes darting back and forth to me and then to April.

"No," he said.

"What about that?" Detective Franks said, pointing to the wall behind us.

We all turned around.

"What?" My hand flew to my mouth.

Spray painted on the wall was "X3" in graffiti bubble writing.

"Looks like someone tagged your wall," Detective Franks said. "Know anything about that, young man?"

Sweat was beginning to glisten on José's forehead.

"No, sir."

Detective Franks eyed him carefully.

"You can wait outside, but I'm going to want to talk to you later."

José left, while Detective Franks turned to the other officer.

"Keep an eye on him."

The officer nodded and left.

April touched my shoulder.

"I'll be in the bakery."

She left as Detective Franks wandered past the table to the office door and glanced inside. Then he surveyed the pile of books on the floor. "Do you have any idea why someone would do this?" he asked quietly.

"I *had* an idea," I exhaled, shaking my head. I was close to tears and was straining to hold it together. "Until that," I said, indicating the graffiti.

"What do you mean?" he asked, his eyes holding mine.

I showed him the inventory tag.

"This tag was taped to this table," I said, nodding to the pile of rubble at my feet. "It's the only one completely destroyed. And it was Martha's. I picked it up the other night from her home. Mr. Garth, the man who refinishes our furniture, set it up and began to work on it yesterday."

He glanced down at the table. "But why would the table be significant?"

I looked down and used my toe to sift through the debris. A brass drawer pull caught my attention, and I leaned over and picked it up.

"Maybe because it had a drawer," I said, showing him the drawer pull. "Probably a hidden drawer. That's not unusual in these old pieces of furniture. Maybe there was something in the drawer." I looked back at some of the other furniture that had been turned over. "It seems like whoever did this came in through the side door and worked their way back, looking for tables with drawers in them. If you'll notice, all the drawers have been pulled out. They didn't know which table was Martha's, until they found this tag," I said, holding up the tag again.

"And then they struck gold," he said.

"But if they found the drawer and whatever was in it," I said with a frown, "why did they destroy the table and bother with the bookshelves and the office?"

Detective Franks followed my gaze towards the bookcases.

"My guess is that they *didn't* find what they wanted in the drawer," he said. "And they thought maybe you had."

He shifted those gorgeous brown eyes my way.

"That can't be good," I said with a slight tremor to my voice.

"No," he agreed. "But the graffiti may change all of that. It could be gang-related. Or maybe your maintenance man has some enemies. Do you know much about his background?"

"No," I shook my head. "Other than he grew up in Southern California. But, Detective, he doesn't belong to any gang. I'm sure of it."

"You wouldn't be the first one to be fooled, you know. We'll have to do a thorough background check on him, and frankly, everyone else. But right now, let's see if anything was stolen and how they got in. Then we can try to figure out what, if anything, this has to do with Mrs. Denton's death or local gang activity."

Just then, April appeared at the back door to the bakery.

"What is it?" I asked, seeing the stricken look on her face.

"You'd better come with me," she said to both of us. "They also broke into the bakery."

We followed her into the back of the bakery, passing shelves that stored ingredients, a large refrigerator, set of commercial sinks, a commercial oven, and two counters. So far, everything looked normal–until we got to her office. April had a floor-to-ceiling bookcase filled with cookbooks in her office—or, she used to. Now the majority of the books had been thrown to the floor. Her desk had also been swept clean and the drawers emptied. Her office looked hauntingly similar to what's left behind after a hurricane, minus the water damage. And April looked like she was ready to supply the water. Tears were streaming down her face.

"What in the world would anyone want with my cookbooks?"

Detective Franks was glancing around the small enclosure, then out to the commercial kitchen.

"You're the cook?" he said to April.

She flashed a look in his direction.

"She's my partner," I corrected him. "April runs the bakery, and yes, she does much of the cooking."

"So you normally come in first thing in the morning and start cooking."

He was scrutinizing April as if he thought he was about to catch her in a lie.

"Normally, yes," she said.

"So why didn't you notice this when you came in?" He nodded to the office mess.

So, there it was. He really did suspect she was hiding something and, unfortunately, April didn't look like she was going to be much help in clearing it up. Her eyes kept darting over to me, and her expression looked like she'd inadvertently swallowed a fly.

"I…uh…I went into the warehouse first this morning, looking for an old cookbook I saw in there. I was thinking of duplicating a recipe."

That sounded perfectly reasonable to me. I glanced Detective Frank's way, wondering what he thought, but Sybil's foghorn of a voice split through the growing tension in the room.

"Julia, are you okay?" she called from the warehouse.

Before I knew it, my nosey neighbor had waltzed her way past the ovens and was at my elbow, her eyes wide.

"Oh my stars! What happened? I saw the police car pass my house and thought maybe someone had died again. But *this* is tragic. All of your antiques…"

"The bakery and the warehouse were broken into last night," I said, barely controlling my temper. "We've lost a lot of the antiques, and we're just trying to find out if anything was stolen. We're kind of busy…"

"Why would anyone want to steal anything from in here?" she said, hands on her hips. "It's just a bunch of…"

"Sybil!" April barked at her.

Sybil stopped mid-sentence, those marble blue eyes staring out from behind her glasses.

"We need to finish here," April said.

April's message was clear. She wanted Sybil to leave. So, of course, Sybil didn't. She turned to me and merely shifted gears.

"Why don't I go and get the puppies, Julia? You have too much to deal with here. I'll just take them to my place and you can get them in the mornin'. Then you can tell me all about it."

I had to admit, I thought that was a good idea since I hadn't even fed them, yet.

"That would be great. Thanks. You know where their dog food is. They haven't eaten."

"Oh, stars," she waved me away. "Don't worry about that. I have plenty of food and Pepsi will be thrilled."

Pepsi was her Chihuahua. I hate Chihuahuas.

"Call me if you need me. Mornin', Libby."

As she exited out the front, I saw that that Libby had arrived.

"Julia, Mr. Stillwater just said he'll be leaving, and Ms. Jenkins is in the breakfast room..." She stopped and her eyes grew wide when she saw April's office.

I turned to April, who seemed to have left this planet for a moment. Her eyes were glazed over as she just stared at her office. I gave her arm a squeeze, bringing her out of her reverie.

"Okay if we take some pastries over from the bakery for breakfast? You can stay here with the police and I'll be back over as soon as I can."

"Of course," she said numbly.

"C'mon, Libby," I said, steering her away. "Let's load up on some stuff."

Her eyes lingered on the mess in April's office as we moved to the display cases. Libby and I gathered up the pastries and a load of donuts and put them into a big box. Before we headed back to the inn, I glanced back at April, who looked like she was about to cry again. I thought if we didn't solve this mystery soon, I could start losing staff and business partners as fast as I seemed to be losing guests.

CHAPTER EIGHTEEN

Detective Franks called for a forensics officer to dust for fingerprints and take pictures of everything, including the graffiti. There were no broken locks or windows, raising all sorts of questions as to how the intruders got in. He forwarded everything to Detective Abrams, who was off for the day, and then spent a good forty minutes interviewing José and then April. But the only piece of evidence they found was a can of black spray paint that had rolled behind a desk.

Once the forensics people were gone and a police van had picked up what was left of Martha's table, I went back over to the carriage barn to begin cleaning up and taking inventory. José stayed to help, and we called in Crystal who was off for the day. April worked to clean up her office, while Libby remained at the inn. Anything we weren't able to salvage was hauled to a big dumpster we had out back.

Around noon, Detective Franks called to say that they had gone to Martha's home to look for anything out of the ordinary. He must have agreed with me about the hidden drawer in the table. While they were there, Sybil came over and confirmed that everything looked the way it should. I had no doubt Sybil could have inventoried Martha's house down to the flatware.

The inn was normally full this time of year, but while we worked in the carriage barn, Mrs. Devonshire and Mr. Stillwater both checked out early. I suppose even the potential thrill of seeing a ghost would be overwhelmed by the real danger of encountering a murderer. That left only one guest, Ms. Jenkins, who was scheduled to leave on Tuesday.

By three o'clock, we'd completed the bulk of the work and were all exhausted. Libby said she would stay on duty until five o'clock to make up for her sick day, but I let Crystal go, while José and I locked up.

"I don't know anything about that graffiti, Ms. Applegate," José said to me, his dark liquid eyes betraying his anxiety. "Besides, it's not really graf…"

"I know," I replied. I put a hand on his arm. "Don't worry, José. This is all going to work itself out."

"No, Ms. Applegate," he said. "What I meant was I'm not sure it's even gang graffiti. Have your detectives check it out. I don't think that tag means anything."

He nodded and left. April had offered to make us a late lunch, so I walked back to my apartment to clean up. I changed clothes and then grabbed my mother's cell phone on the way out the door again. I'm not sure why. I just thought keeping her close to me under the circumstances might be a good idea.

When I joined April in the kitchen, she had things laid out for sandwiches. As we each made a sandwich, I asked how she was doing.

"I don't know," she said, squeezing the bread in her hand hard enough to leave fingerprints. "I've never been through anything like this before."

"But something else is bothering you."

She sat down and looked at me. "I'm not a psychic, Julia. You know that. I don't hear voices or see things. I get feelings, impressions. So why didn't I feel anything last night? It was my space that was broken into."

The first glimmer of fear I'd ever seen flashed in her eyes.

"Someone was in my space, *my* space, and I didn't feel a thing."

"Maybe you're too close to it," I said.

April just stared at the bread in her hands and then finally finished making her sandwich.

"Maybe," she said under her breath.

"Look, April, this has all of us upset. But we've got to keep our heads."

"I know," she said. "I know." She took a deep breath and then looked at me. "I'm so sorry about all of your antiques, Julia. And what in the world was that thing spray painted on the wall?"

I shook my head. "I don't know."

"Do you think it was a gang? Something to do with José?"

I shrugged. "No. Not José at least. And he says it's not even a gang tag. But, why would a gang break in and damage a bunch of antiques on Mercer Island, anyway?"

"Maybe it was meant as some kind of message to José. We don't really know much about his background."

Now I was staring at my sandwich. "I don't want to think about that. This is where I have to have a little faith."

We each took a bite and ate for a moment. As I wiped my mouth with a napkin, I asked her, "By the way, why were you even here this morning? You weren't supposed to come in. It was your day off."

She glanced up and then away.

"I just had some things to take care of. You know me, even when I'm not here, I'm thinking of here, so I might as well *be* here."

"Okay," I said a little confused. "Look, ignoring the graffiti for the moment, I've been trying to figure out why Martha's table was smashed. Out of all the pieces of furniture in there, that one piece was completely destroyed. Why? By the way, I found a drawer pull when I was standing there with Detective Franks. I think the table may have had a hidden drawer. If so, perhaps there was something —"

April stood up, nearly knocking her chair over.

"Oh my God." She wiped her hands on a paper towel. "You need to come back to the bakery with me, right now!"

"Hunh? Why?" I muttered.

"I have to show you something."

CHAPTER NINETEEN

I dropped my sandwich and followed April out the kitchen door. Considering the events over the past few days, I held my breath as we crossed the drive into the bakery. Rather than going to her office though, she went to a horizontal coat rack mounted on the wall next to one of the counters. Three commercial aprons hung there, along with the denim one I'd given her when she first opened the bakery. She grabbed the denim apron off its hook and reached into the large pocket that stretched across the lower third of the apron, stenciled with her name. She pulled out a small binder.

"What's that?"

She paused and looked around as if someone might be listening.

"Let's go into my office."

My anxiety ratcheted up a notch as I followed her into the small enclosure.

"April, what's going on?"

She closed the door before speaking.

"Mr. Garth gave this to me yesterday evening when he was getting ready to leave. He said that he'd found this when he was setting up Martha's table and didn't know whether it was valuable or not."

She handed me the thin volume. It was a 5x7" three-ring binder, probably sold at any office supply store, except it had a purple paisley cover. Inside, the loose leaf pages were divided into a series of columns, which were filled in with a bunch of letters and numbers. There was nothing to identify who owned it. I frowned.

"What do you think it is?"

"I don't know," April said. "I didn't really look at it. I was busy and just dropped it into my apron."

"Why didn't you tell the police?"

She stepped over to the small conference table and sat down.

"Because I forgot about it until you mentioned the secret drawer just now. I guess I was so focused on my own office that it just didn't occur to me." She looked up at me. "Do you think this is what they were looking for?"

I came to the table and sat across from her, looking suspiciously at the notebook and reading the entries. Across the top of the columns were capital letters that appeared to be abbreviations for something. Down the left hand side were initials and numbers, like RC/19 and TR/18.

"I have no idea," I said. "I don't know what it is."

She furrowed her brow and leaned into me. "Think about it, Julia. Whoever broke in seemed to be looking through tables with drawers. And then they rummaged through desk drawers and bookshelves. Doesn't it make sense that they were looking for a book?"

I glanced up at her, feeling my heart rate pick up a notch. "I guess so. They were certainly looking for *something*."

"I think they were looking for this book," she said, pointing a finger at the book.

I looked at the book again. "Martha's mother originally owned that table. This could have been hers, or maybe it belonged to Robert." I lifted my eyebrows. "Do you have a hunch?"

"No," April shook her head. "Nothing like that. But I don't think it could have been her mother's. The notebook is too modern. But I suppose it could have been Robert's, although paisley doesn't seem too much like him. Maybe it's some political information someone wants to get hold of. Do you think we should give it to the police?"

"Probably," I said. "But I'd sure like to know what it is first. Whoever broke in could have just as easily have been kids hyped up on drugs and finally just smashed the table because they couldn't find any money. Maybe that's why they left the graffiti—because they were angry." I sat tapping the book, my mind racing.

"I think we should wait and show it to the girls later tonight. See what they think."

"But shouldn't we just give it to the police?" April said. "That way it's out of our hands."

I kept tapping my thumb on the book, stalling for time. There was a big part of me that knew I needed to hand it over to the police. But a bigger part of me wanted to know what the book was first.

"Look," I said. "Angela is coming over soon to leave Lucy with me. I'll show it to her and ask her what she thinks."

"So, what do we do with it now?" April was clearly scared to have it in her possession. "If this little book is worth killing for, I'm not really comfortable having it around."

"Why don't we put it in a box and address it to Graham," I said. "No one will bother a box addressed to the Governor. That will give us time to figure this out."

April's eyes lit up. "Good thinking. I'll get a box."

CHAPTER TWENTY

April found a small box in the back of the bakery, and we slipped the book inside. I folded over the flaps and took the box back to the inn, thinking I'd tape it up and address it to Graham when I got to my apartment.

We normally locked the front door at five o'clock, so I was heading for the front door, when a familiar, "Yoo hoo!" broke the silence.

"Julia," Sybil drawled, coming through the door. "I came to get a few toys for the dogs. But first, how are you doing? Was anything stolen after all? Do the police know who broke in? Do you need any help cleaning up?"

She moved into the foyer like a steam engine, forcing me back to the registration desk, where I had to put a hand up before she bowled me over.

"Too many questions all at once, Sybil. I'm doing fine. Nothing appears to have been stolen. And, no, the police don't know who did it."

She slouched against the counter. If the horse I rode out in Sammamish could look like people, then he had a twin. Sybil had a long face with a wide mouth, large teeth and a broad forehead. To top things off, she wore her hair in some sort of top knot. All she was missing was the bit in her mouth, which right now I felt like supplying. Her husband was the president of a local bank in the area and was gone much of the time, leaving Sybil with entirely too much time on her hands. She'd tried several times to join our book club, but all the spots had been filled. Now, with Ellen and Martha both gone, I scrambled to think of an excuse if she asked again. But she was already on to different topics.

"So, Julia," she said, pursing those big lips, making me think she was about to whinny. "Do you really think someone tried to poison Senator Pesante and killed Martha instead?"

I set the box on the corner of the registration desk and sat down on the stool.

"Look Sybil," I said with all the patience I could muster. "I don't know who was trying to kill who...whom...whatever." I shook my head. "And frankly, murder is just too horrible for me to contemplate right now. I have to deal with the break in at the warehouse and the fact that someone was also at Martha's home the other night when José and I picked up her table."

You would have thought I'd started a fire.

"Oh, my stars!" she squealed, interrupting me. "I know. I saw the police over there this morning and so I walked over. When I told them I took care of Martha's place when she was gone, they asked me to help identify anything that might be missing. But everything looked normal," she said proudly. "Who do you think it was?"

"I don't know," I replied. "I never saw his face. But José thinks it might have been someone who knew the house was empty."

"And now your place was been broken into, too," she said with false sympathy.

"Yes. I just wish they hadn't destroyed so many of my antiques," I said wistfully. "They ruined some really beautiful pieces, not to mention the table I bought from Martha. I'd promised Emily I was going to keep it."

"I'm truly sorry, Julia," she said, frowning. "You love your antiques. How could anyone be soooo cruel? I mean, if they didn't steal anything, why would they do that?"

"I don't know." I sighed. "It seemed like they were looking for something."

"Oh for heaven's sake, what in the world would you be hiding in your antique shop?" she snorted.

"I wasn't hiding anything," I shot her an angry look. "That's the point."

I glanced at the box sitting on the end of the counter. Sybil ignored me.

"The police said it could be a gang thing," she said, continuing unabated. "I didn't know we had any gangs on Mercer Island. I'm going to tell Henry we have to add security. You know, he didn't want me to get Pepsi. He said Chihuahuas aren't really dogs at all. But now I bet he'll be glad we have her."

I didn't like Henry any better than I liked Sybil. But now that I knew he had been against getting Pepsi, I decided I should get to know him better.

"How are the puppies, by the way?" I asked, hoping to change the subject.

"Oh, I...uh...they're fine. You know how they love to play with Pepsi. That's why I thought I'd get a couple of toys."

"Okay, give me a second and I'll grab a couple."

I went to the cupboard in the kitchen and grabbed a couple of the loudest squeaker toys I could find, hoping against hope that they would drive Sybil nuts. When I came back to the registration desk, she was perched on the stool behind the counter, drumming her fingers. The box with the ledger sat right next to her.

"Julia," she said, slipping off the stool. "You don't think they're connected, do you?

Your break-in and the person lurking around Martha's? Well, of course, they must be. I wonder what's going on. I..."

I stuck the squeaker toys in her face and said, "Here you go. These are their favorites."

"Oh, that'll be fine," she said. "But Julia, I don't think you're sufficiently concerned about this. These people could be targeting the entire neighborhood."

As if a light bulb had just gone off in her big head, she quickly stepped back to the other side of the counter.

"I'd better go," she said nervously.

"I'm sure you're perfectly safe, Sybil. You have Henry, and..."

"And Pepsi," she said quickly. "Pepsi is an excellent watch dog, you know. She could wake the dead when she gets going, I tell you. Your two little dogs are pretty good, too."

She referred to Mickey and Minnie like they were smaller and less robust than her Chihuahua. I admit that my Dachshunds don't weigh more than ten pounds each, but with their long snouts and sharp teeth, they could pulverize her little Taco dog.

"By the way, Sybil," I said, changing the subject, "I'm checking with everyone who has a key to the inn. Has yours ever been out of your possession? Anyone ever ask to borrow it?"

She thought for a moment and then whipped out her jailor-size ring of keys again. "No. As you can see, I have your key right here next to Corinne's."

Corinne was another neighbor, and from the looks of it, Sybil had keys to most of the homes on Mercer Island.

"Where do you keep them?"

"On a hook in my kitchen," she said happily. "That way I always know where to find them. And since I'm home most of the time, I don't see how anyone could have gotten them. Oh," she held out her big hand, "and I'll need to get Martha's back."

"Oh, yes," I said, "I'm sorry. Hold on."

I quickly ducked into the office and grabbed my key ring from the desk drawer and removed the one she'd loaned me to Martha's house.

"Here you go," I said, handing it over. "So, back to my key. No one has asked to borrow it, have they?"

She shook her head, and I couldn't help but picture a bridle slapping against her jowls. "Of course not. I would have told you," she said.

"Okay, thanks," I said. "I'm just trying to figure out how someone might have gotten into the inn, if in fact that's what happened."

"What a scary thought," her eyes stretched into large marbles again. "Do you think someone actually broke in and poisoned the fudge? Oh, my stars, there might be a murderer sneaking around the neighborhood, too?"

She took a deep breath, and I could see that she was beginning to hyperventilate. I reached over for the box with the ledger in it.

"Listen, I've got a ton of stuff to do."

Sybil spied the box. One flap had popped up.

"What's this?" she asked, pulling it over and glancing inside.

I quickly drew the box to the far edge of the counter. "It's just … um… something Graham wanted me to send him."

"I have to stop at the post office myself tomorrow," she offered brightly. "I'd be glad to drop it off for you. You have enough on your mind."

"Thanks, but I've got it," I said, as I began to usher her out the door. "I have a few other things to mail, so I'll just take it all tomorrow morning on my way to the shelter."

"All righty, then. You look exhausted, Julia. You need to get some rest. I know you don't like pills, but a couple of Advil PM would do wonders for you tonight. I'll bring the puppies back tomorrow morning. Or if you want, I can always keep them for a couple of days in case you need a longer break."

I stretched my shoulders, feeling the strain of the past few days catch up to me. I'd miss the dogs, but decided that Sybil was right; I needed some good old-fashioned rest. And who knew what tomorrow would bring.

"Thanks. I'll pick them up tomorrow, though. I'll get them on my way back from the shelter."

She grinned. "That would be fine. Now you take care and get some rest," she said, turning to go. "I know most of your guests have left," she said over her shoulder. "So it should be pretty quiet over here. I suppose having a murderer lurking about can't be good for business."

Like so many of Sybil's comments, that little barb was meant to wound me—if only a little. While I mostly found Sybil annoying, she had a bit of a mean streak that I really didn't like. I thanked her, said goodbye and closed and locked the door. When I turned around, I nearly jumped out of my skin. Libby was standing right behind me.

"Sorry," she said.

"Um…that's okay," I said, taking a deep breath. "I didn't hear you."

She was beginning to remind me too much of the ghosts that inhabited the place.

The sound of a door closing echoed down the stairs and then Ms. Jenkins, my one remaining guest, appeared at the head of the stairs. She was a petite woman in her thirties, with shoulder-length black hair, a decent figure, and dark brown eyes accented with dramatic eye makeup.

"Excuse me," she said to both of us, as she descended the stairs. "But I don't seem to have gotten any clean towels today."

She nodded and raised an eyebrow as if she was annoyed by this oversight.

"I'll take care of it," Libby said.

Libby started for the laundry just as the front doorbell rang. We all stopped. I left the box on the counter and crossed the foyer to open the door. I found a man standing under the porch light, wearing dark pants and a black bomber jacket. He had a small rolling suitcase by his side. What gave me a start was his shocking white hair, which hung just below his ears, and a set of piercing blue eyes off set off by a lack of eyebrows.

"I...uh, was wondering if I could get a room for tonight," he said.

"Of course," I said, stepping back to let him in.

"I'm in town visiting my sister, who just had a baby," he said, closing the door behind him. "But I'm afraid the baby won't let me sleep. Colic or something like that," he said with a shrug.

He gave me a full smile, exposing a set of crooked, yet gleaming white teeth. As I studied him briefly, I realized that he actually did have eyebrows. They were just so light that they disappeared against his skin. I wondered if he was an albino.

"I'm sorry I didn't call," he said, peering at me through a pair of wire-rimmed glasses. "We just finished dinner and the baby started up again. I thought I'd better find a place before it got too late. I was heading downtown for a motel when I saw your sign and thought I'd just stop in and ask." He smiled again.

"No problem. Please, come in," I said.

I backed up and turned abruptly towards the registration desk, hitting the box with my elbow. It flew off the counter and landed on its side. The small ledger book slid half way out onto the floor.

"Let me get that for you," the new guest said, moving forward promptly to pick it up.

I beat him to it, almost knocking him over as I bent down.

"Thank you," I said, grabbing it and pushing the book back inside. "Just a little something for my ex-husband." I folded the box flaps into place.

"I'll get the towels," Libby spoke up, bringing attention back to her.

"Thank you, Libby," I said as she turned and left for the laundry.

Ms. Jenkins stood there with one hand on the bannister, looking like Marlene Dietrich. She stared at the new guy as if waiting for him to notice her. I stood holding the box watching her and waiting for her to leave. Our new guest stood awkwardly looking back and forth between us.

Count to three.

"Well!" I said, finally breaking the silence. "Let's get you checked in."

I crossed behind the counter and put the box on the shelf underneath. As I pulled out the guest book, I glanced over at Ms. Jenkins, who was still regarding the new guest as if he were something she hoped to order off a menu.

"I'll have Libby bring the towels to your room," I said to her.

She looked up at me as if just waking from a dream and then took the hint and retreated up the stairs.

"Well, you're in luck," I said, opening the book. "We have a room with a private bath for $225 a night, and one that shares a bath for $175."

"I'll take the one with a private bath," he said.

Just then, Ahab let out a loud whistle. His cage sits in a direct line with the reception desk, so he can see people when they come in. We both flinched.

"Sorry," I said. "That's Ahab. He gets excited when new people come in."

"Willkommen, bienvenue, well...come!" he sang in his best imitation of Joel Gray.

I chuckled "Just ignore him." I turned back to the registration book. "Okay, that will be $225."

"Houston, we have a problem," Ahab squawked again. "Houston, we have a problem."

"He's cute," the new guest murmured, his eyes narrowed in Ahab's direction.

He pulled out a money clip, glancing back to Ahab, who by now had shut up. As I watched him peel off the required amount, I couldn't help but wonder why someone would carry so much cash, especially if they were just visiting family. But then I decided I didn't really care.

"I just need your name here," I said, pointing to the space provided on the registration form, "and your license plate number."

"I'm driving a rental," he said.

"That's okay. We can just put that number down."

"I'll have to go out and check. Just a minute."

He went back outside, leaving the front door open. Since it was December, it was already dark outside, but I caught a glimpse of a large, dark truck or SUV in the first car slot. Then he returned with the license number. I explained the meal schedule and glanced at his name.

"Well, Mr....Brown, we have a nice library," I said, indicating the room across the entryway. "We have a refrigerator in the breakfast room stocked with sodas and fruit juices. And of course there is always coffee. Breakfast is served between 7:30 and 9:30, although I'm afraid that on the weekends we only serve a continental breakfast. And if you'd like to take a walk in the morning, there's a lovely trail just north of the beach."

"Thanks," he said. "I should only be here the one night. I'm scheduled to go home tomorrow afternoon."

Libby appeared behind him with the towels. When he turned, she averted her eyes, as if his appearance had startled her. I introduced them, and she nodded politely and offered to take him up to his room.

As they trudged upstairs, my cell phone jingled and I saw that I had a text from Angela. I'd forgotten all about her bringing Lucy over. She was at the side of the house. I grabbed the box and hurried to my apartment to unlock the side door.

Lucy greeted me by sticking her nose in my stomach. Angela was behind her holding a 20-lb bag of dog food. An enormous dog pillow leaned up against her leg.

Lucy is what they called a Harlequin Great Dane, which means she's covered in black and white splotches. Her face is divided almost in half—half black, half white—making her look as if she's wearing a mask.

Since she comes up to my waist, she stuck her big nose into my stomach a second time, clearly asking for some recognition. I reached out and stroked her head.

"Hello, Luce," I said.

"Hey, Mom, thanks for this," she said. "Where are the puppies?"

"Sybil has them."

"Great. You and Lucy can be best buds tonight. You want her bed in your bedroom again?"

"Yes, on the other side of my bed so I don't kill myself tripping over her if I have to get up in the middle of the night."

I took the dog food, while Angela grabbed the dog bed and went down the hallway to the master bedroom. After placing the pillow on the far side of the bed, she came out and put a comforting arm around my shoulders.

"Okay, so, how are you really doing? I heard about the break-in. Losing all those beautiful pieces must have been horrible. Have the police learned anything yet?"

I sighed and patted her hand. We were about the same height, but that's where the similarities ended. Obviously, no one would ever mistake us as relatives by birth. Besides her Asian heritage, she was a size 2, another dress size I had no acquaintance with. She had beautiful, long straight blue-black hair while mine was short and artificially dyed auburn. She still had perfect eyesight, while I was forced to use reading glasses. And, she had an easy, outgoing, even gregarious personality, while I bordered on being shy.

"No, we're not even sure how someone got in there. There were no broken windows or doors. And to see Martha's beautiful table completely destroyed like that, well…it was just heartbreaking. I felt like they'd taken Martha from us all over again."

"I'm so sorry, Mom. You know, I could stay here for a couple of days instead of going to Phil's. I could help out a bit. Give you a rest."

"No, no," I patted her hand again. "I'll be fine. It's just good to see you. Can you stay for a cup of tea?"

"Sure, but you sit. I'll make it."

She made the tea, while I grabbed the box with the ledger book off the counter and placed it on the table.

"What's this?" she said when she placed a steaming mug of tea in front of me.

"It was hidden in a secret drawer in the table Martha sold me," I said, sitting down and sliding the book to her. "The one that was

153

destroyed. When Martha sold it to me, we arranged to have the table picked up Friday morning. But, of course, she died first. So, if she meant to remove the book before I took the table, she didn't have time."

"But maybe she just forgot about it." Angela sat down, sipping her tea. She opened the ledger. "Do you know for a fact that it belonged to Martha, and not some other member of the family?"

"No. But consider this... Martha died Thursday. Friday night someone was lurking inside her house when we went to pick up the table. Then our workshop and bakery were broken into last night. All the tables that had drawers had been turned over and the drawers pulled out. And all of the bookshelves were swept clean. Even in the office, things were tossed about, as if someone had rummaged through drawers looking for something in particular. But when we found Martha's table—which by the way was labeled with her name on it—it had been completely demolished. I think someone knew that I'd bought a piece of furniture from Martha, but didn't know which one it was. So, they came here looking for it, either thinking—or perhaps knowing– that something was hidden inside."

I stopped, allowing Angela to absorb it all. She sat thoughtfully, tapping her fingers and taking a moment to study the open ledger in front of her.

"What about the gang tag?" she said.

"So, Mr. Wonderful gave you all the news, even though it's a weekend?"

She shrugged. "He's the lead detective. And he called me to give me an update."

"I bet," I said.

She lifted her eyes to mine. "What about José?"

I slapped both hands on the table. "Why does everyone immediately think of José?"

"Because he's Hispanic, from Southern California, and in case you haven't noticed, he has a couple of gang-related tattoos on his arms."

"He doesn't have anything to do with this, I'm telling you. Leave him out of this."

"Okay. But do you have any idea what this book is?" she asked, still scanning the pages.

"No. I was hoping you might."

She shook her head, sipping more tea. "I've never seen anything like it. It seems innocent enough, though."

"April wants me to give it to the police."

She looked up at me. She had high cheek bones and wore a thin line of eyeliner that extended beyond the tips of her eyes. Right now those beautiful almond-shaped eyes were clouded in thought.

"She's right."

"But it might be nothing, Angela. I already accosted your boyfriend with the pen." I smiled, but she scowled at me. "I don't want to be accused of sending the police on a wild goose chase. You saw how they looked at me when they highlighted that incident with the attorney general in Olympia. I think I should figure out what this is first. If it seems important, then by all means, we should turn it over to the police."

I finally just shut up. I knew the more I tried to talk her into it, the more she'd pull away.

"Here's the deal, Mom. If you don't give this to the police and they discover that it really *is* evidence and you withheld it, they *will* arrest you."

I sighed, knowing I didn't really have a leg to stand on here.

"Okay, I'll take it down to Detective Franks first thing in the morning. But I'm telling you, it could be some sort of shipping ledger, or just some personal notebook. It might even have belonged to Martha's husband."

"Yes, but you need to let the police figure it out. Then you'll be off the hook."

She stood up, taking a final sip of tea. "I have to go. Hey, Luce," she called out to the big dog, who had already made herself at home on my sofa. "I gotta go, girl." Lucy stepped off the sofa and ambled over. "You be good," she said, giving the big dog a kiss on her broad head. "Try not to get in Mom's way." She turned to give me a kiss on the cheek, "I'll call you tomorrow. And do NOT keep that book," she said, pointing a finger at me.

CHAPTER TWENTY-ONE

As tired as I was, I had called a meeting for seven o'clock that night to fill the girls in on the day's events and to find out what progress they'd made on our investigation. For privacy's sake, I told everyone we would meet in my apartment. The weather report said a storm front was coming in, so I cranked up the gas fireplace. April arrived first, bringing with her freshly sliced banana bread. I couldn't believe she'd baked after all that had happened that day, but I'd also never known her to be idle. Maybe baking was her form of therapy.

Lucy wandered out from the bedroom just as April placed the plate on the counter in the kitchen. April gave the big dog a pat and a brief smile, but the circles under her eyes gave me concern. Her face was drawn, and she seemed to move on autopilot.

"This will all work itself out," I said, giving April an encouraging hug. "Angela talked me into giving the book to the police. I'm going to take it to Detective Franks tomorrow."

"That's good," she said, nodding. "I'm glad. At least we won't have to worry about that."

My back door opened and Rudy came in with a burst of wind and leaves blowing in behind her.

"You look like you hit a wind tunnel," I said.

"It's really blowing out there," she said, running a hand over her hair. "What do I smell?"

"Banana bread," I said, "thanks to April."

"God, I love coming here for meetings." She headed straight for the counter. She was dressed in dark green wool pants and a black turtleneck sweater. She threw her wool coat over the back of a counter stool, smoothed down her hair again and lifted a slice off the plate." I've been on the phone all afternoon and haven't had dinner. Tough to get hold of people on a Sunday."

The door opened again and Doe came in, her beautiful salt and pepper hair standing straight up. Doe was the tallest among us, at about five-foot ten, and looked elegant even in a pair of jeans and a tapestry jacket.

"My goodness, it's like a tornado out there," she said, trying to flatten out her hair.

As tree branches scraped against the building, I took their coats and began to sing quietly, "The wind began to switch, the house to pitch. And suddenly the hinges started to un-hitch…"

I threw a backward glance at Rudy who scowled at me, but I just smiled and disappeared into the bedroom.

"Oh, yummy. I'm starving," Doe was saying as I came back out. "I only had lunch today." She reached for a slice of banana bread. "I can't get the board to budge, by the way. We may be headed for a strike, and I might have to refresh my memory on how to drive those trucks."

"Would you really do that?" I asked.

"If I had to," she said, breaking off a piece of the bread. "That's why Greg taught me in the first place. In the old days, we only had a few drivers, and he made sure every single person on the payroll was licensed to drive a truck. Of course, it's been about twenty years since I've done it," she rolled her eyes. "But if push came to shove…" She popped a piece of banana bread into her mouth.

Lucy wandered over to where Rudy was sitting on one of the counter stools. The dog was so tall that her head was almost level with the counter. Rudy pushed the plate back.

"Don't you dare, Luce, or you and I will have words."

Lucy looked up at her, her eyes pleading for a treat. Rudy only looped her arm over the dog's neck.

"God, you're just a big lug of a dog, aren't you?"

"Careful," I said with a chuckle. "She doesn't know she's a dog."

"God, but with that face, she could try out for *Phantom of the Opera*."

A brief flash of lights swept across the window and a moment later Blair breezed in.

"Whoo," she said, "I think Katrina just made landfall."

Her blond hair looked like it had been whipped by an egg beater, but other than that, the spandex was holding firm.

"I smell something wonderful," she said almost immediately. She moved to the counter and looked like she was going to grab a slice of the sweet bread.

"Yes, sorry, Blair," April said. "It's not sugar-free."

"Oh, right," she said, retracting her hand. "That's okay. But God, it smells good."

"If you're going to drink wine, though," I said, "I have some nuts here."

I showed her a bowl of mixed nuts I'd put on the table. Blair had long ago instilled in me the importance of eating something if she drank wine.

"Thanks, Julia," she said with a smile.

I had brewed a pot of coffee and opened a bottle of chardonnay, and we took both into my small living room. Once we were all settled, I told them about the break-in and the destruction of my antiques.

"That's really scary, Julia," Blair murmured, pouring a glass of wine and grabbing a handful of nuts. "Aren't you a little freaked out?"

I sighed as I considered her question.

"Yes, but I'm more heartbroken about Martha's table and the other antiques. Fortunately, no one was hurt. In fact, no one even saw anyone lurking around the barn."

"But aren't you a little afraid they might break into the inn?" she asked.

"I have the dogs," I said with bravado. "Well, dog," I corrected myself, looking over at Lucy who had curled up by the fireplace. "Sybil has Mickey and Minnie. So maybe I should ask José to stay over here tonight."

Doe nodded. "That's not a bad idea. Isn't he a black belt in something?"

"Yes. Tae Kwon Do, I think. Wait a minute while I give him a call."

I ran to the phone and called José. He agreed immediately and said he'd take one of the guest rooms.

"Okay, that's done," I reported. "So what did we find out?"

Blair got up and went to the door of the apartment, opened it and wandered down the hallway towards the registration desk. I glanced after her, but she passed out of view.

"I talked to Philippe, one of my drivers," Doe began. "He said that Carlita is so broken up about Martha's death, she can't stop talking about it. She'd cleaned Martha's house for three years and liked her. She says that Martha had been acting strange lately, though. She was really uptight and jumpy around the house and kept going to the Mercer Island Library for some reason."

"The library?" Rudy said.

"She also spent an unusual amount of time online, something she normally never did unless she was looking for recipes. Pretty soon, she was complaining that she wasn't sleeping. That went on for several days, until she said she got one of those self-help tapes. Carlita said she had this MP3 player she carried with her everywhere the last few days. Martha said she was sleeping better, but according to Carlita, she didn't look much better and started eating a lot of sweets even though she was trying to lose a few pounds." Doe shrugged. "Weird, hunh?"

"I wonder what she was doing at the library," I said.

"Can't you go down and ask?" Rudy asked. "You're on the board."

"They don't keep records of what people search for. I could ask one of the librarians if she asked for help, I suppose."

"Wait, there's more," Doe continued. "Carlita also overheard Martha on the phone the Tuesday after Thanksgiving. She doesn't know who Martha was talking to, but she said, 'I need your help. Something is really wrong here.'"

"Wow, that doesn't sound good," Rudy said.

"It sounds like she was frightened of something. Thanks, Doe." I glanced over at Rudy. "What did you find out?"

Rudy settled back and crossed one leg over the other. "I called a lot of my contacts and finally found a beat reporter down in Olympia who knew something. She told me that Senator Pesante chairs the Senate Judicial Review Committee, and it's rumored that he's about to start an investigation into allegations of bribery at the highest levels of the state Republican Party."

There were gasps around the room.

"Whoa, that would make him unpopular," Doe said.

"Yes, very unpopular," Rudy agreed. "I also talked to Elliott. Pesante used to be the prosecuting attorney in Walla Walla. He has a reputation for being relentless, which means he doesn't give up. Elliot's heard he's received threatening emails. That's not uncommon for politicians, but I guess some of these have been pretty specific."

"And the big donors are shying away from him, too," Blair said as she sauntered back into the room, closing the door behind her. "Mr. Billings says Pesante is toxic right now. No one will give him money. He's too much of a lightning rod. He'll launch an investigation into anything her perceives as wrong and something he can get attention for."

Blair made a left turn and floated into my kitchen.

"That's weird. Graham called him a lightning rod, too. Maybe Pesante was the target after all," I said.

"Did Martha know Pesante?" Rudy asked.

I had to think. "Yes, I mean probably as well as I do. We've both met him, and of course Robert would have known him. In fact, I think he was at Robert's funeral."

Rudy settled back into her chair, sipping her wine, a thoughtful expression on her face. A noise made me look up to where Blair was opening and closing a cupboard in the kitchen. Everyone else tracked my gaze. The kitchen was open to the living room, and we all watched Blair turn and look under the counter. I exchanged quizzical looks with Rudy and Doe.

"But if the senator was the target," April began, not really paying attention to Blair, "then why were *we* targeted for a break-in?"

That brought everyone's attention back to the question at hand.

"I suppose it all could be a coincidence," I said. "A rash of neighborhood thefts."

"But nothing was stolen," April said.

We heard the refrigerator door open and all looked up to watch Blair rummaging through one of the shelves. A moment later, she found what she was looking for and reached in and grabbed it. She turned around ready to open a box of my fudge, only to find all of us staring at her. She stopped with the lid of the box halfway off.

"What?" she said. "I'm hungry."

I got up and came slowly around the counter.

"But, Blair, you can't eat that."

Suddenly, the other girls were there, too.

Doe said, "What's wrong, Honey? What's going on?"

Blair just stared at us and then looked at the box in her hand. All of a sudden, she dropped it and April caught it.

"Oh my God! Is it poisoned? Is it the same fudge?"

"No, no," I said, drawing her out of the kitchen. "I've had that fudge for several weeks."

Rudy stepped in and took her by the shoulder. "C'mon, Blair, let's go sit down."

She steered Blair to the sofa, while April put the fudge back. Blair was practically hyperventilating, so I grabbed a glass of water.

"Blair, are you feeling okay?" Rudy placed a hand on her forehead.

"Yes, of course. I'm fine. I was just…"

Her eyes glazed over as she turned inward, thinking.

"What is it, Blair?" I asked, handing her the glass of water. "What were you looking for?"

She turned to me, her eyes clouded. "The fudge. I wanted the fudge."

"That specific fudge?" Doe leaned in to ask her.

Blair rubbed her forehead and closed her eyes as if thinking. When she opened her eyes again, she said, "No. I couldn't find the right box." She took a drink of water, her eyes staring straight ahead as if she was in a trance.

We all sat back, harboring our own thoughts. It was April who finally voiced what we were all thinking.

"Just like Martha," she said.

Blair suddenly seemed to re-engage.

"I have a headache," she said, rubbing her forehead again. "Maybe I could go lie down?"

"C'mon, Blair," I said, taking her into my bedroom.

I helped her lie down and put a throw over her legs and then returned to find a very somber group of women in my living room.

"Wow," Doe exhaled. "She really did act just like Martha."

"If I believed in voodoo," April said, "I'd say both Martha and Blair had been hexed."

"Seriously?" Rudy said, giving her a critical look. "Voodoo?"

April merely shrugged. "Do you have any better ideas?"

No one responded.

"Wait a minute," Doe said rather quietly. "Remember what Carlita said about Martha not being able to sleep?"

We all nodded.

"Blair told me that she's been having trouble sleeping, too. I guess Mr. Billings has been gone a lot, and she doesn't like staying in that big house alone."

Rudy rolled her eyes. "If having trouble sleeping was the trigger for eating poisoned fudge, we'd all be dead."

Good point, I thought.

"Yes, but remember Carlita said that Martha started listening to self-help tapes all the time," Doe continued. "Blair told me she'd gotten one, too. I was with her at the gym yesterday morning, and she was listening to it while she was on the exercise bike."

"Actually," Rudy said, standing up, "I noticed her take something out of her ears when she came in tonight." She walked over to where Blair had dropped her purse on the floor. Rudy reached down and lifted up a small MP3 player and a set of ear buds.

"So they were both listening to MP3 players. What could that mean?" I asked.

"It depends on what it was they were listening to," April said.

"When I asked Blair about it yesterday," Doe said, "she told me it had subliminal messages that would help her relax enough at night to go to sleep at night."

The room seemed to get significantly brighter as everyone's eyebrows shot up. Rudy got up and ran into the bedroom. A moment later, she emerged with a strained look on her face. We all waited expectantly.

"Well?" I asked.

"I asked Blair where she got the MP3 player." She looked around the room, allowing the anxiety to rise. "She got it from Martha."

There was a collective gasp. Doe even fell back onto the sofa.

"What are we thinking?" April asked a moment later. "That somehow the tape has a hidden message on it?"

We all looked at each other with questioning expressions.

"Why not?" I shrugged. "Subliminal learning tapes are very popular."

Rudy sat down again. "But if it was commercially made, why would it have some weird message about eating your fudge?"

No one had an answer to that. Suddenly, Doe sat up straight.

"What if she didn't buy it? What if someone gave it to her?"

"Do you know what you're saying?" Rudy said with raised eyebrows. "That someone purposely recorded a subliminal tape with a hidden message to eat poisoned fudge and then gave that tape to Martha."

"That sounds pretty fantastic, doesn't it?" Doe said, flopping back again.

"Let's just say for a moment that Doe's right, and that's how it happened," I said. "If it did happen that way, then Martha was the target all along."

They all turned and looked at me. Finally, April grabbed the teapot and stood up and went into the kitchen.

"Something tells me she was."

"But why?" I said to her with exasperation. "Why would someone want to kill Martha?"

"We need to find out if that tape has a hidden message on it," Doe said. "We're kind of stuck until we know that. If it doesn't, then we're barking up the wrong tree."

"And if it has a hidden message on it?" Rudy asked.

"Then we focus like a laser on Martha," Doe said with the tenacity of a CEO.

"But how do we find out what's on it?" I asked. "Isn't the whole point about subliminal messages that you can't hear the message?"

"I think that sort of thing is done in layers," Rudy said. "I'm sure you can pull the layers apart. I know the dean of the IT Department at University of Washington, I could…"

163

"Wait a minute," April said, holding up a hand. "Shouldn't we just give it to the police?"

We all paused.

"Yes, I think we should," I said. "We already have something else to give them." I glanced back at April, who was filling the teapot with hot water again.

"What?" Doe asked. "What are you talking about?"

"Wait a minute."

I got up and went to my study and got the ledger. I brought it back.

"You want to tell them, April?"

She shrugged, coming back into the room with the teapot. "Mr. Garth gave me this ledger yesterday after working on Martha's table. I put it in my apron and forgot about it until late today, after the table was smashed."

"I'm going to give it to the police first thing tomorrow," I said. "It may have nothing to do with Martha's death, but if it does, they'll figure it out."

"But what is it?" Rudy asked.

I opened the book on the coffee table and everyone huddled around.

"We thought it might be some kind of shipping ledger," April said.

"But for what?" Doe asked skeptically. "It doesn't indicate any kind of product. It has dates and what looks like ports or something."

"You think shipping ports?" I asked.

"Or maybe airports," she answered.

"It's weird," Rudy decided. "It's not an official ledger. These aren't ledger pages. Someone has turned a stupid-looking notebook into some kind of ledger."

Just then, Blair appeared at the bedroom doorway.

"I think I'd better go home," she said quietly. "I have a pretty bad headache."

Her face was pale and her hair tousled. I got up and went to her.

"Are you sure, Blair? You could stay in the extra bedroom tonight."

"No," she said, shaking her head. "I'm fine. I heard what you guys were saying about the tape, though."

164

"Do you know where Martha got it?" Rudy asked.

"No. She just told me that it had started working pretty fast, so she gave it to me to try."

"When?" April asked her.

Blair had to think a minute. "Um…Wednesday night. I stopped by her house."

"So, you've only been listening to it for a few days?" April said.

She nodded. "Yeah. But she told me to listen as often as I could. What's that?" she asked, nodding toward the book.

She wandered over and glanced down at the first page of the ledger.

"We think Mr. Garth found it in Martha's table," I told her. "But we don't know what it is. Or why someone may be looking for it."

She studied the pages for a moment and then shrugged.

"Well, I'm going to go," she said, heading for her purse.

"Blair, maybe you should see a doctor," Rudy said.

"No, really, I'm fine. I just want to rest."

"Well, I'm driving you home," Doe said, standing up. "We can pick up your car tomorrow."

"Okay," she said weakly.

"I've got to go, too," Rudy chimed in. "What about the MP3 player, Julia? Are you going to give it to the police along with the book?"

I glanced at April and she nodded. "Yeah, I'll drop it off first thing in the morning. They'll be able to find the right kind of technicians to deal with it."

"I think that's a great idea," Rudy patted my arm. "Let the professionals worry about it."

Ten minutes later, everyone was gone, and I was left to clean up, while the adrenalin dissipated from my system. I was in the kitchen wiping down the counter, when I felt a cold spot and glanced up. Elizabeth was hovering on the other side of the counter, her hand to her throat again. The adrenalin surged through my veins.

"Yes, I know. Martha was poisoned," I said, hoping she would stop. "Now, we just need to figure out how and why."

Elizabeth withdrew her hand from her throat and suddenly pushed her palm across the counter toward the book. She didn't touch it, and yet the book flew off the counter onto the kitchen floor.

"What?" I gasped. "Why did you do that?"

I bent over and picked up the book. When I stood back up, she was gone.

I spun around, looking for her, but she had vanished. Now my heart rate was pumping hard. What had that meant?

I glanced at the small book in my hand. Elizabeth had done that on purpose. But why? Like my mother, could she see things I couldn't?

I immediately marched down the hallway to my study and slid the book into the inside pocket of my purse. I was determined more than ever now to get it to the police in the morning.

When the adrenaline had slowed, I let Lucy out in the backyard, got into my pajamas, and then went back to the kitchen to grab a glass of warm milk before going to bed. Blair'sMP3 player was sitting on the counter next to my Wicked Witch of the West cookie jar. It made me think about Martha and Blair. They had both listened to the tape and then gone looking for the box of fudge. Was that how it had happened? Had someone programmed a subliminal learning tape and then given it to Martha? I fingered the MP3 player—tempted to pick it up and listen to it. But then I changed my mind. Let the police deal with it.

I took the ear buds and wrapped them around the body of the small device and left it on the counter next to the cookie jar so that I wouldn't forget it in the morning. Then I downed a couple of Advil PM with the warm milk and went to bed, thinking only of a good night's sleep.

Boy, was I wrong.

CHAPTER TWENTY-TWO

The grandfather clock in the inn's entryway had just struck ten when my head hit the pillow. Like a miniaturized version of Big Ben, the deep, rich bells sounded throughout most of the building. It was a comforting sound, and many guests swore that it helped them sleep.

Lucy had gone to the far side of the bed, where Angela had placed the dog's donut-shaped pillow the size of Hawaii. She circled a few times and then finally plumped down with a groan. I listened to her settle in, remembering that she was a heavy sleeper. I wouldn't see her again until the morning.

I put my mother's phone on the night stand before lying back for my own well-deserved rest. Ever since my mother had contacted me, I felt the need to keep her close.

I slipped into a deep sleep. Sometime later, I was on stage in my high school production of *Grease*. John Travolta was there and had just finished belting out, "*You're The One That I Want*," when suddenly Bill Haley and the Comets began singing "*Rock Around the Clock*." My eyes fluttered open as I slowly became aware that my mother's phone was ringing next to the bed.

The room was dark except for a faint light spill from a nightlight in the hallway. My eyes were only halfway open, as I reached out blindly for the phone. As I groped in the darkness, a hand appeared from nowhere and slapped a cloth over my mouth and nose, pushing my head back into the pillow before I could resist. I tried to cry out, but couldn't and grabbed a pair of thick wrists, scrambling to pull them away as a suffocating, acrid smell set off all sorts of alarms in my head. I remembered that smell. I'd had my tonsils out when I was seven. The cloth was drenched in chloroform!

I gagged and my head began to spin. I tried flipping to my side, but my attacker was too strong. The world began to swirl, and I was about to succumb to the horrid fumes clogging my nostrils, when Lucy came awake with a start and made herself known. From the depths of that big, hollow chest, came a deep, rumbling growl. The attacker hesitated, and my gaze darted to the other side of the bed.

What appeared out of the darkness was straight out of a horror movie.

Lucy's black and white harlequin face emerged from the shadows like some grotesque gargoyle. Her left eye seemed to float in space, while the other side was completely visible, right down to her curled lip and spit-covered, alligator-sized teeth. Her entire body vibrated with rage, and she began to move slowly around the end of the bed, stalking her prey.

That's all it took. The man fled.

He ran from the room, and Lucy lunged after him. He had just enough time to pull the bedroom door closed behind him. Lucy slammed up against it, eliciting a chilling howl. The door bounced open again, and she ran to the front door, throwing herself at the closed door and barking a high pitched alarm.

Meantime, I rolled out of bed and onto the floor, gasping for air. When she realized her pursuit was cut short, Lucy abandoned it and came back to lick my face.

I stumbled to my feet and heard a car engine start up. Tires screeched as a car peeled out of the gravel driveway. I made it back to the bed and grabbed the bedside phone to dial 911. With a raspy voice, I reported the assault. The operator told me to stay on the line, and that's when I heard loud knocking at my outer door. It was José. I hadn't thought to give him a key to my apartment and so had to make the arduous trip down the hallway.

"Ms. Applegate, you okay?" he said in alarm when I opened the door.

He helped me to my chair and knelt down beside me.

"What happened?" he said, his face twisted in concern.

I was still coughing, and I must have looked a wreck. He got up and went to the sink and got me a glass of water, which I took gratefully.

"I heard the dog and then a car," he said.

Lucy watched José with little interest. He clearly wasn't a threat, so she climbed up on the sofa and stretched out, completely relaxed now.

"Someone…attacked me." I wheezed and then coughed.

Libby appeared in the doorway behind José, her hair in curlers and dressed in a long nightgown. When she heard I'd been attacked, her eyes went wide, and her hand flew to her mouth. This might be getting to be too much for my shy and retiring housekeeper.

"I'll call the police," she screeched.

"Already done." I squeezed the words out, holding up my cell phone.

My throat burned, and my head was swimming. I hadn't inhaled enough of the chloroform to knock me out, but enough to make me groggy. It was hard not to just put my head down and go to sleep. Just then, we heard the distant wail of a siren, and I was able to hang up on the 911 operator.

By the time the two patrol cars rolled into our driveway—again—Ms. Jenkins appeared in the hallway, only to be pushed aside as the emergency personnel burst in. Just great, I thought. Even the ghosts of Christmas past wouldn't keep her here now. The place would be empty by morning.

Right behind the police cars was an ambulance, and before long my apartment was filled with enough emergency personnel to staff a natural disaster. Amidst the EMTs checking my blood pressure and the police asking me questions and looking for clues, Ms. Jenkins reappeared a second time with her suitcase in tow.

"I'm leaving, Mrs. Applegate," she nearly shouted from just inside my door. "Mrs. Applegate?"

There were so many people milling about, I only saw flashes of her as she tried to get my attention. So I nodded and waved her away. Meanwhile, Lucy was up again, wandering around sticking her nose into everything, while Ahab chattered nervously down the hall—running through his repertoire of movie quotes.

"Here's looking at you, kid," Ahab called out. "Go ahead, make my day! Squawk! You talkin' to me? You talkin' to me?"

I called José in from the kitchen, where he was talking to Ms. Jenkins.

"José, can you go and try to calm Ahab down?"

"Sure, Ms. Applegate," he nodded.

The police collected the chloroform cloth from the bedroom and looked for how the intruder had gained entrance. They found no broken windows or locks, which meant that whoever it was may have had a key. That was as unsettling as the intruder himself.

As one of the officers was taking my statement, Detective Franks appeared in the background, looking a little bleary-eyed. After all, it was the middle of the night.

"You okay?" he asked, stepping forward, his face pinched with concern.

"Yes, just shaken." I rubbed my throat, which still burned.

He lingered for a moment, watching me, and then said, "Okay, just give me a minute. Let me talk to the officers and I'll be right back." He left to confer with the other officers on the scene. Within a few minutes, he was back.

"When you're up to it, we'd like you to walk through the apartment and let us know if anything is missing. What chased the guy off?"

"The dog," I said, nodding toward Lucy, who was now sitting by my side, watching an EMT take my blood pressure. "Whoever it was wasn't counting on Lucy."

"Your other dogs are still gone?" he said, looking around the floor for the little wieners.

"Yes, they're still with Sybil. Remember? She wanted me to get some rest," I scoffed. "Fat chance."

He looked thoughtful. "Did anyone else know you had the Great Dane here?"

I stopped massaging my throat for a moment. "Yes. All the girls from my book club were here for a short meeting tonight. But I don't think anyone else knew."

José and Libby were both hanging about in the hallway in case they were needed. But they were out of earshot.

"What about your staff?" he asked, nodding in their direction.

"Um, no. They didn't know. My daughter brought the dog in through the side door."

He wrote a note in a small notebook.

"It had nothing to do with either one of them, Detective," I said.

He put up a hand. "I'm not making any accusations. But we'll have to talk to them, nonetheless. How many guests are still here?"

I rolled my eyes in exasperation. "Well, until a few minutes ago, I had two registered guests."

"What do you mean?" he asked.

"My last long-term guest just checked out. I think having the police show up every five minutes was more than she bargained for."

"I see," he said apologetically. "Look, it appears that whoever this was had to have had help. Which means that…"

"They had to have had a key," I said, finishing his thought. My stomach tightened.

"Not only that, whoever attacked you didn't expect the dog, not this dog anyway," he said, indicating Lucy, who by now was sprawled across the floor, snoring. "And so far, it appears that only three people were unaware of the dog. And one of those people just suddenly left."

My eyes opened wide. "You think Ms. Jenkins was the inside person?"

"I don't know. But do you have her license plate number and contact information?"

"Yes, of course."

I called Libby in and asked her to get it. When she returned with the information, Detective Franks called one of the uniformed police officers.

"Put a BOLO out on this Ruth Jenkins. Here's her license plate number."

As he gave direction to the officer, I thought about Mickey and Minnie. Normally, they would not only have been with me, they would have been sleeping on my bed. Had they been there, I doubt anyone would have gotten within six feet of my bed without alerting them, which made me agree that whoever it was knew my dogs were going to be gone, or perhaps didn't know I had dogs to begin with. Detective Franks turned back to me.

"So, do you have any idea who might have attacked you?"

"No," I said, shaking my head. But then something occurred to me. "Wait a minute. Actually, I might," I said, picturing a head of white hair in my mind.

Libby appeared with a mug of hot tea. I took a sip. It felt good trickling down my throat. Detective Franks waited patiently.

"Who?" Detective Franks asked.

I looked up at Libby. "Libby, please take Detective Franks to Mr. Brown's room and see if he's there. I don't think he will be. Nor do I think you'll find his car in the driveway."

They did as I asked, while the EMT's finished giving me some advice for my throat and left. Libby and the police officers came back a few minutes later to report that not only was Mr. Brown gone, his bed hadn't been used, and there were no personal belongings left behind except for his suitcase, which was open but empty. And his car was gone.

We gave the detective a detailed description of Mr. Brown, including the license plate number he'd given us. Once I was feeling better, Detective Franks asked me to walk through my rooms to see if anything had been taken. The apartment had two bedrooms and a small study that included a desk, file cabinet, and computer. The study was a mess. Someone had thrown the box addressed to Graham on the floor and rifled through my desk. I checked the inside pocket of my purse.

"Well, I can tell you one thing that's missing," I said.

"What's that?"

"A book. Mr. Garth, my furniture refinisher, found a small ledger book in the drawer of that table of Martha's when he was refinishing it. He gave the book to April, who dropped it into the pocket of her apron and forgot about it. She remembered tonight and gave it to me. I was going to bring it to you first thing tomorrow morning."

"What was in it?"

"A bunch of numbers and abbreviations," I said. "It didn't make much sense. I showed it to my daughter when she was here earlier, and she had no idea what it was, either. But apparently it meant something to whoever broke in here, because it was in the side pocket of my purse and it's the only thing gone." Then I remembered the MP3 player. "Wait, there's something else."

I led him into the kitchen.

172

"I was also going to bring you this MP3 player Blair had with her tonight. Martha gave it to her just before she died…"

The end of my sentence froze in my throat. The MP3 player was gone as well.

"Damn!"

I looked around the floor and behind my flour and sugar canisters, but it was nowhere to be found.

"It's gone, too."

I leaned out into the hallway and called José.

"José, did you see a small MP3 player sitting on the counter earlier when you got me that glass of water?"

He thought a minute. "Maybe," he said. "I think there might have been something there. I'm not sure."

"Thanks, José," I dismissed him.

I looked over at Detective Franks, feeling sick to my stomach now.

"Let's go back and sit down," he suggested.

He helped me back into the living room and into the chair.

"Don't tell me," I said. "If the MP3 player was there when José got me the water, then someone other than the intruder took it. And that means it had to be someone who was in here within the last…oh…twenty minutes."

He nodded. "Unless José was mistaken, or took it himself."

José had gone back into the hallway.

"Listen," I said, bristling. "There were probably fifteen people in and out of here, including *you*. It could have been anybody."

"Touché," he said, with a lift to his eyebrows. "Did the Jenkins woman actually enter the apartment?"

I had to think. "Yes, at least by a few feet. But it was so busy and crowded that I couldn't see her very well. But all she had to do was look into the kitchen and she would have seen it lying on the counter."

"Actually, Ms. Applegate." José interrupted us, stepping back in from the hallway. "She did go into the kitchen. When she came to tell you she was leaving, she stepped into the kitchen. I came in behind her as she was just getting something out of her purse. When I interrupted her, she turned around and said she just wanted to leave you a note to let you know to mail her the bill. She didn't want you to think she wouldn't pay."

"Could she have been putting something *into* her purse instead of taking something out of it?" Detective Franks asked him.

José shrugged. "Sure. I guess."

"By the way, where were you when Ms. Applegate was attacked?"

José paused and glanced at me. "I was upstairs. Ms. Applegate asked me to sleep over here tonight after the warehouse was broken into."

"That's right, Detective. I did."

Detective Franks looked at me, his brown eyes cautious. Then he shifted his gaze to José. "We found your fingerprints on that can of spray paint today, the one that was used to paint graffiti in the warehouse," he said.

José wasn't surprised by this information, but his dark features tensed. "There are several more cans in the garage with my finger prints on them, too," he said. "I can get them for you, if you'd like. We don't lock the garage."

José was an inch or two shorter than Detective Franks, and yet he stood straight and tall. He knew he was under suspicion and was fighting back. Detective Franks took a moment to contemplate his response, and then relented.

"That's okay. Just stay close. I may want to talk to you again."

José frowned and left. Detective Franks dropped onto the end of the sofa.

"I think you're far too trusting when it comes to your staff," he said. "They have access to everything here at the inn."

"I understand, Detective," I said, a thin edge to my voice. "But I think we should focus on Mr. Brown and Ms. Jenkins. She could have easily taken the MP3 player."

"We'll catch up to her," he said. He looked at me with caution. "I think it would be a good idea if you slept somewhere else tonight. I'd like to get a forensics team out here to dust for prints first thing in the morning. I doubt we'll find any, but it's worth a try."

"I can use one of the guest bedrooms. I have plenty...now," I said with a grimace.

"Does José have a key to your apartment?"

"No. In fact, I had to let him in after I was attacked."

"Okay. Just the same, I think I'll post an officer here tonight," the detective added. "Just in case this guy decides to come back."

"Thank you, Detective. I appreciate that."

He really was a nice-looking man, and I felt suddenly exposed sitting there in my nightgown. I crossed my arms over my chest and stood up.

"I should get some things to take upstairs."

I quickly got my robe and slippers, a change of clothes, a few bathroom items, and my mother's phone. I called Lucy from where she'd commandeered her favorite spot on the sofa, and we all paraded down the hallway to the front desk. Detective Franks had one of the police officers string yellow crime scene tape across my doorway as we left.

"I'll have a forensics team out here first thing in the morning," he said. "Do you mind if Officer Barnes sits inside here tonight? It's pretty cold outside."

"Of course not. I'd feel better if he did." I turned to Libby. "Libby, could you bring him a cup of coffee?"

She nodded as Detective Franks turned to speak to the officer. When he was finished, he turned to me.

"I'm really glad you're okay," he said quietly. "I'll talk to you tomorrow."

I nodded and he left. I locked the front door tight and climbed the stairs.

"I'll sleep with the door open," José said to me from the door to his room.

"Thank you, José. I'll see you in the morning."

As I organized my things a few minutes later, I pulled my mother's cell phone from the pocket of my robe. I was beginning to think it was a necessary part of my attire, and I couldn't help wondering why my mother had called me tonight. Had she wanted to warn me about the intruder? I'd have to ask her next time she called. And thank her, because she may have saved my life.

CHAPTER TWENTY-THREE

The next morning was Monday, and I awoke with a headache. I grabbed a glass of water and slammed down a couple of aspirin, cringing as the pills slid past my raw throat. My rooms were still blocked off, and Detective Franks called to say the forensics team would be out by nine o'clock. The thought of having another team of police officers in my home turned my stomach to lead. So I decided to go to the shelter for my normal day of volunteering and leave oversight of my apartment to Elizabeth.

Officer Barnes was gone when I came downstairs. I offered to make José breakfast, but he declined and returned to the guest house. The tension in his facial muscles told me he was feeling the stress of constantly being under suspicion.

I woke Ahab and greeted him.

"Good morning, Juuulia," he said, stretching my name out as Sybil might.

When Lucy lumbered over to the cage, Ahab squawked and jumped to the top perch, singing, "Who let the dogs out? Woof. Woof. Woof."

"She won't hurt you," I said, smiling. "She's more gentle than you are. C'mon, Luce," I said, leading her into the kitchen.

April was already busy making breakfast when I finally appeared with Lucy by my side. The moment she saw me, she came over and embraced me with a hug.

"Damn, Julia! Why didn't you call me last night?"

"I'm sorry," I said, disengaging myself. "But I'm fine. I take it you heard all about it."

"The police officer stopped in. You know, the one who slept here last night?" she said with raised eyebrows.

"I know. Sorry, but it was really late by the time everyone left. I wasn't hurt, though," I said quickly. "Lucy saved the day. I never thought I'd be grateful for this big lug of a dog," I said, patting her on her head. "Give me a minute. I have to take her outside. My apartment is blocked off as a crime scene."

I rolled my eyes as if it was no big deal, but of course, it was. I took Lucy out the back door and across the drive to a lawn area. With my arms wrapped around me to ward off the cold, I stood there while she did her business. We returned to the kitchen, me rubbing my hands together and exhaling frosty breath, while Lucy merely lumbered over to where April stood at the counter making waffles. I went to the pantry and found an extra bag of dog food.

"Lucy, c'mon over here."

She was tall enough to threaten to steal one of the waffles off the plate sitting at April's elbow.

"Don't even think about it," April warned her.

"C'mon, girl," I said, pouring half the bag into a big mixing bowl.

Those big mournful eyes darted from the waffles and then back to me, while a big blob of drool slipped from the corner of her mouth. Finally, she abandoned April and came over to me. Having her in the kitchen was like having a pony over for breakfast.

"I don't think you'll have to make too many of those," I said, indicating the waffles. "Ms. Jenkins left last night, as did a new guest, a Mr. Brown," I said gravely. "So, we have no guests, and in case you didn't hear, the police are looking for Ms. Jenkins. She may be the one who gave a key to my attacker, who by the way was probably Mr. Brown."

"You're kidding? How would she have gotten a key to your apartment?"

"I don't know. But it had to be an inside job. There is an extra key to my apartment in the office. Maybe she snuck in there when no one was around. We were all pretty much preoccupied with cleaning up the warehouse yesterday."

"I didn't meet this Mr. Brown," she said. "What was he like?"

"Creepy," I replied, remembering his shocking white hair and albino look. "Remind me never to let a creepy man check in again," I said, grabbing a cup of coffee.

April unplugged the waffle maker and came to the table with the plate.

"I don't mind saying that this is beginning to get very scary, Julia."

I grabbed the butter and syrup from the refrigerator and sat down with a deep sigh.

"Well, perhaps it's all over now."

"What do you mean?" she asked.

"Whoever attacked me last night stole the ledger book and the MP3 player. They got what they wanted," I said, spearing a waffle.

She slumped into a chair with an audible exhale. "So all the evidence is gone."

I paused. "Yes." I dropped the waffle onto my plate. "But maybe that means at least that we—the inn—won't be the target anymore."

April had begun wringing her hands. "Let's hope so."

Libby showed up at the doorway, looking very gray.

"Are you okay?" she asked quietly.

"I'm okay," I said, with my hand to my throat. "But I'm won't be yodeling today. Come sit down and have some breakfast."

"I'm not really hungry," she said. "I think I'll get started on turning the Jenkins room."

"I don't think we have anyone else checking in until this weekend, when we're full," I said. "So, maybe we can all take a break and catch up on other things."

"Would you mind if I took the afternoon off, then?" Libby said. "I...haven't done any Christmas shopping."

Poor Libby was one of the blandest individuals I had ever known. She had mousey gray hair that was thinning at her hairline, a weak chin, a long, spindly neck, large, boney hands, and sallow skin. But after the last couple of days, she looked worse for the wear, if that was possible. She now had dark circles under puffy eyes.

"I think that would be fine," I told her. "I'm going to the shelter this morning, so maybe you could hang out while the forensics guys are here to keep an eye on Lucy. Detective Franks said they'd be here by nine. Once they leave, you can lock up and take off."

"Sure," she said weakly. "I'd be happy to. I'm going to go get started on the room," she said, and left.

"I'm worried about her," I said to April, while I poured syrup on my waffle. "She doesn't seem to be taking this in stride."

April looked over her glasses at me with a furrowed brow. "And you are, I suppose? Someone attacked you last night, Julia. Yet you're acting like nothing happened."

I stopped with my fork poised to take a bite. But I put it down and stared at my plate for a moment.

"No, I know it happened," I said with a sigh. "But when I think about Ellen's death, and then Martha's death, the break-in at the carriage house, and now the attack on me...if I don't find a way to compartmentalize it all, you might find me huddled in my bathroom screaming."

"Maybe a few moments of screaming might do you good."

"That's why I'm going to the shelter today for my regular shift. I need to be around people who need me...to be around someone whose life might just be worse than mine right now. You understand, don't you?"

She nodded. "Of course, I do. But I also like your idea of a break. Maybe a few days without guests will force us all to slow down and just..." she stopped and just stared into her coffee.

"What?" I asked, wondering why she'd stopped.

"I don't know," she said. "It's like there's something here, staring us right in the face, but I can't put my finger on it. Maybe a break in our routine would allow us to get centered, regroup, and figure out what's going on."

"Okay, look, when I get back this afternoon, let's get in the car and drive up to the place where Ellen died."

"Why?" she said, with a twist of her head.

"I don't get impressions like you do, but I've been thinking a lot about Ellen lately and how she died. I drove up there after her funeral, and there's something about her suicide that doesn't ring true. I just have a feeling that somehow this is all connected. And I can't get it out of my head, because Martha was convinced that Ellen didn't kill herself. And now Martha is dead, too."

April looked skeptical, but shrugged. "Okay. Why not? Crystal will be in by 10:00, so she can man the phones. I could use some things from the store anyway. Maybe we could stop there on the way back."

I smiled. "Done."

÷

I pulled out of my driveway about forty-five minutes later. The day was clouding over, and I could smell rain in the air, so I'd dressed in jeans, a heavy sweater and my red wool coat. As I passed Sybil's house, she came running down the driveway waving her big flabby arms. I merely slowed down, rolled down my window and called out, "I'll pick the puppies up this afternoon. Gotta go!"

And with that, I drove on. I glanced in the rearview mirror and watched her stop at the end of her drive with her hands on her ample hips. I knew she'd heard the sirens the night before and wanted to pump me for information, but this well was empty.

It was just a few minutes before nine o'clock when I came through the back door of the shelter. I locked up my purse and went straight to the children's room, where I found Emma coloring with the two little girls, Sierra and Samantha. Rosa was doing puzzles with Julio. Emma left to do other chores, and I took over. Rosa seemed in a better mood and smiled at me, but we didn't broach the subject of her baby. Since it was so close to Christmas, we shifted gears and spent the rest of the morning helping the children dye macaroni shells to use making necklaces to give to their mothers as gifts. Emma came in at 11:15 and took the kids to the kitchen for lunch, giving me a few moments alone with Rosa.

"How are you doing?" I asked her.

She dropped her head and pursed her lips. "Okay," she said. She placed her hand on her belly. "The baby, she is growing."

Then tears suddenly threatened to overtake her. I got up and put my arm around her.

"Rosa, you're positive you heard those women talking about you?"

She nodded, sniffling. "Si. They use my name."

"Has anything else happened since Friday?"

180

"No," she said. "But Ms. Kramer say they may move me."

"Move you? Where?

"To another shelter."

"Oh," I said with relief. "They often move the pregnant women to the Enumclaw Shelter when they get close to their due date. It's practically next door to the birthing center up there. That's good. You'd get very good care."

She didn't look convinced, but merely nodded.

"You need to go get some lunch, now," I said, helping her to her feet. "You're eating for two, you know."

"Thank you, Ms. Julia."

After Rosa left for the kitchen, I went back to the office, wondering if Faye was still there. Perhaps I could engage her in some way to discover the name of the woman Rosa had overheard outside the laundry. But Faye was gone. I glanced at my watch and realized that she would be at her weekly Rotary club meeting, where she was the incoming president.

As I stood in the office wondering what to do next, a thought occurred to me. I could look at Rosa's file. Maybe I could discover who brought her to the shelter. Once I had that information, maybe I could backtrack to find out who it was who brought her into the country in the first place. A nervous flutter tickled my insides at the thought of doing something so outlandish (and wrong!), but I was determined to try and help.

I scooted down the hallway to check Matt's office, but it was closed and locked. He usually went out to have lunch with his girlfriend. So far—so good. Since Emma was with the kids, I thought I might be safe.

I slipped back into the main office and went to the file cabinet, where I'd seen Matt access resident files. I had to open and close two or three drawers until I found the drawer for current residents. I didn't know Rosa's last name, and so had to go through them one-by-one. I finally found a Rosa Cordero. She was pregnant and nineteen years old. Something niggled at the back of my neck as I read her file, but I didn't know why. The file said she'd been found at the back of a restaurant going through a dumpster and brought to the shelter with no ID. Rosa had told the shelter that she had lost her apartment for an undisclosed reason. A woman by the name of

Monica Garrett had brought her in. I knew Monica Garrett. She was a member of my church.

All of a sudden, my mother's phone rang again. I pulled it out of my pocket and snapped, "What?"

"I don't know," she said. "I just got a sudden feeling that you have to be careful."

I looked up when she said this and froze. Emma was watching me through the windows in the playroom where the children were napping.

"Uh...yeah. You're right. Um...I'm going to pretend I'm talking to you, and..."

"Well, that's just about the stupidest thing I ever heard," she said. "You *are* talking to me. So, whatever you're doing, stop acting like an idiot and just act natural."

I grimaced. "Thanks. I'll just do that. Then what?" I asked to keep the conversation going.

"I don't know," she said. "I don't know what the hell you're doing."

"I'm holding a file I shouldn't be holding."

"Where are you?"

"A homeless shelter where I volunteer," I replied.

"Is someone watching you?"

"Yes."

"Okay, put the file away and pretend like you're checking something off a list. Like you're doing inventory or have been asked to complete a task of some sort."

"Good idea," I said. "Thanks."

Sometimes my mother wasn't so bad. Before I could say anything else, though, she hung up. Damn! Why did she keep doing that?

I replaced the file and did as my mother had suggested. I went over to the volunteer desk, picked up a pencil and pretended to check something off on a clip board. When I glanced up again, Emma was gone.

My heart was still hammering in my chest. I'd had enough espionage for one day. It was time to go home. I shook my shoulders, trying to relieve the tension and grabbed my purse off the desk. I turned to leave and stifled a scream. I came eyeball to eyeball with Dana Finkle. Her small beady eyes were glaring at me through folds of flesh.

"Can I help you, Julia?" she said, her putrid breath clogging my nostrils.

I backed up a step and chanced a reply, my hand to my chest, my heart beating rapidly.

"No...I'm fine, Dana. What are you doing here?"

Her bloated features seemed to puff up even more, if they could.

"I've just joined the board of directors here," she said proudly. "I think the question is what are *you* doing here?"

Since Dana and I are not exactly friends, she probably wouldn't know that I volunteered at the shelter.

"I volunteer. Martha and I began last spring, after Ellen died. I watch the children and talk with the women."

"Ah," she said, "I see. So you're just a volunteer. Then what are you doing here in the office?"

My heart skipped a beat.

"Um...just putting some things away. And what do you mean, *just* a volunteer?"

"I just meant that you're not in a position of authority, that's all."

"No. I volunteer. I help out around here." My temperature was rising, right along with my anger. "When did you join the board?"

I had to get her off the subject of what I was doing in the office.

She tossed her head, putting into motion the folds of flesh at her neck.

"Father Bentley contacted me when Martha died. He needed someone he could count on."

That made me bristle. "You say that like Martha was being irresponsible by dying."

"Of course not," she stuck her chin in the air. "You're always taking things out of context, Julia."

"That wasn't out of context, Dana," I said with a snap. "That *was* the context. And since you just joined the board in, oh, let me see...the last couple of days...and probably haven't even been to a board meeting yet, what exactly are *you* doing here?"

She inhaled—her beady eyes defiant.

183

"When I accept a responsibility, I take it very seriously. People's lives are at stake here, and I find that spot checks can sometimes produce interesting results."

"Spot checks? You've got to be kidding. So you're here to catch the staff off-guard, I get it." I threw the straps of my purse over my shoulder. "I'll be sure to let Faye know you were here checking up on her."

Her mouth dropped opened, but I marched past her without another word, hoping to put an end to any speculation about my presence in the office.

As I stepped into the hallway, feeling giddy that I had just dodged another bullet, I glanced across the indoor courtyard and saw Rosa's door open. I made a quick decision and glanced behind me to make sure Dana hadn't followed me into the hallway. Then I hurried around the front end of the building to intercept Rosa.

I stopped her just as she was about to go out the front door to the van that would take her to her weekly doctor's appointment. I gestured for her to follow me back to her bedroom for a moment. A quick check of the hallways guaranteed that we weren't being watched. Once we were inside her room, we closed the door.

"Rosa, I checked your file. Tell me why you were kicked out of your apartment."

She hesitated before answering. "The woman who brought me to this country found me the apartment. I was there…hmmm…two months," she said, hunching her shoulders as if she was just guessing. "But the man there, he found drugs and kick me out."

I was shocked. "Were they your drugs?"

"No. No," she shook her head vehemently. "No drugs. I don't know where they from."

"And the apartment manager didn't believe you." I said it as a statement.

She shook her head.

"How were you paying for the apartment?"

"They got me job at a bakery. I wash dishes and help with the baking."

"But you were living on the streets when they found you. What happened to your job?"

Tears filled her eyes again. "The man who own bakery accuse me of stealing money and he fire me."

"And you didn't steal any money." I said it again as a statement, not a question.

"No. I no steal anything, Miss Julia."

"And this all happened within a few days?"

"Yes," she said, sniffling.

"And then you lived on the streets for how long?"

She shook her head. "Maybe two days." She held up two fingers. "I find food and sleep in the alley."

"And then Mrs. Garrett found you and brought you here?"

Her eyes grew very wary and she inhaled suddenly.

"Rosa, was it Monica Garret who was talking to the woman who brought you into the country?"

I heard the front door open and the chatter of the kindergartners, returning from their half day at school. I quickly turned to Rosa.

"Do you have a cell phone?"

She shook her head no. I made a quick decision. My mother would have to forgive me. I reached into my pocket and pulled out her God-awful pink phone.

"Here, take this. If you press right here," I said, pointing to the contact list button, "and then touch my name here," I said, showing her, "you'll dial my cell phone. Call me for any reason, Rosa. ANY reason. I want to help you. Do you understand?"

"Si," she said, nodding yes.

She grabbed my wrist. "I am scared," she said, the fear reflected in her eyes.

"I know," I said, putting my hand over hers. "But you need to go now. To your doctor's appointment. You need to take care of your baby."

I wanted to get her mind off the dangers she might face and onto the one lifeline she had—her baby.

She smiled. "Yes, thank you."

"Be strong, Rosa. I'm going to help you. Let me go out first. I'll go out the back to my car, while you go out the front."

She nodded, and I opened the door and slipped into the hallway. A mother and her six-year old daughter passed me going to their room, the girl chattering loudly. Out of the corner of my eye, I saw Emma in the courtyard talking to Dana. She glanced my way just as one of the boys hit another boy over the head with a toy truck, grabbing her attention. I took the opportunity to leave.

I made it safely to the parking lot without further detection. It had begun to rain, so I used my key fob and unlocked the car from twenty feet away. I jumped in as quickly as I could and threw my purse onto the passenger seat before starting the car.

I'd only been on the road a few minutes when I made a snap decision. The shelter was only about ten minutes from St. Martin's Church, which sat at the north side of Queen Anne Hill in Seattle. If I was lucky, I could catch Father Bentley on his lunch break. I wanted to ask him about showing a video at Martha's service.

I pulled off 15th Ave. onto Dravus Street and wound my way up towards Mt. Pleasant Cemetery. About halfway up, I made a sharp left turn onto a winding road that would eventually climb to a steep hill that ended at the back of the cemetery. St. Martin's church was nestled at a bend in the road about half way up, on a shelf of land that overlooked Ballard Bridge and Salmon Bay to the west. The property had once been a small high school. While the main building had been razed when the church was built, the old gymnasium remained on the north side of the parking lot, with the remaining road extending up the hill directly in front of it. The church included a chapel on the south side, a large meeting room, a community room and kitchen, the teen center, the children's room, and several offices. The main floor of the gym had been turned into a daycare center, while the basement at the back was used for storage and a small food bank.

I parked and entered the church through a door on the north end of the building, which took me to Father Bentley's office. I passed bulletin boards with notices for the Santa's breakfast and Christmas Eve service, and then a glass case that listed church classes and services. Several people waited in the assistant pastor's office, while two women were just coming out from meeting with the youth minister.

I turned into Father Bentley's outer office and greeted Cora, his administrative assistant, a woman who never failed to irritate me, because she never failed to pry for information on other parishioners.

"Oh, Julia, how are you?" she gushed. "I'm so sorry to hear about poor Mrs. Denton. You must be devastated."

Twiggy and Kate Moss had nothing on Cora. She was thin as a rail, her bony cheeks sticking out like something from a Halloween mask.

"I'm okay, Cora. I was wondering if Father Bentley might be free."

The tight skin over her face contorted into a look of disappointment.

"Oh, he's on the phone right now," she said, her long fingers curling around her pencil. "But he shouldn't be long. Why don't you have a seat? I want to hear all about what happened with Mrs. Denton. We're all just devastated around here."

Talking about Martha's demise was the last thing I wanted to do.

"By the way, I was surprised to run into one of the Mercer Island City Council members at the shelter," I said, purposely changing the subject. "She just joined the board over there. Her name is Dana Finkle."

Cora's eyebrows shot up. "Oh, yes, she met Father Bentley last year at the auction for the Pacific Northwest Ballet. Father Bentley was a guest at Faye Kramer's table and so were the Finkles. I think she and Mrs. Kramer are good friends. Anyway, when Martha died, Father Bentley thought immediately of Mrs. Finkle for the board."

I couldn't imagine why anyone would immediately think of Dana Finkle for anything, unless they were staging the Wizard of Oz and needed someone to play a fat Wicked Witch of the West.

"Well, if the community room is free, maybe I'll wander down there to see how we'll set up after Martha's service."

"Oh, sure," Cora said. "I'll let Father Bentley know where you are."

As I turned to go I glanced down to her desk, which was piled high with stacks of loose papers, folders, and binders. A blue paisley binder sitting on top of a stack of papers caught my eye and made me search for air, because my lungs seemed to deflate.

"Where did you get that?" I asked, pointing to the book.

She looked over at the notebook. "My brother has a stationery supply company in San Diego. He gets them for us. I'm sure I could get you one if you'd like. They come in several different colors."

187

"No," I said. "I don't need one. I…it's just very pretty…"

"Hello, Julia."

It was Father Bentley's soft New Orleans drawl. I looked up with a smile.

"Hello, Father," I said, turning. "I needed to check on a couple of things for Martha's service."

"Of course. Cora could help you, you know. She's very good at events."

"No! I mean, that won't be necessary," I said, nodding to Cora, whose eyes had lit up like candles at the suggestion. "The girls from our book club will help. And Martha's daughter will be here."

Father Bentley was in his late forties, medium height with a broad chest, square jaw and a pepper gray beard trimmed close. He was nice enough looking, if you liked dark eyes that seemed to sink into his head.

"I was wondering if we could show a video during the service. The girls want to put some family photos together. Martha's daughter suggested it."

"What a nice idea," he said. "If you'd like to create a soundtrack, I can ask Jeremy to help you."

"Jeremy?"

"He's a volunteer in the teen center downstairs. We've created a small recording studio down there for the after-school program. It gives the kids a place to come and hang out in the afternoon…keeps them off the streets."

"I had no idea. I bet they love it."

He grinned. "Yes, weekday afternoons around here are a bit noisy. Once a quarter, we even have a battle of the bands. This has become quite the place for young people to come and hang out. Anyway, Jeremy could help you pick out some music and record a background tape. He's very good. I'd offer to do it, but I don't really know how to use the equipment."

"I think a soundtrack would be nice," I said, a tear forming. "Maybe I can come over tomorrow afternoon."

We started out of the office and he put a hand on my shoulder.

"How are you doing, Julia? This must be a very difficult time for you."

I reached for a smile, but came up short. "I'm okay. I keep busy with the inn," I said, not wanting to say anything about the break-ins or my attacker. "I want to make this service all about Martha. She deserves it."

"Yes, she does. I want you to let me know if I can help," he said, smiling and showing a set of perfectly straight teeth. "She was a good woman and she'll be missed."

I nodded, feeling it difficult to speak.

"Why don't you come around one o'clock tomorrow," he said. "The kids won't be out of school yet, and that way you and Jeremy will have the studio to yourselves."

As we strolled back down the hallway, I thought of Martha's last question to me.

"Father Bentley, I was just wondering...did Martha come to confession shortly before she died?"

He stopped and gave me a curious look. "No," he shrugged. "I can't remember the last time she came to confession. The police stopped by and asked me the same question, though. Why?"

"She sold me a table a couple of weeks before she died. And before she left, she asked me if *I* had been to confession lately."

He tilted his head at me and smiled.

"Yes, yes, I know," I said, blushing. "I haven't been to confession in years. That's what I told her. But I thought that maybe she was asking because she felt the need to confess something."

"Well, you know, Julia," he said with his hands behind his back. "Even if she had come to me, I couldn't tell you what she said."

"Oh, I know that, Father. It just seemed so curious. I was just wondering." I said with a sigh. "You know she was poisoned, don't you?"

He seemed to inwardly cringe. "Yes. I heard about it." He shook his head. "She was one of the nicest women I know. For the life of me, I can't understand why anyone would do something like that."

"Well, the police don't know yet if she was the target. They think Senator Pesante may have been the target. He was supposed to be at the inn for a reception the day before." Tears pooled in my eyes again and he reached out a hand.

189

"It wasn't your fault, Julia. There is evil in this world, sometimes hidden right before our eyes. You were a good friend to Martha. She knows that, even now."

He started ambling down the hallway towards the entrance, drawing me with him.

"I really do wonder what our society is coming to sometimes, though," he continued." Every day there's another burglary, a shooting, or a murder. I wonder what happened to 'love thy neighbor'?"

"That's what I'd like to know, too," I said. "I did love my neighbor, and then someone killed her."

A young man came through the front door and Father Bentley stopped.

"Oh, there's Jeremy now. Jeremy!" he called.

The young man ambled toward us. He was medium height, thin, with a funny goatee.

"Yes, Father," he said.

"This is Mrs. Applegate. She'd like to have you help her make a soundtrack tomorrow for a video honoring a friend of hers that died. Can you do that?"

He glanced at me and smiled.

"Sure. I'd be happy to."

"Fine. I told her to stop by about one o'clock."

"That should work." He nodded to me. "I'll see you then."

He continued past us, strolling along as if the world functioned on a slow clock.

"He seems like a nice young man," I said.

"He is," Father Bentley said. "He's had a tough life, but I think he's finally getting it together."

"Father," Cora called from the office doorway, "Mrs. Moore is on the phone. She says she needs to speak to you immediately."

"Sybil?" I asked, surprised. "Is she a member of the congregation now?"

Father Bentley took a deep sigh and smiled with forced patience.

"You haven't been around much, lately, Julia. Lots of things have changed around here. Mrs. Moore is not only a member of the church, she's a Deacon. God help me," he said, giving the sign of the cross. "Now you know why I know so much about Martha's death. We don't even need a newspaper around here." He winked at me and then patted my arm. "I'm sorry. I'll have to take the call. Please phone me if you need anything. I'm always here for you. We loved Martha very much."

And with that, he walked away.

CHAPTER TWENTY-FOUR

The heavens had split open by the time I left the church, flooding the sidewalks and parking lot with a torrential rain. I practically ran to the car, jumping in and shaking water off like a dog. I pulled out of the parking lot and carefully wound my way down to 15th Avenue again and pulled out onto Elliot Avenue, which runs along Puget Sound just west of downtown Seattle. There wasn't much traffic, but I flipped on my headlights for good measure and got over into the right lane. I was heading for Interstate 5, which would take me home. I cursed myself for not bringing the van. The Miata didn't do well in heavy rain. It was so low to the ground that when other cars passed, they threw buckets of water onto my windshield, making it hard to see.

I crept along at thirty miles an hour, passing Elliot Bay Park on my right. It suddenly began to hail, and I swore softly and slowed down even more. I was so focused on the road that I didn't notice when a large, black SUV pulled up behind me, until its headlights glared into my rearview mirror.

"Shit! Just go around me," I said to the car.

But the car didn't move. It loomed over my rear bumper like some hulking monster. I refused to be intimidated and shifted my focus back to the road, murmuring, "Asshole!"

A few moments later, the monstrosity of a car pulled out from behind and came up next to me, dwarfing the Miata. It was like having a military tank driving next to me as it blocked what little visibility I had out that window. But within a block, it began to pull away, and I relaxed.

Traffic was unusually light all over that day. As I neared the turnoff to Western, the SUV put on its right directional and then veered directly into my lane.

"What?" I shouted.

I slammed on my brakes, but not in time.

The SUV slammed into my left front fender, sending the Miata skidding to the right. I heard a horrible ripping noise as I flew over the curb and into a small parking lot, coming to a stop by slamming into the corner of a building. The airbag released, hitting my face with the force of a jack hammer.

I sat for a moment, having trouble catching my breath. Tears filled my eyes, and my hands shook uncontrollably. Finally, I pushed the airbag aside to glance out the window, trying valiantly not to fall apart. The SUV was gone.

I reached for my purse and struggled to find my cell phone with shaking fingers, just as someone startled me by pounding loudly on my window. A woman wearing a hooded coat stood outside my door. The hail had stopped, but it was still wet and dark out there. I gave up on the phone and just grabbed my umbrella and purse, and stumbled out of the car.

"You okay? We're calling 911," she said.

I nodded and she took my elbow and helped me around the back of the car and up the steps. I glanced over to my car and cringed. The Miata's front end was wrapped around the cement column at the corner of the building. We hurried inside, where a young man and woman waited anxiously.

My good Samaritan introduced herself. Apparently I had demolished the front column of her insurance company. She put me in a chair and handed me a tissue to wipe my nose where a small trickle of blood had appeared. The young man brought me a glass of water, and I took a drink as I touched my eye with my fingers. It was going to swell, I just knew it.

"I'm so sorry," I said, nearly weeping.

My left eye was closed and watering, a result of the airbag, and my head was throbbing. My chest felt like someone had dropped a cement block on it, making it a little difficult to breathe.

"That car...that car just ran me off the road. Did you see it?"

"Yes," the woman said, placing a hand on my shoulder. "I was just coming out to my own car when I heard it hit you. I looked up as you came off the road and headed for…well…me," she said awkwardly. "It scared the hell out of me. I jumped back onto the steps. But I'm glad you're okay. Actually, I'm glad we're all okay."

"It was a Hummer," the younger woman said.

I glanced up. She had short, dyed black hair and was perched on the edge of a desk, popping Peanut M&Ms into her mouth.

"It pretty much pushed you off the road," she said with a crunch. "And then just drove on. Do you have insurance? Cuz, if not, we could help you with that." Crunch.

The wail of a siren announced the arrival of a police car. As it pulled into the small parking lot and the door opened, I wondered briefly if I would know the officer. After all, men in uniform were beginning to feel like family.

CHAPTER TWENTY-FIVE

An hour later, I was sitting on a gurney in the emergency room at Swedish Hospital. Angela was there, along with Detective Abrams. I had called Doe and Rudy, who were on their way. Blair wasn't answering her phone, and April was taking care of the inn since Libby had left to go shopping. The doctors had given me a clean bill of health, other than some bumps and bruises. My Miata, though, not so much. Angela kept touching me, as if to make sure I was still there and okay.

"So, there's no way you could ID the car," Detective Abrams asked, his blue eyes searching my face.

He had perched his lanky frame on a windowsill, his broad shoulders blocking most of the light coming through the window.

I shook my head. "No. It was hailing at the time, so I was concentrating on the road. The other car just plowed right into me. I never saw a license plate. I just know it was a big black SUV. But the young woman at the insurance office said it was a Hummer."

"And you never saw the driver?" he asked.

"No. The car was too big. All I could see was its bumper and the door."

"Do you think it was on purpose, Mom?" Angela asked quietly. "Hitting you, I mean."

"I don't know," I said, touching the swelling around my eye. "He put on his right directional, so maybe it was just an accident. I think that's what the police thought. The weather made it hard to see. Maybe he couldn't tell how close he was to me."

"Your car *is* pretty small," Detective Abrams said.

I looked up at him with my good eye. "*Was*," I said.

He shrugged. "Sorry."

"But then why didn't he stop?" Angela asked.

"Maybe he didn't even notice," Abrams said. "Those rigs are so big that hitting a little Miata was probably like swatting a fly."

"José said there was a Hummer parked outside of Martha's home the night we picked up her table," I said. "The night the intruder pushed me into the study. When José chased him down the driveway, the Hummer was gone."

"That's convenient," Detective Abrams said with a raised eyebrow.

"What do you mean?" I asked, picking up on his remark.

"I'm not sure José is a good source of reliable information," he replied with a tilt to his head.

"I still don't know what you mean," I said, my hackles rising. "I trust José."

Detective Abrams sighed. "You know that we found his fingerprints on that can of spray paint."

"Yes. So what? He works there. He sprays things." I said.

"How can you be so sure he didn't have anything to do with what happened in your warehouse?"

"Because I know him," I said, sitting up straight.

"Do you?"

"What's that supposed to mean?" I demanded again.

"Mom, José has a record," Angela interrupted us. "He's been arrested several times."

"That doesn't surprise me. He had a rough time when he was young. I already know that," I said, feeling my temperature rise. "That doesn't mean he would steal from me."

"There's something else," Angela said, glancing at Detective Abrams.

She took a deep breath, and I braced myself.

"I'm not sure this is the right time, but you've got to hear it sooner or later...Mr. Garth is dead."

For the second time in just a few days I felt as if a bomb had gone off and my hearing had failed. Mr. Garth. My friend and loyal employee.

"Whaa...?"

Angela reached out and grabbed my hand. "He was found by a neighbor this morning. It happened either Saturday night or early yesterday morning."

"He was murdered?" I almost shrieked.

Tears plopped over the rims of my eyes.

"He was hit with a fireplace poker," Detective Abrams said quietly.

A sob escaped my throat, and I dropped my head to cry unabashedly. Angela put her arm around me. It took some time to finally compose myself.

"I'm so sorry, Mom."

"I...I should..." I stuttered, not knowing what to say.

"No, Mom, you shouldn't do anything. You need to stay put. Something's clearly going on here, and we need to figure it out."

"You think this is all connected?" I looked up through a clump of wet lashes.

"We don't know," Detective Abrams said. "Mr. Garth's death could have been a robbery gone bad. But we also learned today that Senator Pesante was in a hit and run accident this weekend. He's in a coma in Walla Walla."

I inhaled quickly as my brain stalled.

"So...you think Senator Pesante was the target all along? Not Martha?"

"I don't know that, either," Detective Abrams said. "But Pesante was run off the road, just like you," the detective said, pausing. "Unfortunately, his car went into a ravine and burst into flames."

The saliva in my mouth had turned sour. "Oh, God," I exhaled. "This is awful." I shook my head, trying to get my brain around what was happening. "But if he was the target, why would Mr. Garth have been killed?" I asked, wiping my eyes.

"The book, perhaps," Abrams said, shrugging. "We just don't know. It feels like fingers are pointing in every direction right now. But I don't believe in coincidences. Besides, phone records show that your friend, Martha, called Senator Pesante the week after Thanksgiving. We just don't know why."

My eyes opened wide. "Oh my God! Martha's cleaning woman overheard Martha on the phone saying something like, 'I need

197

some help. Something's really wrong.' It was the week after Thanksgiving. I bet she was talking to Senator Pesante."

"Well, I definitely think it's all connected," Angela said. "And we'd better find out how before someone else is killed."

"I'll have to have a talk with this Carlita," the detective said.

"But what about Ms. Jenkins and this Brown character?" I asked.

"We haven't found either one," Abrams said."

"But the book would connect Martha to the break-in at our warehouse and Mr. Garth," I said.

"Yes," he said, nodding. "We just don't know why."

"Did Detective Franks tell you about the subliminal recording?"

"Yes, but we don't have it," he said, throwing up empty hands. "It's hard to prove something like that without the tape."

The detective's cell phone chirped, and he reached into his pocket to get it.

"Abrams," he said, answering it.

He listened for a moment, glanced up at me and then said, "Okay, I'll meet you there."

When he hung up, Angela and I just stared at him.

"Well?" my daughter said.

He shifted uncomfortably on the window sill, finally clearing his throat.

"Detective Franks has just taken your maintenance man into custody—for the murder of Mr. Garth."

I stopped breathing and just blinked at him.

He continued to talk, but I couldn't seem to hear what else he was saying. His mouth was moving, and he kept glancing at me, but it was like watching TV with the sound turned off. Angela suddenly shook my shoulder. "Mother, are you listening? José has been arrested."

"Yes, I heard that part," I muttered, tears filling my eyes again. "Why?"

Detective Abrams glanced at Angela with caution, as if he wasn't sure I was capable of hearing the rest of it.

"Go ahead," she said. "Tell her again."

"A soda can was found on Mr. Garth's kitchen table, but his daughter says he never drank soda, so we fingerprinted it." He paused. "They just confirmed that José's fingerprints were on the soda pop can. Detective Franks has officers at your guest house now, searching it. I'm sorry, Ms. Applegate. I really am."

I couldn't respond. I just sat and stared out the window, wishing I could turn back the clock to the day before Martha died. I wanted this all to end. But as Detective Abrams pushed off the window sill, I stopped him.

"I don't understand," I said. "Why would José do this? What reason would he have for any of this? And the graffiti—why would he announce himself like that?"

The detective shrugged. "I agree the graffiti doesn't make sense. For one thing, it wasn't a typical gang tag. Graffiti is an abbreviated language all its own. The tag in your warehouse was a combination of symbols that we can't match to anything."

I brightened up. "He told me that. José told me that it wasn't a normal gang tag."

"But we can't ignore the fingerprints," the detective said. "I'm very sorry."

For all of his confidence, Detective Abrams seemed genuinely saddened by this turn of events.

"I need to get going," he said. "I'll let you know what I find out."

"Mom, I can take you home."

"No, we've got her," a voice rang out.

We all turned to find Doe and Rudy coming through the curtain. Rudy enveloped me in a hug, making me wince as she compressed my chest.

"Oh my God, Julia. I'm so glad you're okay."

When I groaned, she backed off.

"Oh, dear, I'm so sorry," she said.

My left eye was swollen shut by now, so I peered at her through my right.

"It's okay," I inhaled, feeling my ribs expand through sore muscles. "But I'm ready to go home, if that's okay," I asked, looking up at Detective Abrams.

He just nodded. "I know how to get hold of you if I have to. But actually, it wouldn't be a bad idea if you all took precautions. If this book you mentioned was important enough to kill over, you could all be in danger. You all saw it, right?"

Doe and Rudy hadn't met Detective Abrams. Rudy turned to him with an obvious look of appreciation.

"You must be the tall drink of water," she said with a grin. He frowned in confusion.

"Never mind her," Doe said. "What's this about taking precautions? We both live alone."

"This case has gotten suddenly very complicated, and we don't know who the targets are anymore," he replied.

"Mr. Garth was murdered," I told them.

Both women blanched, and Doe's hand went to her mouth.

"Why don't you guys stay with me at the inn?" I suggested. "I don't want to be alone, anyway."

Detective Abrams nodded his approval. "I think that's a good idea. I can also have Detective Franks increase police patrols in the area."

"I think having an officer spend the night again would even be a better idea," Angela said.

He nodded and pulled out his cell phone and stepped through the curtains to make the call.

Doe glanced at Rudy. "We can pick up overnight bags on the way back."

"I'll call Blair," Doe said. "Maybe she should come over, too. I think Mr. Billings is going out of town again."

"Okay," Detective Abrams said, coming back to the bed. "Officer Barnes will stay there again. I've got to get back. Call us if you need us, but please…lay low."

CHAPTER TWENTY-SIX

My comfortable world was unraveling, making the trip home a blur. Two people close to me were dead. A roomful of my cherished antiques had been destroyed. I'd been attacked in my own home and almost lost my life on the road. And now everything seemed to tie to a person who worked for me and for whom I had affection. Where was this all going? And when would it end?

Once April had fussed over me like a mother hen, Doe and Rudy ushered me to my room and insisted I rest. While they helped April make fried chicken and corn bread for dinner, I fell into a deep sleep. At some point, Sybil brought the dogs back; thankfully, I missed her. But according to April, they were forced to fill her in on the details of the past twenty-four hours. She was sent scurrying from the inn when Lucy lumbered into the kitchen and stuck her nose between her legs. Lucy—my hero.

I woke up with a headache and stiff muscles, but generally, I felt okay—until I looked in the mirror. Even make-up wouldn't help the face looking back at me. My left eye was still swollen shut and had turned an ugly black and blue. And my lips were just two inflated inner tubes stuck to my face.

April had opted to join the slumber party. I had a sneaking suspicion it was because she wanted to keep an eye on me. She knew how much I cared about Mr. Garth *and* José, and now I might lose them both. I planned to try and see José the next day, maybe even arrange for bail.

Libby had texted me just before dinner that she would be staying the night with a friend. So, it was just us girls—and the dogs—and Ahab—and Officer Barnes, who had set up camp in the library again after two helpings of fried chicken.

I joined the girls in the living room, where April had built a fire to ward off the cold. It didn't help; I felt a chill that went all the way to my bones. We spread out around the room. Lucy commandeered some blankets in front of the heat, while the Doxies tucked themselves in at my sides on the sofa. The dogs' presence was comforting and felt like the only thing holding me together.

The mood was somber, and everyone was doing a lot of staring into the fireplace. April concerned me. She had deep circles under her eyes, and her natural exuberance had been replaced by a quiet detachment.

"It feels as if things are spinning out of control," Rudy said as she settled into one of the upholstered chairs with her glass of wine. "I mean, someone really did try to kill you today, Julia! You don't think it was José, do you?"

"No! He was here all afternoon," April said with a stern look.

Rudy flinched at the rebuke.

"I wasn't accusing him," she said quietly.

April started to say something and then stopped. "I know," she said with a deep sigh. "I'm sorry I snapped."

"Do you remember anything about the Jenkins woman, Julia?" Doe asked, changing the subject.

I looked up, trying to remember the overly made-up woman.

"No. She was hardly ever here and when she was, she stayed in her room."

"Did she make the reservation in advance?" Doe asked.

"Yes, but only the day before. She said she was in town for a conference."

That surprised April. "Don't you usually book conferences in advance?"

"Yes, you do," Rudy said. "Well in advance."

"Did she ever say what kind of conference it was?" Doe asked.

I thought a minute. "No, and I never asked."

"Wait a minute!" Rudy said, stopping us. "What organization schedules a conference two weeks before Christmas?"

"Good question," Doe said.

April turned to me. "Maybe you should mention that to the police. They could check to see if there really were any conferences in town this week."

Just as she said this the doorbell rang. April answered it and came back with Detective Abrams. He glanced around the room, nodding in approval.

"I'm glad you're all here," he said.

"Well, Blair isn't," Rudy said. "She's coming later."

"I wanted to let you know that we tracked Ms. Jenkins to the Canadian border," he said. "But it appears that she may have crossed into Canada already."

"I see," I said, disappointed. "So, that's that?"

"No. We've contacted the Royal Canadian Police in Vancouver and may get a lead on her tomorrow. We also talked with a kid who lives up the street from Mr. Garth. He said a black Hummer almost hit him around 4:00 a.m. Sunday morning when he was leaving for work. He said it was parked near Mr. Garth's home and pulled out directly in front of him. He couldn't see who was driving, but I thought you ought to know. We don't know if it's the same car that ran you off the road, but as you know, I don't..."

"...believe in coincidences," I said.

"Right," he said.

"Detective," Rudy said, "we just thought of something you should check out."

She told him about Ms. Jenkins' conference and he nodded again.

"Good thinking," he said appreciatively. "I'll have Detective Franks check it out tomorrow. I'll be off duty tonight, but if you need anything, call Detective Franks. I'm going to check in with Officer Barnes, and then I can let myself out."

We thanked him and he left.

"Damn, too bad we can't switch him for Officer Barnes," Rudy blurted. "I wouldn't mind camping out with him tonight."

Everyone laughed except me. I had pulled my legs up onto the sofa, trying to feel warm. It wasn't working.

"Has anyone talked to Emily?" Doe asked. "The memorial service is day after tomorrow."

"She called over here this afternoon," April said. "Under the circumstances, she said she would postpone the service until the weekend."

I looked up, feeling like I was living in a fog.

"Um…that box of pictures is in the office," I said. "And Father Bentley said he would have one of his guys record a nice background track for us. He told me to come by tomorrow."

"Blair could do that," Rudy said. "You need to rest."

I nodded.

"You okay, honey?" Doe said.

"I can't assimilate all of this," I said, tears forming again. "So much has happened and we don't even know why. And I'm worried about José. He's had such a rough life already."

April was sitting next to me and reached out and grabbed my hand. "At least you're okay."

"Yes, but why Mr. Garth?" I said. "Why in the world would anyone want him dead?"

"It has to have something to do with that damn ledger," Rudy stated flatly.

"But by the time Mr. Garth was killed, he didn't have it anymore," I sobbed. "April had already given the ledger to me."

"But no one knew that," Doe reminded me quietly, getting up and handing me a tissue. "He was killed Sunday morning, wasn't he? And you said he worked on the table Saturday afternoon. My guess is that whoever broke into the warehouse was looking for the book. When they didn't find it here, they went directly to his home, thinking he'd taken it with him."

I used the tissue to wipe the tears from my face and sighed loudly. "I wish I'd given it to the police right away. Maybe if I had, he'd still be alive."

"I doubt it," Rudy countered. "Whoever did this wouldn't necessarily know if you gave anything to the police."

"So," Doe began, "it's the ledger that's causing all of this?"

"We don't know that for sure," April countered. "Remember that Senator Pesante is in a coma."

"There are just too many tangents in all of this," Doe said, frustrated. "Julia, do you still have that big whiteboard you let companies use when they hold meetings here?"

I nodded. "Yes, it's under the stairs."

I started to get up, but April stopped me.

"You sit tight. I'll get it."

As she and Doe rolled in a large, hinged whiteboard and set it in front of the fireplace, careful not to disturb Lucy, Blair arrived with a small duffle bag.

"I'm here for the slumber party," she announced. "Where's the wine?"

She dropped the bag, tossed her coat over a chair and went directly to the table that held the wine.

"What did I miss?" she said, eyeing the whiteboard. "It looks like you're about to start class or something."

We explained what we were doing and caught her up. She came and gave me a big hug and asked how I was feeling, and then grabbed a handful of nuts and plumped down in a chair.

"Okay, I'm ready," she said, taking a sip of wine.

Doe lifted a marker from the tray. "Let's get it all down," she said. "Start at the beginning, Julia."

I rubbed my eye again, trying to bring myself back to life.

"Martha told her daughter a couple of weeks ago that she was thinking of quitting the shelter, and then almost immediately stopped going. Let's start with that."

"Do we think the shelter is important to all of this?" Rudy asked with a tilt of her head.

"Yes," I said. "I'll tell you why in a few minutes."

Doe nodded. "Okay, I'll write it down."

"And when I bought the table from Martha, she asked me about going to confession," I said.

"Not only that," Rudy said. "She said something about taking something that belonged to someone else."

We all looked at Rudy like deer in the headlights.

"You're right, she did," I said, slightly stunned. "It's the book again. She must have been talking about the book."

"She said she took something 'for the greater good.' Maybe she was trying to protect someone." April was thinking out loud.

"Or *save* someone," I said, my mind beginning to sort through a number of memories from over the last few days.

Doe wrote that down and said. "Let's stick to what we know for the moment. According to Martha's cleaning gal, Carlita, Martha began listening to the MP3 player and then Carlita overheard that phone conversation."

Doe wrote as she talked.

"And at some point, someone poisoned Julia's box of fudge wrapped for Senator Pesante," Blair said, jumping in. "We just don't know when."

"Hold it. Can we back up a bit?" Rudy said. "We need to know when the MP3 player was given to Martha, because it would have taken a couple of days for the messages to have worked."

"Well," Doe began, reaching over and taking another sip of wine. "Carlita said she saw the device for the first time last Tuesday."

"But that still doesn't give us the exact day that she got it," Rudy said.

"I think I can narrow it down," I said, feeling my energy slowly returning. "When Martha stopped by on Saturday to get the check for the table, I asked her how she was feeling, since she'd missed a couple of days at the shelter. She said she was having trouble sleeping and asked me about sleeping medicine. I forgot all about that," I said, shaking my head. "Anyway, she couldn't have had the tape then or she would have been using it. So she must have gotten it sometime between Saturday and Tuesday."

"Dang it!" Blair said, suddenly sitting up straight. "All this talk about sleep just made me remember something, too. I saw Martha at Safeway just after church on Sunday. I was just coming back from the gym. She loved *Downton Abbey*, right?" The girls nodded in agreement. "I asked her if she was going to watch the new episode that night, but she said she didn't know. All she knew was that she was going home to take a nap because she was exhausted. When I asked her why, she said she had a lot on her mind and couldn't sleep."

"So, she didn't have the tape on Sunday, either," Doe said, writing it down. "That means she probably didn't get it until Monday. Did anyone talk to her that day?"

It was quiet for a moment as we all thought.

"Actually, I did," I said, looking up. "That's the day I called to ask her if I could borrow her chafing dish for the Christmas Eve party, and she said no, she'd already offered it to someone else. We talked for just a few minutes, and frankly, she was kind of curt

206

with me. Then the doorbell rang and she said, 'That must be Jeremy. I have to go.'"

"Who's Jeremy?" April asked.

"I have no idea...I just...oh, shit!" I said, nearly coming off the sofa. Both dogs rolled onto the floor as I sat forward. "Father Bentley introduced me to him today. He runs the church's recording studio. He's the guy I'm supposed to meet tomorrow afternoon to make the background tape for Martha's memorial service."

"Wow, so you think this Jeremy gave Martha the tape?" April said somberly.

"Yeah. Maybe," I said.

"What was he like?" Rudy asked.

"A skinny kid. Not much to look at. But Father Bentley said he'd had a tough life and was finally getting it together. And he's the only one who knows how to use the equipment."

"A recording studio," Blair said. "The perfect place to make a subliminal recording."

Her expression betrayed her anger at the memory of her own experience with the MP3 player.

"So, Martha *must* have been the target," Rudy said, leaning forward onto her knees. "But if they knew Martha had the ledger book, why didn't they just kill her in her own home and then tear the house apart until they found it? Instead, they killed her in a way that threw suspicion on everyone else and then went looking for the book, anyway."

"Maybe they didn't know she had the book," Doe said.

"I think they did," April said. "Because they started looking for it pretty quickly. In fact, that could be why someone was at Martha's home the night Julia and José picked up the table."

I looked over at April as the proverbial light bulb went on over my head.

"Of course. It wasn't just a thief—it was someone looking for the book! It didn't make sense at the time, but when we got there, Martha's three hand-blown glass bowls that usually sat on the table had been moved. I thought she'd moved them getting the table ready for me to take."

"Sounds more like you interrupted them," Rudy said.

A cold chill ran the length of my spine. I'd had too many close calls.

"Then that's why they broke into my warehouse," I said. "They *knew* I had the table. But since they hadn't gotten as far as taking the tablecloth off, they didn't know what the table looked like. When they didn't find the book anywhere else in the house, they came to our warehouse looking for the table. When they found the secret drawer, they found the hiding place, but no book, because Mr. Garth had already removed it. So they went through our offices and bookshelves and then went to Mr. Garth's house, thinking he may have taken it."

"But doesn't that prove that José didn't kill Mr. Garth?" Blair said. "He would have known exactly which table it was, since he helped you pick it up. And he could have gone in there at any time Friday night and found that book before Mr. Garth started refinishing the table."

"You're right. Thank you, Blair," I said with a grateful smile.

"But none of this explains why they attacked you today," April said.

"Because they didn't find the book at Mr. Garth's, either. And by Sunday afternoon, everyone and their brother knew that I had it."

"What do you mean?" Rudy asked.

I glanced around the room, knowing that my occasional ineptness would not be news to anyone there. And yet, it was still humiliating.

"April had put the book into a box because I was originally going to make it look like I was sending something to Graham—so no one would disturb it," I said. "When I brought the box back here to the inn, I put it on the reception desk. Sybil showed up to get toys for the dog and stuck her big nose into the box at one point." I sighed. "And then when that Mr. Brown checked in, I knocked the box off the counter right in front of him. The book slid out. Libby and Ms. Jenkins were both standing there, so all three of them saw it."

Other than Rudy murmuring, "Wow," they were kind enough not to groan out loud, but I could tell that inwardly they were cringing.

"But there's that Ms. Jenkins again," Blair said.

"And then later that night, you think Mr. Brown broke into your apartment?" April said.

I looked over at her. "Because he knew I had the book."

"What kind of car did he drive?" Rudy asked.

I closed my eyes for a minute and thought back to when Mr. Brown went back outside to get his license plate number.

"I'm not sure," I said. "It was dark outside and all I saw was a big black bumper."

The room was quiet for a moment, making me look up.

"What?"

"A black bumper, Julia?" Rudy said with an incredulous tone.

I stared back at her blankly.

"Maybe a Hummer?" she said, prodding me.

I gasped as I realized she was right. Minnie suddenly climbed up onto my chest, sensing my despair. I wrapped my arms around her and moved her down to my lap.

"It's okay, girl," I murmured to her.

"But we still haven't figured out how he got into my apartment. The key is different than the one to the inn."

"Who has keys to your apartment?" Doe inquired.

"April," I said, nodding in her direction. "Libby and... Sybil."

"Sounds like somehow he got one of those keys," Rudy said.

"Mine is with me all the time," April said, fingering her pocket.

"There's also a spare key in the office," I said.

"How long has Libby worked for you?" Blair asked.

"About two years. But..." Suddenly Libby's face flashed through my mind. "You know, I noticed something weird just before Libby took Mr. Brown to his room. For a moment, I thought she knew him. It was just something about how she looked at him and then looked away, as if she recognized him."

"Libby?" April looked skeptical. "She couldn't hurt a fly."

"I wouldn't think so, either, but..."

"If I had to vote for anyone, I'd vote for Sybil," Rudy said. "You said she saw the book, and she's a pain in the butt." Rudy wrinkled her nose in distaste.

"I don't know," I said, skeptically. "I wouldn't think Sybil had the brains to do anything criminal."

"Yes, but she did know that the dogs would be gone, so the burglar could get in more easily," April said.

"True," I said. "But I'm pretty sure Libby did, too. I think she heard Sybil suggest taking the dogs when we were out in the bakery."

"Who didn't know Lucy was coming?" Rudy asked.

I thought for a moment. "I think just José and Libby. Well, Sybil didn't, either."

"So, what have we learned?" Doe said, bringing us back to the whiteboard.

Rudy got up and stared at what Doe had written on the board. "That there's a whole bunch of arrows pointing in different directions," she said. Then she poured herself more wine.

"Julia, you said you were going to tell us how this might be connected to the shelter," Doe reminded me.

I took a deep sigh before I began, thinking that this was far more complicated than I had ever imagined.

"When I was at the shelter on Friday, I heard one of the young women crying. Her name is Rosa, and she doesn't speak any English, or at least I thought she didn't. She was in the chapel. When I came in, she was talking to herself, saying something about someone taking her baby. But she was saying it in English. When I asked her about it, she almost came out of her skin. She was terrified I would tell someone. She told me that she met a woman in Venezuela at a medical clinic who said she knew someone who could bring her to America for a new life. But they wouldn't take anyone who spoke English. So she lied. And then she overheard two people outside the laundry room at the shelter. These people mentioned her name and something about taking her baby."

"Any chance she just misunderstood?" Rudy's face betrayed her skepticism.

"I wanted to think so. But I looked at her file, and Monica Garrett is the one who found her on the street and brought her to the shelter."

"Monica Garrett...from the church? I didn't know she had anything to do with the shelter," Doe said.

"And now this Jeremy from the church may have made the tape that killed Martha," April said, putting a period at the end of the sentence.

"Right," I said.

"Someone should talk to Father Bentley," Blair said, grabbing a handful of nuts from a side dish.

I looked over at her. "And say what? We don't have any proof. And there's one more thing." I looked down and stroked Minnie's head. "When I was at the church today, I saw a notebook exactly like the one Mr. Garth found in the table. You know, with that paisley cover? It was just a different color. I asked Cora where it came from, and she said that her brother-in-law owns an office supply company."

"That's a weak thread," Rudy said. "They're probably sold in all the office supply stores."

"I know. That's what I thought at the time. But I'm like Detective Abrams... I don't believe in coincidences, and I think there are too many when it comes to the church and the shelter."

"You think Martha found something out about the shelter, something having to do with that book, and she was killed for it?" April said.

"Yes, I do."

There, I'd said it. All the thoughts that had been swirling around in my head had now been put out on the table—or the whiteboard. And I felt oddly relieved, as if I'd just turned in a major term paper.

Everyone sat quietly for a few moments. Rudy swirled the wine in her glass. Doe absent-mindedly corrected something on the whiteboard. Blair munched on a cashew. And April stared into the fire, while I stroked Minnie's long nose.

"So, if we follow that thread," Rudy began, lifting her eyes to mine. "Then it all goes back to the shelter."

"I'd bet on it," I said. "That must be what Martha meant when she told Emily that volunteering there wasn't what she thought it would be. The shelter had let her down."

"But this Rosa said someone was going to take her baby. Do we think they're stealing babies?" Doe said, the tone in her voice betraying her doubt.

"I don't know," I sighed, shaking my head. "It's hard to believe. But it's certainly done in other parts of the world."

"But how would Monica Garrett play into all of this?" she asked.

"That's what I'd like to know. Supposedly, Monica just found Rosa on the streets of Seattle, and like a good Samaritan, brought her to the shelter. But if that was her having a conversation about Rosa's baby outside the laundry, then she actually *knows* the woman who brought Rosa into the country."

"It smells wrong," Blair said. "In fact, I think it stinks."

"There's one more thing that stinks," I said. "I saw Dana Finkle today at the shelter. Apparently she's joined their board of directors."

"God! I knew it," Rudy said, slapping her leg. "That woman is the devil in disguise."

"Maybe it's time to call that good-looking detective back," Doe said, lifting her glass as if in a toast. "We could offer him a glass of wine and then explain what we know."

"What good-looking detective?" Blair said, her eyes alight with interest.

"I just wish I knew what Martha found," I said, ignoring Blair. "What is it about that book?"

"Can you remember what was in it?" April asked.

"No," I shook my head.

"I can," Blair said with a nonchalant toss of her head.

We all looked at her in surprise.

"You only saw it for a brief minute last night," Rudy said.

"That was enough. Get me a piece of paper and a pencil," she said.

April got up and retrieved what she'd asked for. When she returned, Blair came over and kneeled down on the floor on the other side of the coffee table in front of me. She moved my anniversary picture book of *The Wizard of Oz,* spread out the paper, and closed her eyes for a moment. When she opened them, she began to draw the chart she'd seen from memory. Rudy and Doe came up behind her, looking over her shoulder.

A few minutes later, she said, "That's it!"

Doe said. "Jeez, Blair, I knew you had a good memory for things like shoes and handbags, but..."

"I know...but I'm just a ditz," she said without a hint of irritation.

"No, Blair," I said, turning the paper around so that I could see it, "we've never thought you were a ditz. We just thought you didn't care about things like this."

"I don't," she said, leaning forward with her elbows on the table. "But once I see something, I don't forget it."

"Why haven't you ever said anything?" Rudy asked.

"She has, in a way," Doe said. "Think about it. Who do we go to when we need the name of something...a perfume, a restaurant, a street? Or if we need the date of something that happened six years ago..."

Blair smiled gently. "I've been able to remember things since I was little. But I can't help you figure out what all of that means," she said forlornly. "Sorry."

Doe and Rudy were looking down on the chart. I turned it around again so they could see it.

"Wait a minute," Doe said, leaning over. "What's Rosa's last name?"

"Cordero."

"Look there. RC," she said. "That could stand for Rosa Cordero."

I twisted around to see the columns better. The RC was sitting right next to the number 19.

"Yes, it could. And she's nineteen years old," I said, pointing to the number 19.

"What if these are ports?" Rudy said, pointing to the second column. "SEA must stand for Seattle. Which would mean Rosa came into Seattle, while some of these other girls came into, what? I don't recognize any of the others."

"Maybe SEA isn't the airport" April said.

"It's gotta be," Doe said. "What else could it be?"

"Hold on," Rudy held up a hand. She pulled out her smart phone and spelled something out on the keyboard. "Ha!" she said. "SEA is Seattle, and IAD is Dulles Airport in Washington, D.C. MSP is Minneapolis."

"So then TPA is Tampa," Blair said. "Mr. Billings and I flew in there a few months ago."

"Right," Rudy agreed, putting her phone away.

"So, what do we think?" Doe said, pulling over one of the chairs.

"If we're thinking pregnancies, what if DD stands for due date?" Blair spoke up. "What if they're *all* pregnant?"

That shut us up for a moment.

"Oh my God!" I said as a chill rippled down my back. "If they're all pregnant, then maybe Rosa is right. God, I wish Libby was here. She used to be an obstetrics nurse. If they're tracking pregnancies, she may know what some of these other initials mean."

It got suddenly quiet again, forcing me to look up a second time.

"What?" I said, as I realized everyone was staring at me.

"Libby used to be an obstetrics nurse?" Rudy said, the sarcasm dripping from her lips.

"What? No," I shook my head. "I refuse to believe Libby is involved in anything. She's not like that."

"Julia," April said, putting a hand on my forearm, "We don't know anything for sure. We're all just speculating."

Rudy had come over and sat on the arm of the sofa. "Yes, but if we don't believe in coincidences, then we have to accept the possibility that Libby could be involved."

Rudy nodded at me, making me see the logic.

"I think US could stand for ultrasound," Doe blurted out, still looking at the sheet.

We all looked at her in surprise and then down at the paper.

"Of course," I said. "I just naturally thought it meant the United States. But it could mean ultrasound. And the numbers below that are the dates they had the test. So, someone is keeping track of their pregnancies. And then the Bs and Gs in the next column indicate whether it's a boy or a girl. But what about these over here? They look like more abbreviations."

I pointed to where there was a column with things like M/M T.P., M/M A.L., M/M C.R. followed by a five digit number. Everyone studied it for a minute. Finally, it was Blair who spoke up again.

"I think it's the people who are getting the babies. The numbers are their zip codes," she said solemnly. "The M and M probably stands for Mr. and Mrs."

I stared at Blair like she was a genius.

"I think you're right, Blair. Oh, my God," I whispered. "It's real. This is all real."

I pulled a throw over my legs as I began to shiver.

CHAPTER TWENTY-SEVEN

We tried calling both Detective Abrams and Franks before going to bed, but couldn't reach either one, so we left messages. There was nothing else to do that night, so everyone headed to their rooms. It was almost midnight when my head finally hit the pillow. I was exhausted and fell asleep almost immediately. Several hours later, a distant ringing once again pulled me from an awkward dream. I pried my eyes open and reached over and answered my cell phone, which I'd left next to the bed.

"Mrs. Applegate!" a hushed voice said. "Please, you can come?"

I raised myself up onto one elbow. "What? Who is this?"

"It's Rosa, Mrs. Applegate. Please, you can come?"

I shook my head to get rid of the cobwebs and the pain medication. It sounded like Rosa, albeit a little garbled.

"Um...Rosa, where are you?"

"I...they moved me. To the other shelter. I'm all alone."

Rosa began to cry and mumble something. I sat up on the edge of the bed.

"Okay, they took you to Enumclaw. Are you having labor pains?"

"No. Baby no come, yet. Not for many days. I just...I just feel so alone. I understand if you no want to come."

I was up now, rummaging through a drawer, looking for my jeans with my one good eye. "That's okay, Rosa, I'll come. I'm sure everything is fine. Like I said, they often take the pregnant women to the Enumclaw shelter because it's so close to the hospital. But I believe you, Rosa, about what you heard. I'll come be with you now, and then I'll have someone come and sit with you twenty-four hours a day until your baby comes, if I have to. No one is going to take your baby. Okay?"

"Okay. Si, Mrs. Applegate."

"I can be there in about an hour. Watch for me, okay?"

"Yes, Mrs. Applegate. Thank you," she said, sniffling.

"Do you need anything?"

"Uh…they forget toothpaste and no shampoo."

"I can bring you those things. You hang tight."

"I will watch for you. Thank you, Mrs. Applegate."

She hung up, and I struggled to get dressed. My body was sore and I had trouble finding things. Then I snuck into the corridor, making sure the dogs stayed behind. We kept small bottles of shampoo and tubes of toothpaste for guests in a cupboard behind the registration desk. I tiptoed past the library, where Officer Barnes was stretched out in a chair, snoring. Then, as quietly as possible I hurried to the registration desk and opened the cupboard and grabbed what I needed. I was just about to return to my apartment, when a sharp voice stopped me.

"Where the heck are you going?"

I spun around to find Blair standing in the breakfast room with a chicken leg in her hand.

"It's like four a.m. or something," she said.

I stopped like a guilty teenager.

"Actually, it's three a.m.. I have to go out for a while," I said in a whisper.

"What? Where?"

"Rosa called," I whispered. "They've moved her, and she wants me to bring her a few things."

"And you're not calling the police?"

"She's okay—she's just lonely," I said, gesturing for her to keep her voice down. "They've just moved her to the shelter in Enumclaw. They move the pregnant women up there when they're close to giving birth so they'll be near the hospital. Her baby isn't due for a couple of weeks."

"You're not going anywhere without me," she said, throwing the chicken bone into a wastebasket.

I eyed the wastebasket. "Really? I have dogs."

Blair scowled and reached over and picked up the wastebasket.

"Listen, Blair," I said. "I can do this. You stay here."

She threw out a shapely hip and placed her hand on it.

"Really?" she said, mimicking me. "What are you going to drive?"

"I…" and then I remembered I didn't have a car.

"I'll take a taxi, Bub," Ahab murmured from under his cover.

"I'll drive the van," I whispered, drawing her back down the hallway toward my apartment.

"With one eye," she said scornfully.

I turned to her, looking at her through my good eye. "Okay, maybe you're right."

"Damn right I'm right. C'mon. Let's go."

Before I could stop her, she stomped through the door to my apartment, put the wastebasket on the counter, and headed down the hallway to the guest bedroom, where she was staying. I threw the chicken bone away, and a minute or two later, she was dressed in jeans and tennis shoes and carrying her coat and purse over one arm. Blair was close to 5' 8" tall in heels, but in the tennis shoes, we were much closer in height. Without her makeup, she looked a lot younger, and I realized how naturally pretty she really was.

"What are you driving tonight?" I asked with a nervous edge to my voice.

She gave me a mischievous smile. "The Porsche."

My heart skipped a beat. Knowing that we'd have most of the roads to ourselves at this time of the morning wasn't as comforting as you might think. But I didn't have much choice. I'd be on the road with an amateur race car driver.

Blair threw the shoulder strap of her purse over her shoulder, and we snuck out the side door to avoid Officer Barnes.

We took I-405 south on the eastside of the lake until we got to Renton; there we left the freeway. Since Blair was traveling at roughly the speed of light, we thought it would be safer and less likely that we'd run into police or highway patrol on the back roads. The Seattle area was home to an entire landscape of bedroom communities, and we traveled east, following the Cedar River all the way up into the foothills and Maple Valley, a town of 22,000. Here drivers can make a choice to keep going to Enumclaw, or turn west and drop down into the city of Kent.

We headed towards Enumclaw and very quickly left Maple Valley's few lights behind. At this time of the morning, we were alone on the highway. Blair reached out to turn on the radio, when I took a chance.

"So, Mr. Billings is in Vancouver on business," I said.

"Yep," she said with a nod, retracting her hand. "He's thinking of buying a dealership down there."

"His first name is Jacob, isn't it?"

She snuck a suspicious glance my way. "Yeah. Why?"

"Oh, I don't know. I've just always wondered why you call him Mr. Billings, that's all."

"How long have you and the others been scheming to ask me that?"

"Oh, no scheming," I said with a smile. "I really did just wonder."

I tried to seem nonchalant, but in truth I was hoping that by engaging her in conversation, she might slow down a bit. My insides were beginning to feel like a milkshake as she took corners at full speed.

"Jeez, I thought you guys had guessed that a long time ago," she said, pulling her foot off the accelerator to allow the little car to slow down. "I met Jacob when I was in Billings, Montana, four years ago, visiting my mother. He was there to visit one of his rancher buddies. We hit it off and one thing led to another, and...," she smiled coquettishly. "Anyway," she said with a shrug, "I nicknamed his...uh...his...you know...."

I snapped my head around to look at her.

"What?" I almost choked. "You mean like...oh my God...like, 'Oh, hey, Honey, can Mr. Billings come out and play?'" I said in a fake sexy voice.

She nodded with a smirk. "You know he was separated from his wife back then, but he was still married. So when we got back to Seattle, I'd call him at the dealership and leave a message that I was looking forward to seeing *Mr. Billings* that night. Or having lunch with *Mr. Billings* the next day. Afterwards, it just seemed to stick."

"Oh, dear," I said, erupting in laughter. "I don't think I'll ever be able to look at Mr. Billings the same way ever again."

"I know. Isn't it funny how things like that happen?" she said, chuckling. "I've had pet names for several of my other...you know, but I would never utter those nicknames out loud."

That sent us into a new round of laughter.

Within a few miles, we slowed through the speed trap in Black Diamond and then sailed down a sloping curve to a small valley where Jones Lake glistened in the moonlight. We climbed up the other side until the car's headlights illuminated a sign telling us we were approaching the Green River Gorge. The Green River, now famous because of the Green River Killer, flows down from the Cascades through a gorge, where the steep cliffs rise some 300 feet above the river bed.

We dropped down to the darkened bridge that spanned the deep crevice below, and I glanced at my watch. We'd been on the road for thirty-seven minutes, a record by anyone's standards. If I hadn't already digested my dinner, I might have been wearing it, given Blair's propensity for taking curves at high speeds. I also realized I couldn't feel the fingers on my right hand anymore because they were wrapped so tightly around the armrest.

As we came up the other side of the gorge, the road leveled out in a valley rimmed by the dark outline of mountains. We were coming into Enumclaw and began to pass farm houses and barns that appeared only as black silhouettes in the dark. We coasted into the residential part of town where the road began to twist and turn until it took us right into downtown Enumclaw.

Enumclaw is a small, western-style town tucked into the foothills of the lower Cascades. I know my way around the area only because Angela had belonged to a 4H dog club back when she was in middle school, and the club had shown the dogs at the King County Fairgrounds there.

I had Blair turn left on Griffen Street, and we glided past darkened stores and shops until I told her to turn left, and we found the shelter at the end of a short dead-end street.

We pulled into the parking lot at 3:45 a.m. The shelter was a single-level building that looked more like a prison camp than a women's shelter. Only a single lamppost shed light onto the front walkway, leaving much of the entrance in shadow.

We got out and followed the path to the entrance, feeling the crisp mountain air nip at our skin. I pulled a wool scarf tight around my neck to ward off the cold, and then pressed the buzzer, knowing it would take the night manager a few minutes to roll out of bed and come to the door. A minute later, there was a crackle on the intercom.

"Yeah?" someone said with a growl.

"We're here to see Rosa," I said.

"Rosa who?"

"Rosa Cordero. She came in tonight. She's very pregnant and is nervous about the delivery. She asked me to bring her a few things."

"Who are you?"

"I'm a volunteer with the shelter in Ballard," I said, feeling like they might want to consider offering this woman some customer service training. "My name is Julia Applegate. I have my ID." I searched my purse and pulled out my picture ID.

"Just a minute," she said impatiently.

She pushed a button and a buzzer sounded. The door unlatched and she opened the door a crack. I handed her my ID, and she peered at it with a scowl on her face.

"I'm not sure who you're talkin' about," she said, "but come on in."

She let us in and turned and strode toward the office. She was wearing baggy sweat pants, an old sweat shirt, and slippers. Her hair stuck out at odd angles, and she was hunched at the shoulders.

"I just came on at midnight," she said over her shoulder.

We followed her up the hallway and turned right into a small office where three desks were crammed up against one another and piled high with papers and file folders. She went to a chalk board on the far wall that had been divided into twelve numbered squares. In the middle of each square was a hook. Most of the hooks were empty and had names written under them, meaning the room had a resident in it, and the resident had the key. But two rooms were empty, and the key still hung on the hook. There was no Cordero written anywhere on the board.

"Hmmm," she muttered. "Doesn't look like she's here."

"But she just called me and said that she was."

The woman looked sideways at me over her glasses. Then I remembered how awful I looked and I dropped my chin.

"Somebody beat you up?" she asked.

"No. I was in an accident" I told her. "Anyway, Rosa said they brought her here."

"Let me check the computer," she said with a huff.

She went over to a laptop that sat on one of the desks and typed something onto the keyboard. Then she scanned the screen.

"If she was here, she's already gone," she said.

"What do you mean, gone?"

"I don't see that she was ever checked in. You said she was pregnant. Maybe they took her right over to the hospital. But let me check one more thing. If she came in and left quickly, maybe they just dropped her belongings and didn't get her checked in. I'll check the two empty rooms."

She got up and left the office.

Blair followed her to the door and watched her disappear down the hallway. Then she turned to me.

"She could use a little etiquette training. Not to mention a perm."

"No kidding."

I glanced around the room, anxious to get to the hospital if that's where they'd taken Rosa. But my heart stopped when I heard the faint sound of "*Rock Around the Clock*." It was coming from somewhere in the office.

"What the heck is that?" Blair demanded.

We both looked for the source of the sound and followed it to a desk at the far side of the room. In the bottom drawer was my mother's God-awful pink phone, along with a red scarf I had seen Rosa wear. I quickly reached in and grabbed the phone. As I drew it out, I flipped it open, hoping the charge had held. But the moment I opened it, it stopped ringing and went dead.

"Nope, nothing there," the night manager said, rounding the corner into the office.

I whipped around and dropped the phone into my pocket.

"I guess you'll just have to run up to the hospital and see if she's there."

Blair was staring at me curiously, but I began moving past the other woman and into the hallway.

"Well, thanks so much. We'll see if we can find her up there."

We left the building and turned towards the car.

"Okay, spill," Blair said, as we hurried down the sidewalk. "What was all that about with the phone?"

My heart was thumping so hard, I had to take a deep breath to quiet my nerves. I stopped when we got to the car.

"It's mine," I said, exhaling.

"What is?" Blair said, with her hand on the car door.

"The phone," I said. "It was my mother's. I gave it to Rosa this morning so she could call me if she got into trouble."

Blair's eyes grew wide. "So Rosa *was* here!"

"Yes," I said, getting into the car. "Let's go!"

Blair jumped in and started the engine.

"Do you know where the hospital is?" she asked me.

"Yes, it's back the way we came. We passed it on the way here."

"Okay," she said, twirling the steering wheel and backing out of the parking space. "Just tell me where to turn."

She sped out of the parking lot and we retraced our route. A few minutes later, we were pulling into the parking lot of Enumclaw General Hospital. I directed Blair to the ER. Finding out if Rosa was there wouldn't be easy since hospitals don't give out patient information. But I told Blair to just follow my lead. A minute later, we rushed into the waiting room.

"Has Rosa Cordero come in yet?" I nearly shouted as I ran to the reception window. "She's about to deliver."

The girl at the desk looked up in alarm, her eyes opening wide at my appearance.

"I was in an accident today," I said, hoping I could my appearance to my advantage. "I couldn't get here until now," I said, gesturing to my eye. "I hope I haven't missed her delivery."

"No one has come in tonight except a kid with a sprained ankle," she said cautiously.

"But she must have," I said in a strained voice. "She was staying at the shelter, and they said she was brought over here. She called me and needs to know I'm here. It's important," I gushed, leaning over the counter.

The girl backed up a little. "Well, she's not here. They may have taken her to Valley Medical Center. They do that if they think there's going to be any complications."

I began to wring my hands as if the strain was too much for me. "Well maybe she was admitted? Could you check? Please?"

"Um...just a minute."

She picked up the phone and dialed a number, watching me out of the corner of her eye, while Blair pretended to try and calm me down. When someone answered on the other end, the girl turned away and spoke softly into the phone. A moment later, she hung up.

"I'm sorry, but no one has been admitted tonight expecting to deliver."

I stared at her for a moment.

"No one. You're sure?"

"I'm sure," she said patiently. "I'd check with Valley."

The charade was over before it began. My mind was whirring. Where was Rosa?

"Thank you," I said.

As we walked back to the car, Blair stopped me at the curb.

"You okay, Julia?"

I was staring straight ahead, unaware of where I was going. I glanced up at her and shook my head.

"I don't get it. They only have three shelters, and this is the only one near a hospital. Where else could she be?"

"Maybe she really did go to Valley Medical Center. We can go check. Let's not panic until we make sure."

I nodded numbly, and we got back into the car and headed out of town.

We got caught at the light at 416th Street, where the road opens up again to the ranches and farmland. Blair fiddled with the radio as we waited for the light, while I glanced through the window to my right. There was a darkened Stop & Shop on the corner. A black long-bed truck sat in the parking lot facing the street with its engine running and its lights on. It was one of those oversized rigs with running lights across the cab and a winch hooked to the front grill. The windows were tinted, so I couldn't tell if someone was behind the wheel, but it didn't matter. Even though it wasn't a Hummer, I felt my heart beat pick up. What was it doing there?

The light changed, and Blair crossed through the intersection without having noticed it. I decided not to say anything; after all, we were in the Porsche. The truck didn't have a chance at catching

224

us. And it wasn't the Hummer. It was probably just an innocent rancher. But as we pulled away, I twisted around and glanced behind us anyway. When the truck didn't follow immediately, I felt a flood of relief.

"What the heck were you looking at?"

"Nothing. I thought I saw a cop, that's all." I was lying, but I didn't want to alarm Blair. She misunderstood me.

"Okay, I'll take it easier on the way back. You were looking a little pale in there, anyway."

"No, don't slow down. I really want to get to the hospital," I said, clutching my seat.

"Okay, then. Here we go."

She let the speedometer climb back up. As we whizzed through the dark, I prayed a deer wouldn't decide to cross our path. I kept checking the side mirror, but the only headlights were far back, so I began to relax. We were just a little sports car rocketing through space.

I had just begun thinking about the best way to get to Valley Medical Center, when we careened around a curve and dropped down the south side of the hill toward the gorge again. Suddenly, Blair cried, "Shit!" and slammed on the brakes.

The Porsche swerved and skidded to a stop about fifty yards uphill from the bridge. Sitting right in the middle of the bridge was the Hummer, its giant silver grill gleaming in the light from the four pole lamps. Its headlights were on and it was facing us, like a predator waiting for its prey. The only way forward was to go through it or around it. And since it was sitting right on the center line, going around it was out of the question.

I felt my stomach clench.

"Should we get out and make a run for it?" I said.

Blair turned and looked at me. "Are you nuts? I'll just turn around."

But she never had the chance.

Something slammed into us from behind, jolting us forward. Blair looked up into the rear-view mirror.

"What the hell?"

It was the big truck, now pushing us down the hill like a snow plow. Blair slammed on the brakes, but the small tank behind us was too powerful. The Porsche's engine whined in resistance, as I topped it in a frantic scream.

As we slid towards the Hummer, the Hummer started to slowly move forward towards us, and my mind raced. Our fate lay in one of two directions. Either Blair spun the steering wheel so we'd go off the edge of the cliff, or we'd be crushed in between the two monster trucks. Neither seemed like a good choice.

I continued to scream like a silly school girl and snuck a glance at Blair. She wasn't making a peep. Instead, she was completely focused on keeping the sports car on the road. With only twenty-five yards to go before we became a car sandwich, hold the mayo, Blair called out, "Hold on!"

Really? Did she think I wasn't already holding on?

I swallowed my scream as Blair took her foot off the brake and slammed it down on the accelerator. The Porsche's tires screeched as they spun, and then the little car popped off the truck's bumper. It hit the pavement at about fifty miles an hour, racing straight for the Hummer. Seconds before we would have hit it head on, Blair yanked the steering wheel to the right and then to the left, slamming up and over the curb on the bridge, just missing going off the side. The car bounced off the guard rail and back into the side of the Hummer as we screamed past the huge vehicle, tilted on two wheels. I was nearly thrown into Blair's lap. It was over in half a second and we were past the blockade—minus things like side mirrors, bumpers, and my lungs.

As we bounced back off the curb, Blair slowed, and I yanked my head around. The giant truck didn't have time to slow down and hit the Hummer off center, going full speed. The Hummer whiplashed to the left and then slammed through the guardrail. When the truck pushed past it, it pushed the Hummer backwards off the bridge and into the gorge. An explosion of smoke and flame rose into the darkness, and for a moment, I thought I couldn't breathe.

Until I saw the monster truck lurch ahead, coming straight for us again.

Suddenly, I screamed, "Go! Go! Go!"

Blair hit the gas pedal and the Porsche jumped forward. We crested the hill and then she called out to me, her voice not more than a screech.

"Call 911!"

There was a roaring in my ears so that I almost didn't hear her. But I reached forward and scrambled for my purse on the floor, pulling out my phone.

"Tell them there's been an accident on the gorge bridge just outside of Enumclaw," she shouted.

"Shouldn't I tell them someone is chasing us?" I yelled back.

"Sure. Do that, too. Tell them we're a couple of miles outside of Maple Valley."

With my fingers shaking, I misdialed twice, swearing the entire time. When the 911 operator finally came on the line, I nervously relayed the information. The responder wanted to know who was chasing us, but I had to admit that I didn't know. She finally reacted when I reported the accident on the bridge, and said an ambulance was on its way. I told her I wanted to keep her on the phone, but just then Blair swerved to avoid something, and my phone flew into the back of the car.

"Damn," I exhaled, glancing into the back.

"Don't worry about it," Blair said. "We only have a mile or so to go."

"What happens when we get to Maple Valley?"

"We find the police station," she said matter-of-factly.

I wasn't as confident as she was about that. As I looked over the seat for my phone, I glanced through the back window.

"Shit!"

The truck's headlights were about a half mile back, and while they didn't seem to be gaining, they weren't giving up either.

"Dammit!" Blair exclaimed suddenly.

"No, I think we'll be okay," I said, watching the headlights behind us.

"That's not what I mean," she exclaimed. "We're losing gas. Fast. We must have punctured the gas tank."

I returned to my seat and looked over at the gas gauge. It registered less than a quarter of a tank and the arrow was moving down quickly.

"We're not going to make it to Maple Valley," she said with alarm.

"We've got to," I said.

"If we can just make it to an open gas station," she said.

"Are you kidding?" I screamed. "These guys won't let a little thing like having other people around stop them. They'll just get out and shoot us."

Blair shot me a panicked look, and I realized her granite composure was beginning to crack. It spurred me to take action.

"Blair," I barked at her. "Just get us into town. We'll find the police station or a place to hide."

Just then, my mother's phone rang. I reached into my pocket and answered it.

"What? We're a little busy here."

"Mr. Billings," my mother said, and the phone went dead.

I stared at it a moment and then nearly jumped out of my seat.

"Doesn't Mr. Billings have a dealership in Maple Valley?" I said excitedly.

"Yeah," Blair said. "He does."

"Okay, get us to the dealership."

"Okay," she said, turning her attention back to the road. "It's on this side of town. It's close."

"That's good. That'll work. Get us there," I said, encouraging her.

I turned around again to check on our pursuers. The headlights were gaining.

"We're going to do this, Blair," I said. "It's going to be okay."

But a glance at the gas gauge stirred a nervous flutter in my chest. The yellow light was on and it was nearly on empty. It was happening too fast.

The lights on the outskirts of Maple Valley appeared. I crossed my fingers and held them tight. We had to do this.

As Blair steered the battered little sports car forward, I became aware of a clinking sound coming from the rear of the car. Both side mirrors had been snapped off, and from where I was sitting, I could see that the left front fender was caved in. If the poor little car could have limped, it probably would have.

"Okay," Blair suddenly said. "I'm going to turn at the next corner, and I'm not slowing down. As soon as we pull into the parking lot, I'm going to circle around to the back."

"Do you have a key?"

"No, but I know where they keep a spare."

We made it to Kent-Kangley Road and Blair ignored the red stop light. She spun the steering wheel to the right and the car skidded around the corner, sending a hub cap rolling across the road. So much for keeping under the radar. At the end of the block, she cranked the wheel to the left, and we bounced into the dealership's driveway. True to her word, Blair barely slowed down before she circled the building, pulled the car in between two other cars, slammed on the brakes and turned off the engine.

"Let's go," she said.

Once I'd peeled my forehead off the front window, I threw open my door. Blair's door had been wedged shut on impact and she had to climb out on my side. Not so easy in a sports car.

We finally got out, hunkered down and ran for the back door. A framed advertisement for a BMW hung on the brick wall next to the door. Blair pushed the corner of the poster aside and pulled out a key on a string. Within a few seconds, we were inside the darkened dealership, and Blair locked the door behind us.

We found ourselves in the back hallway. I followed Blair through a door to the showroom. In front of us were two automatic doors filled with paned windows looking out onto the car lot. It's how they drove cars onto the showroom floor. Three cars were parked inside facing the front lot—a big Mercedes sedan, a Lamborghini, and a BMW. We crawled up to the Mercedes and hid behind it, peering out the front windows.

"Do you think they'll find us?" I asked, my heart pounding so hard I thought they could probably hear it through the brick walls.

"Not right away. You can't see the back door very well from the street. But we ought to tell 911 where we are."

She turned to me, surprised to find that my hands were empty.

Sheepishly, I said, "That phone is dead."

"How can it be dead? You just got a call on it."

Her face expressed all the suspicion I'm sure she felt. Just then, the damn phone started playing "*Rock Around the Clock*." I smiled.

"Ignore that," I said.

"Isn't that your phone?"

"Not exactly." I paused. "It's my mother's phone."

"Well, can't you just tell whoever's calling to call the police?"

"Um…not really. No," I said, shaking my head.

"Julia! Answer the damn phone!"

I reached into my pocket and pulled out the phone and answered it.

"What now, Mom?"

This time Blair turned to me with her eyes wide.

"Julia," my mother said. "You're not safe."

"Really, Mom?" I sniped. "Do you think we don't know that?"

"No, Julia. Danger is very close!"

Then, she was gone.

"We need to go," I said, nudging Blair.

"Says who? Your mother?"

The look on her face was clear. She thought I was nuts.

"How do we get out of here?"

She leaned over and read the Mercedes' license plate number.

"C'mon," she said.

We crawled on hands and knees towards a desk, and then scurried across the open floor until we were behind the service counter. Blair reached up and opened the office door and we nearly fell inside. She closed the door. Ducking behind the desk, she reached up to a pegboard on the wall that held all the car keys. She found the set of keys she wanted and grabbed them. As she glanced out the window, she swore.

"Shit! They're here!"

"I know," I said without looking.

She shot me a wary glance and then headed for the office door again. We poked our heads above the door window, peering out the front windows of the dealership. Two men in black were weaving in and out between cars in the front, looking for the Porsche. One had iridescent white hair. It was the creepy Mr. Brown.

"How did they find us?" I asked.

"Doesn't matter," she said. "Let's go."

Blair waved for me to follow her. She opened the door and we crawled out of the office again and scuttled back to the Mercedes sedan. She gestured for me to get into the passenger side, while she scurried around to the driver's side. We each carefully opened the doors and ducked inside, keeping bent over so as not to alert our attackers. I glanced over and saw that steely expression on Blair's face return. She was back. What was it about putting her behind the wheel of a car that gave her so much confidence? She turned to me with an almost gleeful look of determination.

"Put on your seatbelt—tight. And then hold on."

"How many times am I going to hear you say that tonight?"

I donned my seatbelt and pulled it tight. Then I grasped the armrest and braced myself. Blair turned the ignition key and removed the emergency brake. The two men looked up as soon as they heard the engine.

"Aren't we going to open one of the doors?" I asked, feeling my entire insides clench.

She glanced sideways at me. "Why would we do that?"

Blair put the car in gear and pressed down on the accelerator. The car's tires spun on the slick showroom floor, and then it lunged forward. We crashed through the front showroom windows, emerging in a shower of splintered glass and window frames as the car roared onto the lot, heading straight for our attackers. They jumped to either side, ducking glass and bent metal as it cascaded down upon them.

"Whoo, hoo!" Blair hooted as we sped past.

She streaked out of the parking lot onto 242nd Street and made a hard right back onto Kent-Kangley Road.

"I'm taking us into Kent," she said. "I know where the police station is there."

"Okay," I squeaked, barely able to breathe.

"Do you have your mom's phone?"

"Yes," I said, my entire body buzzing with adrenaline.

"Then call 911 again. Let them know where we are," Blair said.

"I was serious before," I said to her. "The batteries are dead."

"Your mother is, too, but she sure seems to be calling you! So call 911!"

I reached into my pocket and got the phone out again. The Mercedes' dash clock said it was now 4:23 a.m. We were alone on the road. We had just passed a small commercial center on the left and were hurtling down a long stretch of highway that led straight into Covington and then Kent—two of Seattle's bedroom communities. I had just flipped open the phone, hoping against hope that it would work miraculously, when the world collided, sending the Mercedes into a 360 spin.

231

The luxury car flew off the road, hit a curb, and flipped completely over, landing back onto its tires. Inside, we were thrown back and forth like rag dolls held in place by the seat belts. This car not only had front air bags, but side air bags, too. When the side one exploded in my ear, I thought a gun had gone off. I flew one way and then the other until the car finally came to a stop and the world went suddenly silent—except for the ringing in my ear.

I opened my eyes, or thought I did. All I saw was the blurry image of a figure standing some distance from me. I felt completely weightless and floated forward, surrounded by hushed whispers. When I got close to the figure, I realized it was my mother, waiting for me. She didn't speak, she just put her fingers to her lips and gestured with her other hand to where a body lay on a table. It was Rosa, her long hair draping off the side, her big belly rising like Mt. Rainier above her breasts. Two people stood over her.

I tried to call to Rosa, but no sound came out. She was in danger, I knew it. I had to warn her. I tried to go over to her, but as I moved forward, the table moved further away. I stopped. How could I help her? I looked up. There was a doorway. Something familiar hung on the wall beyond the door. It was a painting I recognized of an angel hovering over a lake. But before my mind could identify it, the sound of voices drew me out of the blurred haze.

My eyes fluttered open. All I saw was the damn air bag again.

I pushed it aside and turned towards the voice. The concerned face of a young man floated into view just outside my window. He was trying to open the door. I turned my head towards Blair. She was slumped back in her seat and to one side, and appeared to be out cold. A young woman had gotten Blair's door open and was pushing the air bag away from her face. As she did, I gazed past Blair to the young woman, just as a large black shadow passed slowly along the road behind her. As the shadow floated by, a face turned towards me, a helmet of gleaming white hair shining through the darkness.

The predator was still here.

232

CHAPTER TWENTY-EIGHT

I woke to a white glare and thought that perhaps I was with my mother again. This time, however, there were the sounds of people talking and moving about. I heard wheels rolling along a hard floor, and I was lying on something that was shaking as it moved. As I jostled along, I watched lights above me pass one by one. When I was wheeled through a door, it dawned on me that I was in a hospital. Again. Why did my life seem suddenly like Groundhog's Day?

I didn't feel pain, which was odd because I knew I'd been injured. What I did feel was weightlessness—like I was floating. I had some trouble breathing, which frightened me, and my eyes popped open as bodiless hands lifted me and then gently put me down again.

"Hold still," someone said.

There were a lot of clicking noises and readjustments. Then I faded away.

÷

"Julia, are you awake?"

I opened my eyes. The world came slowly into focus, and I was looking at a white ceiling. I turned my head and Doe's lovely face swam into view. Her brows were furrowed with concern, and she was holding my hand.

"Julia," she said with a tear in her eye. "You're okay. Banged up, but okay."

"Blair?" I asked.

"She's okay, too," Doe replied. "Just a broken leg and some cracked ribs."

I nodded. "Thank God. What happened?" I was muttering with not much more strength than an afternoon breeze.

"You were hit by a truck... some kids out joy-riding and drinking."

"Where am I?"

"Valley Medical Center," she said.

"You've already been taken down for x-rays and a CAT scan," a new voice said.

Rudy's face appeared next to Doe.

"Blair is right here next to you," she said. "Right now, you're in the ICU until they make sure there are no head injuries."

I twisted my neck to look for Blair, which actually made me cry out. My entire body was screaming with pain. The curtain was partially closed around the bed next to me, but I could just barely see Blair's blond head and Mr. Billings sitting in a chair on the opposite side of the bed.

"Mr. Billings?" I asked with the hint of a smile.

Doe pulled a chair up closer to my bed. "He just got here a few minutes ago. The rest of them are on their way."

I nodded, understanding that she meant the rest of Blair's ex-husbands.

I had survived with a wrenched shoulder, a turned ankle, and a bunch of cuts and bruises. I could also tell my face had taken another beating, because the skin felt tight and my lips wouldn't work quite right. When I swiped my tongue across my bottom lip, I winced at a stinging sensation. My right shoulder ached something fierce and when I looked down at my right hand, I realized why my hand throbbed. Two of my fingers were in finger casts.

"They're going to keep you both...probably for 24 hours."

Doe was talking to me, but I had trouble focusing.

"A nurse was just in here and they're waiting for beds to open up. I guess it's been a busy night," she said.

That reminded me why Blair and I had been out so early in the morning in the first place.

"Doe, did anyone check to see if Rosa is here in the hospital?"

234

I kind of slobbered when I spoke. Doe used a tissue to wipe dribble away from the corner of my mouth before answering.

"That's why we went up to Enumclaw," I continued.

"She's not here, Julia."

The new voice was April's.

I looked up and saw my best friend's face appear through the curtain, her face pinched in concern. I reached out my injured hand and she stepped forward and grabbed it, careful to avoid squeezing the injured fingers.

"I just talked to the nurse. She said you kept asking about Rosa when you were brought in. But they checked, and there's no one here by that name."

"Then we have to go," I said, starting to get up.

"Noooooo way," Doe said, putting a restraining hand on my arm. "The doctor wants you to stay here."

"I can't."

The curtain parted, and Angela stepped in with Detectives Abrams and Franks. It was a party. But I noticed that Detective Franks actually averted his eyes, as if it was difficult to look at me.

"Mom," Angela, said putting a hand on the blanket covering my legs, "you stay put. They're trying to find you a room where you and Blair can be together, and Detective Abrams said they'll leave an officer here to stand guard."

"We don't need someone to guard us."

She gave me an incredulous look. "Mom, we checked with the 911 operator and know about the chase and what happened in Maple Valley at the dealership. Someone has tried to kill you twice. And they're still out there somewhere."

"I know that. But I have to find Rosa. I promised her."

"Rosa? Who is Rosa?" she asked, her eyes narrowing.

"She's a girl at the shelter. This is all about the shelter."

I felt my head begin to clear, although my speech was still garbled.

"Rosa is about to have her baby, and she overheard someone at the shelter say they were going to take it," I explained as clearly as I could manage.

"Whoa," Detective Abrams held up his hand. "What are you talking about? Who is taking whose baby?"

235

I gestured to Doe to put an extra pillow behind my back so that I could sit up straighter. I winced as I scooted up, but continued.

"Rosa lives at the shelter where I volunteer." I had to speak very slowly. "No one there knows she speaks English." I kept going, struggling to move beyond the pain of breathing. "She says she's heard things that have frightened her before…" I took a shallow breath. "But she was afraid to say anything because she might be kicked out. The other day, she overheard someone mention her by name. They were talking about taking her baby. She was terrified. I gave her my mother's cell phone to call me if she needed me, and she called early this morning."

I had to stop and take another breath.

"Is that why you were out in the middle of the night?" Angela asked, the look in her eyes scolding me.

"Yes. Rosa said they moved her to the shelter in Enumclaw and that she was scared to be alone. She asked me to come and bring her some things. But when Blair and I got up there, she wasn't there. We checked the Enumclaw Hospital, but she wasn't there, either. On the way out of town…"

I had to stop again, because tears suddenly filled my eyes.

"It's okay, Julia." April stroked my arm. "We're here now."

I nodded. "I know. Okay. When we were at the shelter in Enumclaw, I found my mother's cell phone. That means Rosa had to have been there."

Everyone was silent for a moment. When no one said anything, I said, "Why would they take her cell phone away and nothing else?"

Angela exchanged a look with Detective Abrams.

"Still not much to go on," he said with a shrug.

"Something occurred to me when we were whizzing around in the car, though," I said. "The woman on the phone kept calling me Mrs. Applegate. Rosa never called me that. She always called me Miss Julia. And there's something else. The woman Rosa overheard at the shelter talking about taking her baby was Monica Garrett."

"From the church?" Angela eyes had grown wide.

"Yes," Doe replied. "We tried to call you guys last night to tell you all of this, but couldn't get a hold of you."

Angela shot Detective Abrams a cautious glance, while Detective Franks stuck his hands in his pockets.

"Sorry. I was on duty, but there was a boating accident right off the marina last night. We were so involved with all the emergency personnel that I guess I missed your call."

He looked so guilty, I let it pass.

"According to Rosa," I said, "Monica Garrett was talking to the person who helped get her into the country."

"So?" Detective Abrams shrugged again.

"Don't you see? Monica Garrett supposedly found Rosa in an alley, as if she had never heard of her before. But in fact, she knows the woman who actually brought Rosa into the country."

"And Monica works for the church, and the church owns the shelter," Doe said quietly.

"What about Father Bentley?" Angela asked. "How does he fit into this?"

"I don't think he has anything to do with it," I said, slowly working my mouth. "But it has everything to do with that subliminal tape Martha gave to Blair. I was at the church yesterday afternoon. Father Bentley was going to have me meet with a young man named Jeremy who works in their recording studio; he was supposed to help make a tape for Martha's funeral. I suddenly remembered last night that a few days before Martha died, I was on the phone with her, and she had to get off because someone was at the door...someone named Jeremy."

"So you think it's this Jeremy who made the tape with the subliminal message and gave it to her?" Detective Abrams asked.

"Don't you?" I asked him with a raised brow.

Suddenly, Detective Abrams was all movement and energy.

"I'll put an APB out on this Rosa. What's her last name?"

"Cordero," I said. "She's nineteen years old."

He had his phone in his hand. "We'll also pick up this Jeremy. Don't know a last name, do you?"

"No."

÷

Once the excitement died down and Blair and I had been moved to a double room, we were left to rest with an officer posted outside our door. Blair had been sedated, so I couldn't talk with her.

I fell into a deep sleep and woke a couple of hours later. The bedside clock said 7:12 a.m. and the early morning light was just beginning to break through the curtains. I felt a deep pain in my shoulder, and the details of a very vivid dream were beginning to fade. It was the same dream I'd had in the car. The one with my mother, Rosa, and the painting of the angel.

I opened my eyes to the muted light of my hospital room, barely aware of the muffled noises of the nurses down the hall. I glanced to my right, expecting to see Blair. But the curtain was pulled between our beds. I felt groggy, and I ached all over. I assumed that the pain medication they'd given me earlier had worn off. I reached over and picked up the phone next to the bed; I had to call someone. I finally knew where they'd taken Rosa.

I dialed Rudy's cell phone, and she answered on the first ring. When I said hello, she barked, "Julia! You should be asleep."

"There's something I have to tell you," I said, stopping her. "I think I know where they took Rosa."

Before I let her say anything, I related the dream I'd had about my mother.

"That painting of the angel and the lake," I said. "It's in the basement of the old gym, next to the church. There's a storeroom in the back, behind the food bank. I've been down there several times."

"Okay, hold on, Julia," she said. "There's someone here you need to talk to."

Suddenly, Angela came on the line. "Mom, do you know where April is?"

"No. She ought to be in bed. Like everyone else."

"She's not. In fact, the police came to the inn looking for her."

"Why? What's the matter? Why are you looking for April?"

"Mom, they ran financial checks on everyone. It's a matter of routine. Anyway, April is broke. She's in debt up to her hazel eyeballs."

"What?!" I sat up in bed, feeling the tears forming.

"Not only that, she's been writing bad checks. The bank is after her and her house is in foreclosure, and now…well, she's been

238

emailing José about some book. The emails are kind of cryptic, but now she's gone. No one knows where she is."

My mind felt as if it was finally just shutting down. April. My best friend.

"Mom? Are you okay?"

"I know where they took Rosa," I said through tears, ignoring her. "She's at the church gymnasium. You need to get there, fast."

"Mom, we need to find April."

"You need to get to the church!" I snapped at her.

There was a pause.

"Mom, we can't just go running in there. You know that. It's private property. The police would have to get a search warrant."

"Then get a search warrant!" I said, choking back the tears. "Her life may be in danger. You *have* to find her. I know she's in the basement of the old gym."

"Okay, I'll tell Detective Abrams. But please, they've put an APB out on April. So, if she contacts you, tell her to turn herself in."

"Turn herself in? She's not guilty of anything!"

"I hope not, Mom. I really do. Get some rest. I'll stop by to see you later."

"Wait!" I stopped her. "Put Rudy back on."

I heard the door to our room open and the jiggle of the curtains on the other side of Blair's bed.

"Okay," Rudy said re-engaging with me, her voice barely a whisper. "But I also have something to tell you first."

"What is it?"

I didn't think I could handle much more.

"Doe and I couldn't sleep and needed something to do. We were going through that box of pictures you got from Martha's house, and we found a flash drive."

"A flash drive?" I said.

"We thought there were family photos on it—but Martha had downloaded names, dates, and other information about a bunch of the young women at the shelter. It matches some of the codes in the ledger. But she also downloaded pictures, Julia. There were pictures of babies, and…"

"Go on," I whispered, not wanting the nurse to hear me.

"There were pictures of some of the girls, and they were nude! They looked…as if they were selling themselves."

I felt adrenaline flush my veins as I heard the door open and close again.

"I've got to get out of here. Can you pick me up?"

"Are you sure you're okay to leave?"

"I'm fine. Just come and get me. And don't you dare tell Angela or that damned detective."

"Okay," she said in a hushed voice. "I'll get Doe and meet you out by valet parking in thirty minutes. Can you get past the guard?"

I smiled, feeling my swollen lips stretch until they hurt. "No problem. See you in a few."

I hung up and threw back the covers. Getting out of bed was more difficult than I'd anticipated. I had a terrible headache and was still woozy from the medication. And my body didn't seem to work the same. Everything hurt, making it almost impossible to move. When my feet hit the cold linoleum floor, though, I came fully awake.

I found my clothes in a small closet next to the head of the bed and struggled into my jeans, blouse, and jacket. By the time I was dressed I was out of breath and had to pause. As I reached into the bedside drawer to pull out mother's cell phone, I heard the door open and turned to see the flash of a white sleeve as a nurse stepped into Blair's enclosure again. I froze as I heard some rustling. Then the door opened and closed again and it was quiet.

I slipped into my loafers and exhaled a sigh of relief as I dropped the phone into my pocket. I was just about to reach back into the closet for my purse, when a hand appeared from behind me and covered my mouth and nose with a very familiar-smelling cloth. Within seconds this time, my eyes closed and I was out.

CHAPTER TWENTY-NINE

I woke up lying on my side on a hard cement floor. Dirt bit into my cheek, and I sucked up dust motes every time I inhaled. As my eyelids fluttered open, the blurred outline of a short staircase came into focus. Boxes and paint cans were stacked against it, along with what looked like a jumble of gardening tools.

The sound of muffled voices and loud groaning prompted me to roll onto my back, which forced out a moan as my muscles screamed in protest. That's when I realized that my hands were bound behind me, the bindings digging into my flesh. I rolled into a sitting position, allowing a second involuntary groan to escape my throat. My feet were also bound.

"She's awake," a raspy voice said. "Keep an eye on her."

I blinked several times, trying to shake the chloroform haze that still clouded my brain. Two sets of scoop lights clamped to standing light poles illuminated a gurney positioned horizontally in front of me. The lamps bathed the gurney in brilliant, white light, cloaking the rest of the room in darkness. A little man in a white lab coat stood at one end of the table, while an individual dressed in dark clothing hovered over the table. Someone lay on the gurney, groaning loudly and thrashing about, as if in terrible pain.

I couldn't see anyone else, until a movement to my left made me glace that way. Across the room, a face swam into view that made my stomach turn inside out.

"The great and powerful Wizard of Oz," I muttered.

The bright blue eyes glowed in the darkness, his white hair gleaming under the fluorescent light. It was the elusive Mr. Brown. God, could that guy get any creepier?

"What do you want with me?" I choked on the words.

He cast a furtive glance to his left. My eyes followed his, but I couldn't see anyone.

"You have something we want," he said, coming around the gurney. "And frankly, I'm tired of chasing you down."

He moved to stand over me, his hands clasped casually behind his back.

A woman's scream split the air and the gurney rattled. I peeked around him and realized it was Rosa on the gurney. She was in labor. I tried to rise, but merely succeeded in falling sideways.

"Just sit tight," Mr. Brown said with a snarl.

He stepped forward, looming over me now, his face cast in shadow. But the darkness couldn't hide the gun he pointed at me. I swallowed a ball of spit.

Rosa screamed again. Her labor pains were coming closer together. It wouldn't be long now. The man in the white coat had his hands in between her legs, presumably trying to determine how far she was dilated. Just then *Rock Around the Clock*" rang out and everything in the room ground to a halt.

"What the hell is that?" Mr. Brown said. "Is that your phone?"

I merely shrugged as if I hadn't any idea what he was talking about. He reached down and shoved me to one side and stuck his hand into my pocket as the hit 1950s song kept jingling away. I couldn't help but roll my eyes. Damn it, Mother!

He looked at the readout and frowned. Then he glanced again to his left. Someone was hidden just beyond the ring of light.

"It says 'Out of Area,'" he said.

"Hang up," the voice instructed.

He flicked it off, and dropped it into his pocket.

I tried to place the new voice, but it was unclear whether it was a man or a woman.

The phone rang again, and Mr. Brown pulled it out and flicked it off again. This happened twice more before the voice finally snapped, "Answer the damn thing."

When he did, the look on his face betrayed his confusion. Then he looked at me.

"She says she's your mother."

"What?" a familiar voice said.

I couldn't stifle the gasp that erupted when Libby turned around. When our eyes met, she seemed to shrink back. I thought I saw disappointment reflected there. Or perhaps it was regret. Either way, I was sure we were both in a situation we never thought we'd be in, and there would be no going back.

"That can't be her mother," Libby said. "Her mother is dead,"

"Well, she says it is," Brown snapped. "Here, you talk to her."

He handed the phone to Libby, who clearly didn't want it. She put it reluctantly to her ear and listened. After a moment, her eyes grew wide, and she dropped the phone. Apparently my mother had said something she recognized.

"It *is* your mother," she said in a whisper, a look of fear etched into her bland features. She turned to the voice in the shadows. "I'd know that voice anywhere."

"That's nonsense," the voice said.

And then it all made sense as Sybil stepped into the light.

I felt the blood drain from my face. She stared at me in a way that should have turned my heart to stone, but it didn't; it pissed me off instead. *That bitch!* I thought. She'd played me for years, pretending to be my friend, acting like an airhead.

"Give it to me!" Sybil ordered.

Libby picked up the phone and handed it over.

"Who the hell is this?"

Sybil spoke without any hint of the accent she'd spoken with for years. But even that horse face couldn't conceal the surprise in her eyes when she heard my mother's voice. In an instant, the fear was gone, however, and the steely-edged look was back.

"You're not Cecile, and you don't know where we are. This is all a bluff. Now, I have to hang up so that we can finish here and be gone."

She hung up the phone just as Rosa screamed again.

"The baby is breach," the doctor said behind her.

She turned to him.

"Then turn it," she demanded, as if that were the simplest thing in the world to do.

"No, no," he prattled on nervously. "She needs to be in a hospital. Don't you understand? A hospital."

243

"That baby is already spoken for, which means you'll lose your hefty cut if we can't save it."

The doctor adjusted his glasses nervously. Rosa was groaning in pain. Libby turned back to the gurney and bathed her forehead with a wet cloth. I wondered why Rosa didn't just roll off the table, and then realized she was strapped down.

"Hold her knee," the doctor said to Libby. "Grab her other one," he said to someone on the other side of the table.

When Father Bentley's face appeared from the gloom beyond the gurney, I wanted to cry out in desperation. Was there *no* one I could trust anymore?

The not-so-good Father avoided looking over at me and grabbed Rosa's left knee.

"Let's get this over with," he grunted to the doctor, that insipid New Orleans drawl still apparent. At least he wasn't a complete phony.

The doctor turned to a side table where there were a series of bottles and medical instruments. He grabbed a pair of tongs. I cringed when I saw them, because I knew what he had to do with them. I prayed that Rosa would survive this.

Libby held one knee back, while Father Bentley held the other leg. Then the doctor used the tongs to enter the womb and try to turn the baby. Rosa's screams brought tears to my eyes and I began to shake.

Mother's phone rang again, but this time Sybil threw it to the floor and stomped on it. It kept ringing.

"Shit! I hated your mother when she was alive. But I hate her even more now that she's dead."

Then she returned to the shadows, while her minions worked to deliver Rosa's baby.

It was only a few seconds before a second phone rang. But this time it was Mr. Brown's. With a quizzical look, he reached into his shirt pocket and extracted it, probably thinking it would be someone other than my mother. Too bad for him.

"Shit!" He exhaled, his eyes displaying the first fear. "It's her again."

I smiled despite my situation. Clearly, my mother had increased her ghostly skills and had learned how to dial other people's phones. Sybil strutted over and yanked the phone from Mr. Brown's hand and held it up to her ear.

"Who is this and what stupid game are you playing?"

Suddenly the arc lights flickered and everyone looked around nervously. Sybil glanced up, but wasn't buying it.

"You're not scaring us, and I'm tired of playing along," she said. "You what? Fine. It won't make any difference." Sybil glanced at me. "She wants to talk to you. But if you so much as utter a word that would give her a clue as to where we are, James here will put a bullet in your head immediately."

I looked at him. James Brown? Really?

He moved into position as if to make good on her threat.

"Go ahead," Sybil said to my mother.

She pressed a button, and despite Rosa's groaning, my mother's voice came through loud and clear on the speaker phone.

"Julia, are you okay? I know you're in danger, but I can't see you."

"Yeah, I'm okay, Mom."

"Who is it? Who's there with you?"

"Sybil," I answered.

She exhaled. "Bitch. I should've known."

I was watching Sybil, and she smiled at that.

"I'm not worried, Mom. I'm her only bargaining chip," I said, keeping my eye on her.

The change in Sybil's expression was enough to tell me I had hit a nerve. Keeping the ex-wife of the Governor alive might get her out of a tight spot.

"Say good-bye, Mother," Sybil said, raising her thumb to click off the phone.

"Mom! Find Elizabeth!" I yelled, just before Sybil pressed the off button.

"Don't get your hopes up," Sybil said to me. "As soon as we get that MP3 player, you're the most expendable person here. Did you check her purse?" she said to Mr. Brown.

"It wasn't there," he replied.

"Well, we'll deal with that later," she said as she turned away and started back toward the gurney.

Libby turned and looked at me over her shoulder, but remained silent. Had she been the one to take the player off the counter? If so, would she out me?

"Just the MP3 player?" I said to Sybil's back.

Sybil turned and stared at me for several seconds, causing my heart rate to speed up. I stared back without saying a word.

"What do you mean?" she said in a low, steely voice.

I allowed a smile to slowly spread across my swollen face.

"Rudy and Doe found a flash drive in that box of pictures you so kindly directed me to. Martha must have downloaded the same information that was in the book—along with some pictures."

She advanced so quickly that I flinched back.

"Damn you!" she said, reaching down and grabbing the front of my jacket. "What the hell are you talking about?"

Her face was only inches from mine. The smell of garlic washed over me.

"Ask your hit man over there." I nodded to Mr. Brown. "You were there the whole time, weren't you? In the hospital room? You heard me talking with Rudy just before you knocked me out."

She snapped her head around to look at him. He looked suddenly very uncomfortable.

"She was on the phone with somebody," he said, stammering. "I don't know what they were talking about...but I did hear her mention a flash drive."

She straightened up.

"I'm getting very tired of you, Julia. Don't push your luck."

"You said Mrs. Applegate wouldn't get hurt," Libby said, still holding Rosa's leg. "You said no one would get hurt!"

I began to wonder about Libby's involvement with all of this. She didn't look like a very willing participant.

"Shut up and do your job!" Sybil said, stepping towards Libby. "Don't forget about your darling son who's up to his eyeballs in gambling debt."

Rosa screamed again, nearly wrenching her knee free from Libby's grasp. Her agonizing cries heightened the already razor sharp tension in the room. As Sybil turned away from her, Libby continued to defend me.

"You don't have to kill anyone else," Libby pleaded.

Sybil turned again in a rage.

"Shut up, you moron! Or you might find out who *does* and who does *not* have to die around here."

Suddenly, Sybil's own phone rang, and she yanked it out of her coat pocket, her mouth set in an angry line.

"What? Damn!" she yelled.

"Mother doesn't give up easily," I said with a smirk.

"It's not your mother!" she screamed, throwing the phone across the room. "And I'll kill you if I damn well please!" She suddenly lunged forward and grabbed the gun from Mr. Brown.

"No!" Libby cried, from behind.

Libby spun around and grabbed for the gun. The two women struggled briefly before the gun went off. I flinched and Mr. Brown jumped forward, but it was too late. The bullet tore through Libby's chest. Sybil stepped out of the way as Libby stumbled forwards and crumpled on top of me. Her eyes glazed over as blood bubbled from the open wound in her chest.

I gasped, choking back tears, while Sybil turned to Mr. Brown.

"Shit! One more body to get rid of," she said, nearly throwing the gun back to him. "Shoot that woman if she so much as flinches," she said, pointing at me.

"Mrs. Moore," the doctor called with a panicked edge to his voice. "I can't do it. She needs a hospital."

"No hospital!" Sybil said as if she were spitting. "I told you. She delivers the baby here, or we leave her."

"You can't do that," I cried, tears flowing down my cheeks. "She'll die."

Sybil glared at me. "So what? It's not like her life will be worth much after this, anyway."

"What do you mean?" I blubbered through tears.

She laughed derisively. "What do you think we were going to do? Set nice little Rosa up in her own apartment? She has only one value to us. She's young, and she's pretty."

The weight of that statement settled around me like fog, and I remembered what Rudy had said about the suggestive pictures. "You wouldn't."

"Oh give it up, Julia," she said with a callous toss of her big head. "You're not that stupid."

She sneered as if a human life was worth nothing, and suddenly at least three phones started ringing.

247

"What the hell?" Mr. Brown pulled his out of his pocket again, read the display and dropped it as if it was on fire.

Father Bentley let go of Rosa and practically threw his phone out of his pocket, his eyes wide.

"Who is this woman who keeps calling?" he shouted. "Is it really your mother, Julia?"

"You knew my mother, Father. And you know what she's like when she gets mad."

Mr. Brown looked at me, his intense blue eyes flaring with fear. "Is your mother really dead?"

"Tell him, Father. Tell him how you spoke at her funeral last year," I replied, tears still stinging my eyes. I turned to Brown. "You should have read the brochure when you checked into the inn! It's haunted. It has been for over forty years."

"Don't listen to her," Sybil said, warning them.

"You know it's haunted, Sybil," I said quickly. "Why do you think cupboards always open and slam shut when you're there?"

"Shut up! That's all part of your stupid scam," she screamed, her ugly, misshapen face twisted with rage.

"No scam. Elizabeth doesn't like you. She never has," I said, getting an idea. "Maybe she's here with us now," I said, looking up and around.

Inwardly, I was hoping she really was there. But nothing happened, and my heart sank.

Sybil turned suddenly and stomped towards the stairs where an old shovel leaned against the railing. She grabbed it and turned back to me, her face unrecognizable in her hatred. I cringed.

"I think I'm done with you, Mizzzz Applegate," she said, in her fake Southern drawl again.

She started forward, raising the shovel over her head when out of nowhere an empty paint can flew out of the dark and hit her in the side of the face. She spun in that direction, but there was no one there. Then a rake lifted up off the floor unaided and danced crazily toward her. I could just barely see Elizabeth's hazy outline holding the tool. Sybil backed up, inhaling deeply, staring at it. Mr. Brown looked like he was about to shoot it, while Father Bentley and the good doctor just stared open-mouthed.

Sybil spun towards me.

"Do it," she screamed at Mr. Brown. "Shoot her."

He turned to me and raised the gun, but his hand was shaking and he paused.

"Mom! Get the lights!" I yelled.

The lights buzzed and crackled, and the room was suddenly plunged into absolute darkness.

I tried to roll away so that Mr. Brown couldn't hit me even if he tried, but Libby had me anchored to the spot. Damn! Where were those ruby slippers when you needed them? I ducked my head underneath Libby's shoulder just in case.

It wasn't necessary.

There was an enormous explosion from somewhere above us. It sounded as if a bomb had gone off at the front of the building. There was shuffling and cries all around me in the dark, along with the metal twang of the shovel when it bounced off the cement floor. I pictured them all running into each other like the Keystone Cops, while I was stuck right where I was.

Before I knew it, there were new voices rising above those in my immediate vicinity. And then the lights went back on—all of them, even the room lights. It caught everyone by surprise, and they all froze in momentary flight. Mr. Brown and Sybil had made it to the staircase, while the doctor and Father Bentley had gotten stuck on the far side of the room. The sound of trampling feet on the wooden floor of the gym above us was enough to make Sybil frantic.

"Get out of here!" she screamed.

She ran toward the back door, while Mr. Brown darted up the stairs and out of sight. A moment later, I heard a grunt, and he flew backwards down the stairs, landing with a thud at the bottom. Detective Abrams was right behind him with his gun drawn. He quickly retrieved Mr. Brown's gun. As he did, the doctor and Father Bentley made a run for the back door.

"Don't move!" Detective Abrams yelled, pointing the gun at them. "I'll shoot."

They froze with their backs to him. Two more officers scrambled down the stairs to take them into custody, while Detective Abrams secured Mr. Brown. I suddenly realized that Angela was by my side, trying to lift Libby off me.

"Mom, oh my God! Are you okay?" she said, tears rolling down her cheeks.

Detective Abrams passed Mr. Brown off to another officer and came over to roll Libby to the side. He checked for vitals, but it was a wasted effort. Meanwhile, Angela had pulled me to a sitting position and was hugging me fiercely.

"Stop, you're killing me," I said, wincing. "I'm okay. Just cut me loose."

Detective Abrams drew out a short knife and quickly cut through the zip-tie at my ankles. Angela pulled me to my feet, and he did the same thing to undo my wrists. In the background, officers were marching Mr. Brown and his merry band of mad men out of the room. Sybil was nowhere to be seen.

"Do you need a doctor, Ms. Applegate?" the detective said, real concern reflected in his eyes.

"No, but Rosa does," I said. "Quickly. She needs to get to a hospital."

He turned as if he hadn't even seen Rosa. During the melee, the gurney had been pushed into the corner. She was still tied to the bed, but had stopped groaning and now lay still as a corpse.

"Oh my God," I cried, limping over to her.

Detective Abrams pulled out his cell phone, while Angela and I untied the straps that held her to the gurney. I looked around for some water, but before I knew it, two EMTs were hustling down the stairs with their bags and a stretcher. I looked over at the detective.

"We had them on standby," he said almost shyly. "We weren't positive you were in here, but if you were…well, we had them in case you needed help."

I smiled. "Thank you."

Angela and I stepped back to let them do their work.

"C'mon, Mom," Angela said, drawing me away. "She'll be okay. Let's get you out into the fresh air."

She pulled me toward the stairs, but I stopped her.

"Let's go out the back," I said, moving towards the back door. Besides, I could see puffs of dust floating down the stairs, which I presumed were from the explosion.

We stepped outside into the early morning light, and I squinted, pulling my chin down to allow my eyes to adjust. I heard squeals and then…

"Julia!" Rudy called.

I looked up to find Rudy and Doe rushing for me. Rudy threw her arms around me.

"You're okay. We were so worried."

"I'm okay," I groaned as Rudy let me go and Doe grabbed me.

"We were scared to death, Julia," Doe said.

"I'm okay, really," I said, squirming out of their grasp, pain flooding my body as they squeezed sore spots. "But please stop grabbing me."

They finally released me and I turned to find April, tears in her eyes.

"Damn straight, you'd better be okay," she said. "I am not about to run that damn inn by myself."

"Oh my God, you're *here*," I said to her.

"Yes," she said, grabbing my hands. "I've been meaning to tell you about all my problems. I just..." she started to cry and suddenly, I found myself comforting her.

"It doesn't matter. None of it matters."

I threw my arms around her neck and hugged her, despite the pain. When I finally released her, she stepped back, her eyes wet.

"Stewart died early this morning," she said, a new round of tears flowing for her husband. "He had a heart attack. That's why they couldn't find me. I was out just driving around."

"Oh, April, I'm so sorry," I said, reaching up, stroking her hair.

She sucked up a sob. "But thank God you're okay," she said, holding back the tears. "I couldn't lose you, too."

I grabbed her hands in mine. "You won't lose me. I promise," I said. Then I turned to the others. "My God, you guys. It was Sybil! It was Sybil all along," I said. "But she got away."

"Not hardly," Doe said, nodding behind her.

Doe and Rudy stepped aside. About twenty feet behind them, Blair leaned against a tree, a single crutch under one arm. Her foot was in a cast, and she looked as bruised and battered as I was.

"I wondered when you were going to get around to me," she said with a curled lip.

Sybil lay on the ground in front of her, a police officer standing over her. She was just starting to sit up, her nose and mouth bleeding. The officer quickly stepped in to put her in restraints. Lying a few feet away was Blair's other crutch, a noticeable splatter of blood across the armrest. I laughed and hobbled over to her.

"Blair," I said, "You should still be in the hospital."

"So should you," she said with a smirk. "But when they came looking for you," she said, nodding to Rudy and Doe, "they woke me up. Hell if I was going to let them leave without me."

"You are truly my hero tonight."

"No, no, it wasn't me," she said. "It was April."

I turned with a look of surprise. April merely shrugged her shoulders with a big smile.

"I had a vision…for the very first time, when I was sitting alone in my car this morning. It's never happened before. I saw you…lying on the floor. And I could see Rosa in the background and Sybil. Something deep inside has always told me it was her. So when she came barreling out the door, well…"

"She grabbed my crutch and nailed her," Blair said, proudly.

We heard a groan and turned to find Sybil being lifted off the ground. Her eye was already beginning to swell and as she drew back her lip in a snarl, I could see that one of her big horse teeth was hanging by a thread. She looked at me, her eyes filled with deep hatred.

"Looks like you're going to need a dentist," I said with a demure smile.

"I should have killed you when I had the chance," she said with a slur.

I threw my hands up. "Let the joyous news be spread! The wicked old witch at last is dead!"

This time the girls cheered, even Rudy. As the officer led Sybil away, April put my arm around her shoulder to help me walk.

"C'mon, Julia, let's go home."

We moved slowly toward the parking lot, April helping me, Rudy helping Blair.

"How did you all get here?" I wanted to know as I hobbled painfully along. "And who set off the explosives?"

The girls glanced at each other.

"That wasn't explosives," Doe said. "That was me."

I stopped and gaped at her. "What do you mean, it was you?"

"She means she drove one of her garbage trucks into the building," Rudy said, holding Blair up on her left side.

I looked at Doe, who shrugged innocently.

"Detective Abrams told us they couldn't enter the building without a search warrant because it was private property," she said. "And they were having trouble finding a judge."

"So Doe commandeered a truck from one of her drivers," Blair interrupted her. "Up there."

She used her chin to point to the top of the steep hill, where the road wound around and out of sight.

"Seriously?" I gaped at the hill.

"Hey, I figured that once we were *in* the building, the police could go look for you. Of course, I may be out of a job tomorrow morning," she said with a smile.

"We?" I raised an eyebrow.

"I was with her," Rudy admitted, raising her hand. "I couldn't let her go it alone."

Blair let out a chuckle. "And when she rumbled past that detective, she pretended like she didn't know how to stop the truck.'"

"Wait a minute," I said, turning to Doe. "I thought your husband taught you how to drive those rigs."

"Well, it's been awhile. Maybe I forgot," she said with a shrug.

She smiled that beautiful smile of hers, and I reached out a hand and gave her a squeeze.

"You have no idea how good your timing was," I said, a tear in my eye. "It was a pretty close call in there."

"We're always here for you, Julia. Don't ever forget that."

We'd made it to the front of the building, which looked like a war zone. There were emergency vehicles and personnel everywhere, while the twenty-five ton garbage truck was embedded halfway into the front of the old gym. It had broken a tree in half and there was rubble lying all over the ground, while the entire front façade of the building had been caved in.

"Wow," I said exhaling. "This might be hard to explain to the board of directors."

CHAPTER THIRTY

We learned a lot over the next few days. April's husband, Stewart, had lost all of their money in the early stages of his dementia, and she'd been living on fumes for the past several months. The book mentioned in those emails was going to be a cookbook she hoped to sell, and Jose had offered to design the cover. Both she and José were exonerated.

I found the missing MP3 player when we cleaned out Libby's room, along with a stack of Western Union receipts. For the past several months, Libby had been sending $500 every two weeks to her son in Las Vegas. It's why she did what she did. And it made me cry. While I thought her son was a blood-sucking parasite, I decided that Sybil was much worse. She had taken advantage of Libby's good nature and her love for her son to force her to commit horrific crimes. In my book, that made her a monster of unspeakable proportions.

The police lab was able to deconstruct the subliminal tape. It did, in fact, contain a persistent message to find the gift box for Senator Pesante, open it, and eat a good portion of the fudge. The subliminal message had even told them where to look for it under the reception desk.

Father Bentley admitted to making the tape and asking Jeremy to give it to Martha. He'd instructed her to sleep with it for maximum effect, which meant that for three nights and three days, she'd listened to that message hundreds of times. She never had a chance.

Sybil's husband had also been arrested and seemed happy to supply information now that he didn't have to live under Sybil's thumb. He confessed that Senator Pesante was the original target. Martha had called him when she found the ledger, and he was getting ready to launch an investigation into the shelters. But when he got sick and cancelled the reception, they decided not to let the poisoned fudge go to waste, and came up with a plan to kill Martha with it instead, running Senator Pesante off the road later on in Walla Walla.

While the police continued to sort out the details, April and I readied the inn for Christmas Eve, when we still planned to throw our traditional holiday party. José outdid himself. Tiny white lights outlined every inch of the exterior roofline, while thousands more lit up the trees and bushes that lined the drive. Greeting guests at the front door was the antique sleigh, filled now with weather-proof colorfully wrapped presents and a four-foot high Santa and Mrs. Claus.

Inside, in addition to the three fully decorated trees, were small vignettes of holiday figurines, gingerbread houses, and antique carolers spread throughout the main floor. Even Ahab's cage was laced with red and green ribbons.

Except for Libby's room, the inn was full, and by 7:30 on Christmas Eve, over fifty people milled about, drinking hot toddies and eating a myriad of tasty hot and cold foods created by our favorite caterer. We had tables set up in almost every room to keep people moving about. I'd even hired little Jenny Rayburn to play the harp as background music.

The girls were all there, even Blair, who held court in her favorite leather chair next to the fireplace, her leg still in a cast. Mr. Billings was never far away, attending to her every need. The swelling in my eye had gone down, but it was now a greenish-yellow color, and my fingers were still in casts. Although I still walked with a cane, I was healing nicely.

José had announced that he would be moving into an apartment shortly with his boyfriend, although he wanted to continue working at the inn. So I'd talked April into moving into the guest house and let her house go to the bank. In preparation for the release of April's cookbook, *Vintage Recipes from the St. Claire Inn*, José had created a mock-up of the cover, and we had it on display for

255

advance orders. I'd even forced April to get rid of her apron and join the party. But true to her nature, she kept disappearing into the kitchen to see if the caterers needed help.

Lucy had gone home, but the puppies were all decked out with holiday bows tied to their collars and were weaving in and out of people's feet, looking for the occasional treat that might land on the floor.

At 8:05 p.m., Angela swept in with an entourage, including Detectives Franks and Abrams, a reporter from the *Mercer Island Reporter*, and the Mayor. I surmised that something was afoot. Sure enough, the Mayor briefly greeted me and then stepped up to the fireplace, while his assistant rang a little bell to get everyone's attention.

Mayor Frum was a small man, barely five feet and almost as round as he was tall. He had a nervous tic that forced him to blink his left eye over and over. But he was a jovial man who had served as our mayor for two terms and would be stepping down the following November.

He cleared his throat, and then said, "Excuse me, everyone."

Voices died down, and I gestured to the harpist to stop for the moment. People from the other rooms began to crowd into the living room.

"For those of you who don't know me, I'm Roger Frum, Mayor of Mercer Island."

A few people clapped. He put up a hand to dismiss their signs of appreciation.

"I'm here tonight for a special occasion. To honor five Mercer Island neighbors: Julia Applegate," he said, turning to me, "Blair Wentworth, Doe Kovinsky, April Jackson, and Rudy Smith," turning to each one of the girls as he said her name. "Many of you know that neighbor Martha Denton died recently under suspicious circumstances right here at the St. Claire Inn."

Mayor Frum liked to refer to everyone who lived on the island as "neighbor," as if we were all living as part of a commune.

"While our police department was doing an admirable job investigating her death," he said, nodding in the direction of Detectives Abrams and Franks, "Julia and her friends went even further, looking for that one piece of information that could bring the criminals to justice. And with their help, a human trafficking ring in Seattle was uncovered and shut down, saving many more lives."

There was a joyous round of applause, and then he turned to me and asked me to step forward. He held out a big bronze medallion at the end of a black velvet ribbon.

"I have here, our first ever Mercer Island Hero Award, bestowed tonight on these five brave women. Congratulations," he said.

As everyone applauded, he lifted the medallion over my head.

From the other room came a squawky voice. "I could've been a contender. I could've *been* somebody."

Everyone laughed.

One-by-one, the mayor presented each woman with their award. Then he led the entire room in a final round of applause, as we all smiled broadly and had our picture taken.

"We have one more surprise, Mom." Angela spoke up, quieting everyone down again. She turned to the crowd. "My mother put her life on the line for a young woman staying at a homeless shelter over in Ballard. This young woman had been abducted so that these horrid people could steal her newborn baby and then sell her into the sex trade."

There were shocked murmurs around the room.

Angela turned to me with obvious pride in her eyes. "But my mother couldn't let that happen, and because she wouldn't give up trying to find her, Rosa Cordero is here with us tonight."

Angela gestured to the back of the room and the crowd parted, allowing Rosa to come forward with her newborn baby girl tucked in her arms. Her beautiful face glowed, and her smile lit up the room.

"Oh, Rosa," I said, stepping forward.

I gave her a quick hug and then peeked at the baby in her arms. It had only been a few days since the ordeal, and although I'd been to the hospital once, Rosa had been asleep. This was the first time I'd been able to see Rosa or the baby.

"She's beautiful," I said, smiling.

The rest of the girls gathered around, cooing at the infant, while the crowd clapped.

"Thank you for my baby, Miss Julia," Rosa said with tears in her eyes.

"Don't cry," I said, giving her a hug.

"What did you name her?" Blair asked, tickling the baby's face.

Rosa looked at me shyly. "Her name is Julia. Julia Rose."

My hand flew to my mouth as tears plopped down my cheeks. Doe put an arm around my shoulders and the applause grew louder.

"A perfect name," Blair said with a warm smile.

"We found her a new shelter to stay in," Angela said. "A *good* shelter. Then, we're going to work on straightening out her citizenship."

"No more shelters," I said.

"But Mom, she can't stay in the hospital, and…"

"No," I said with a raised hand. "She'll stay here."

Everyone grew quiet, while Rosa's eyes grew wide.

"No, Miss Julia," she said, shaking her head. "I can't afford to…"

I stopped her. "I'm not asking you to pay. You'll take Libby's room. And, as soon as you're feeling up to it, you can work for it." I turned to April who couldn't hide a smile. "Think you can use some help in the kitchen? Someone with bakery experience?"

"I'd be honored," April said.

"Besides," I said, turning back to Rosa. "I need to be able to see my namesake."

The party went on for another hour and a half, but then people began to leave. I was in the breakfast room where we'd set out the desserts and was just about to grab one of my favorite holiday cookies, when a familiar voice interrupted me.

"Congratulations, Julia."

I turned to find the bloated features of Dana Finkle peering at me. She was dressed in bright green slacks, a green cable sweater accented with a green scarf, looking very much like a giant head of lettuce.

"Thank you, Dana. I'm glad you could make it."

"I'm only here because the Mayor asked me to attend. I think he plans on endorsing my campaign," she said with a slight smile.

"Well, congratulations, then," I said, inwardly cringing.

"Once I'm elected," she said, gesturing to the medallion around my neck, "I don't think we'll continue this 'heroes' idea. I'm not sure it's such a good idea to elevate one person above another. Not that you don't deserve it," she was quick to add. "I suppose you do."

"Dana Finkle is an idiot!" Captain Ahab suddenly cried. "I'd like to kill Dana Finkle!"

Dana's chest puffed up and her face grew red.

"You taught your bird to insult me?" she exclaimed.

Everyone within earshot had stopped and turned to listen. Rudy, Doe, and Blair had also just floated into the room.

"I've never taught that bird to say anything," I said. "Maybe he just doesn't like you, or maybe," I paused, "it was one of the ghoooosts," I said, teasing her.

"Oh, pleeeease," she sneered. "There is no such thing as ghosts and you know it!"

Ahab squawked at that and blurted out, "I do believe in ghosts. I do, I do, I do believe in ghosts."

I glanced at Rudy, who was actually smiling at me.

"Well…maybe I did teach him *that* one."

÷

Two and a half hours later, everyone had left, and Angela and the detectives sat around one of the breakfast tables with us, filling us in on more of the details surrounding Sybil and Father Bentley.

"It appears that Sybil was the ringleader," Detective Abrams said. "Now that we have her husband in custody, he can't seem to keep his mouth shut."

"Probably because he could never get a word in edgewise before," Blair said with a sneer.

Detective Abrams smiled. "Well, he's telling us everything we need to know. He and the missus were part of a trafficking ring that spanned several countries. The Ukraine, along with Bosnia and Venezuela and several cities here in the U.S. They would identify girls who were poor and destitute…but pregnant. They would verify whether the girl spoke any English; if she did, she was immediately cut loose. Those who spoke only their native language would be promised an expedited trip to the United States, where they would be given jobs and a safe delivery in a nice hospital, in return for a small payment of just $5,000, which they could pay back over time."

259

"Of course, as soon as they got here," Angela said quickly, "they had their passports and visas taken away and then would be shipped off to one of the other cities, where they didn't know anyone and felt disoriented and alone. They were given menial jobs and lived in motel rooms or apartments, but after only a few weeks they found themselves broke and living on the streets of a foreign country without any identification and without the ability to communicate with people."

"That's exactly what happened to Rosa," I said.

"Then, lo and behold, a rescuing angel would find them and take them to a nice homeless shelter," Angela continued. "There they would give birth, at which time their baby would be taken away and sold on the adoption black market."

"Why such an elaborate scheme?" Doe asked.

"Because they didn't want the women to be able to identify anyone who had actually handled them during the process," Angela replied. "So they kept them disoriented and cut off from anyone who was familiar to them. This way, they had no place to turn for help."

"So the mayor was right," Doe said, quietly. "They were sold as sex slaves."

"Yes," Angela replied somberly. "It's a lucrative business, and once sold, one working girl can earn the brothel owner upwards of $200,000 a year."

The room had grown quiet and several of us had tears in our eyes.

"You okay, Mom?" Angela asked me, reaching out a hand.

"Yes. No." I sighed. "It's the saddest thing I've ever heard. How could Sybil do something so awful?"

"This is a woman without a conscience," Detective Franks finally spoke up. "She's a predator– someone who enjoys taking advantage of the weak and vulnerable."

"How did Sybil's husband play into this?" I asked, picturing the small, mousy man I'd come to think of as Sybil's indoor carpet.

"He was the banker," Detective Abrams explained. "He laundered the money into off-shore accounts."

"By the way," Detective Franks said, "Monica Garrett is Sybil's cousin and owns the travel agency they used to move the girls from one city to another."

260

I could see eyebrows lift around the room as the logic of this sunk in.

"And Father Bentley is her step-brother," Angela said, with a shake of her head. "It was a family affair."

"The only outsiders," said Detective Abrams, "were Faye Kramer, the albino guy, and the two thugs that went off the bridge in the Hummer. The FBI says the set-up is pretty common. The only difference is that instead of someone owning a string of seedy motels in the ring, this group used a string of homeless shelters. But it served the same purpose and actually provided a better cover."

"I'm just so glad we were able to get Rosa out of there," I said, wiping my eyes again. "The thought of that fate, well..." A sob caught in my throat and Angela patted my shoulder.

"She'll be fine now, Mom."

"What about Senator Pesante?" Rudy asked.

The sugar canister in front of Detective Abrams started to move all of a sudden, and I reached out and placed my hand on it. He gave me a curious look before answering.

"He's out of the coma and they say he'll make a full recovery."

"But how in the world did Martha get involved in all of this?" Blair asked.

"Her niece tipped her off," Detective Franks said. "She finally called us. She's been out of the country. Her husband happens to be Ukrainian," he said with a lift to his eyebrow.

"So...she speaks Ukrainian." Rudy gave voice to the light bulbs going off in our heads. Detective Franks nodded.

"Her niece accompanied Mrs. Denton to the shelter one day just before Thanksgiving. She overheard Faye Kramer on her cell phone talking to the recruiter in Ukraine," he said with a raised eyebrow.

"Wow." I said in surprise. "You would have thought they'd be more careful."

"Well, they've been getting away with this for a long time," Detective Abrams said. "She just got sloppy."

"By the way, Mom, we've talked to the staff at the shelter, and we think Martha volunteered to help do some cleaning the Saturday after her niece was here. There was only the weekend staff on duty, so that's probably when she got the keys and slipped into Faye's office."

"We found a false bottom in one of Faye's desk drawers," Detective Franks said.

"And that must be where Martha found the book," I said.

"Right," Detective Franks confirmed. "And the pictures you found on the flash drive. She knew she had something dangerous. She went to Father Bentley first, but wasn't convinced he would do anything. That's why she called the senator—to get his help. And that's why she couldn't sleep and why you all noticed a change in her behavior. She was under tremendous stress."

"Unfortunately, the moment she spoke to Father Bentley, she sealed her fate," Detective Abrams said.

"She was such a trusting soul," Doe said, shaking her head. "It would never have dawned on her that a priest would do something so awful."

"I'm still having trouble believing it," I said.

"I give her a lot of credit, though," Detective Abrams went on to say. "When she went to see Father Bentley, he tried to get her to give him the book. But she wouldn't, so he had to convince her not to go to the police. He made her believe that by going public the scandal would close down *all* of the shelters, leaving all of those women destitute. He played on her compassion and promised that he would begin an internal investigation in order to send Faye to jail. We have a lot to thank her for. If she'd given the book to Father Bentley, they would have killed her anyway, but we would have never known why."

"But then why did she go to the senator?" I asked.

"As Detective Franks said, she wasn't convinced the priest would do anything, or least not quickly enough. We talked briefly to the senator when he got out of the ICU, and he said she only told him enough to warrant an investigation."

"But how did they find out she'd even talked to him?" Blair asked.

"They bugged her house," the good-looking detective said. "Sybil was going over there during the day when Martha was gone, looking for the ledger and planted the bugs. When they realized she'd spilled the beans to the senator, they knew they had to get rid of both of them."

"Mom," Angela began. "Do you remember that case Detective Abrams and I worked last summer? The girl that was found in the water with her stomach cut open?"

"Oh no," I exhaled. "She was one of Sybil's girls?"

Angela nodded. "Her name was Rita Juarez. That doctor we arrested was a quack. We think he botched a cesarean section on Rita and she died. We think that's why they recruited Libby."

A new round of tears formed in my eyes. "Whatever else she did, Libby tried to save my life. She wasn't going to let Sybil kill me."

Angela put her hand over mine. "I doubt she ever thought anyone was going to get hurt."

"By the way, we'll also be opening Ellen Fairchild's death again," Detective Franks said.

We all stopped and stared at him, as the air in the room seemed to grow heavy.

"We've spoken to her daughter, and she mentioned seeing an MP3 player in her mother's bedroom when they cleaned out the home to sell it. She gave it to her son. She'll mail it back for forensics to take a look at it."

"So they were both murdered," I said.

He nodded. "We think they may have used the subliminal tape on Martha, because it worked so well on Ellen," Detective Abrams said.

It was almost 11:30 by the time we'd finished. I walked Angela and the two detectives to the door. Angela kissed me goodbye, and I watched her walk with Detective Abrams to his car, while Detective Franks hung back. It suddenly occurred to me how handsome he looked all dressed up.

"You clean up pretty nice," I said with a smile.

He smiled back, embarrassed. "Hey, it's Christmas."

We watched the two young lovers drive away, an awkward silence hanging in the air.

"Thank you, Detective Franks," I finally said. "I know you thought I had something to do with this in the beginning."

His brown eyes glinted. "Not really. You seem like far too nice a woman to go around poisoning people. In fact," he said, looking suddenly uncomfortable. "I was hoping you might consider having dinner with me, you know, now that you're no longer trying to avoid a bunch of killers."

It was the first surprise in days that didn't leave me sick to my stomach.

"I'd love to," I replied with a smile.

"Good," he said with a grin. "I'll give you a call in a few days, once you're fully healed."

He gave me a warm smile and left.

÷

April excused herself since she had to be back first thing in the morning for breakfast, but the girls remained to share a final glass of wine before ending the evening.

"I have a present for each of you," I announced.

I pulled out three small boxes from a cupboard.

"It's not fudge, I hope," Rudy quipped.

"Nooooo," I said. "Just open them."

They removed the bows and pulled out wide-mouthed coffee mugs.

"Oh my," Doe said, reading the text on hers with a smile. "This is wonderful, Julia."

"Old Maids Club of Mercer Island," Blair read out loud. "For the adventuresome and young at heart."

"Turn them around," I said.

When they did, there was a collective chuckle.

"The Wiz," Doe said, smiling. "Is that what I am? I like it."

Blair read hers and looked up at me with a big grin. "Catnip. I love it."

Rudy shot me an irritated look. "The Boss? Really? I don't get it."

The three of us cracked up until she finally joined in.

"Okay," Rudy acquiesced, laughing. "I suppose it fits."

"Well, I have something for you," Blair said as she reached into her big purse and pulled out a wrapped box of her own. "This one's for you," she said, handing it to me.

I opened the box to find a door plaque that read "Mayor Julia Applegate."

Rudy and Doe cheered.

"Oh no," I said with a whine.

"Oh yes," Doe insisted. "We need to get started right after New Year's."

I did a face palm. "Damn!"

I let the moment of mirth play itself out and then said, "There's one more thing we have to do. Emily left her mother's ashes with me. She asked me to spread them over the lake on Christmas." I glanced at my watch. "It's almost midnight. I think we should do it together."

"That's a grand idea," Doe said. "She loved it here."

"Isn't it illegal?" Blair said.

"Probably," Rudy laughed. "But who cares? We've just been named the Mercer Island Heroes, and Julia's going to be our next mayor."

"Okay, where's her urn?" Doe wanted to know.

"Over here," I said. I went into the library and pulled a beautiful Cloisonné urn off the bookshelf.

"So, she was here all the time, enjoying the festivities right along with us!" Rudy said.

Rudy looked at me curiously. "Any others you'd like to sprinkle on the lake?"

"Yeah, Julia," Doe jumped in. "Maybe it's time to clean out your garage."

I blushed, knowing that I would be considered a hoarder in some circles when it came to cremated remains.

"Mother wanted me to take her remains back to Illinois. I'll make the trip this summer—no excuses."

"Okay then, let's do this," Rudy said.

We got our coats on and went to the end of the dock, which sits some 100 feet out over the water. Christmas lights twinkled around the lake, and it was beginning to snow. Although there was a light breeze, the lake was quiet and peaceful. Blair stood to my right, leaning on her crutches. Rudy was to her right, in case she needed help, and Doe was to my left as we faced west.

Doe placed a hand on my arm. "Have you thought about what you're going to say?"

"No," I admitted, taking a deep breath. "Does anyone have any thoughts?"

"Just one," Doe said, leaning on the railing. "Martha never got to do her adventure. She always wanted to take up art. I think the next thing we ought to do is to take an art class in her honor."

"What a nice thought," Rudy agreed.

"But what do we want to say about Martha?" I asked.

"That we'll miss her," Blair spoke up. "If I'm the most outlandish one of us, Martha had to be the most conservative. I liked her for that. She was predictable, which was kind of comforting to me. I pretty much knew what she'd wear, how she would react, and what she'd say."

"That's true," Rudy said. "But in her case, it wasn't a bad thing. I think deep down, she knew who she was and had accepted it a long time ago."

"She was our rock, in a manner of speaking," Doe said. "Our anchor, so we didn't get too far off course."

I had to reach up and wipe a tear away. "I wonder if she knew that."

"She does now," Doe said, putting a hand on my shoulder.

"Okay, let's do it, Julia," Rudy commanded. "It's time."

We all turned to the lake as I lifted off the top of the urn.

"Here's to you, Martha," I said. "We'll think of you whenever we look out at the lake."

As I held the urn out over the water and turned it upside down, I felt the girls move away from me on either side. The ashes slid out of the urn just as a sudden gust of wind rose up from the lake. In an instant, the entire clump of ashes blew right back in my face.

Count to three.

"Damn!"

CHAPTER THIRTY-ONE

It was already Christmas morning by the time I had thoroughly cleaned off my face and climbed into bed. I was tired, but I felt better than I had in weeks. As I reached over to turn out the light, my cell phone rang. I answered it, curious as to who would be calling me so late.

"You did good, Julia," my mother said. "I'm proud of you."

I slumped back against my headboard, a warm rush of affection flooding my body.

"Thanks, Mom. And thanks for your help. It was pretty scary there for a while."

"Hey, I wasn't going to let that bitch of a woman do anything to you. You're my little girl."

I rolled my eyes. "Mom, I'm sixty-three. I think I stopped being your little girl a long time ago."

"What about Angela?"

She had me there.

"Okay, I get it," I said with a smile. "I can always count on you."

"That's right, no matter what idiotic thing you're involved in," she said, chuckling. "I have your back."

I laughed light-heartedly. "Thanks. And by the way, this is the best Christmas present ever, being able to talk to you again."

There was a pause, and then she said, "Take me home, Julia."

A tear suddenly welled in my eye. "I will. I promise."

"I love you, Button," she said quickly.

I choked back a sob. She had given me that nickname when I was born because I was so tiny. Hearing it again made me realize how much I missed my own nickname.

"I love you, too, Mom. Merry Christmas."

THE END

Author's Notes

If you enjoyed Detective Abrams in this book and would like to read more about him, check out "A Palette for Murder," a short story in my book, *Your Worst Nightmare.*

Also, human trafficking occurs around the globe and is almost impossible to stop. It strips people of their freedom, their families, their self-esteem, and often their lives. I encourage you to read up on the danger and effects of human trafficking and to see how you might get involved to help stop it.

Thank you so very much for reading *Inn Keeping with Murder.* If you enjoyed this book, I would be honored if you would go back to Amazon.com and leave an honest review. We "indie" authors thrive on reviews and word-of-mouth advertising. This will help position the book so that more people might also enjoy it. Thank you!

Who Was Your Favorite Character?
I thoroughly enjoyed writing *Inn Keeping with Murder* and creating its cast of characters. I would love to know who your favorite character was. I have mine. Who was yours? Let me know by mentioning your favorite character in your review, or by joining me on Facebook @ L.Bohart/author.

About the Author

Ms. Bohart holds a master's degree in theater, has published in Woman's World, and has a story in *Dead on Demand*, an anthology of ghost stories that remained on the Library Journals best seller list for six months. As a thirty-year nonprofit professional, she has spent a lifetime writing brochures, newsletters, business letters, website copy, and more. She did a short stint writing for Patch.com, teaches writing through the Continuing Education Program at Green River Community College, and writes a monthly column for the Renton Reporter. *Inn Keeping with Murder* is her third full-length novel. She has also self-published *Mass Murder* and *Grave Doubts*, as well as two short story books. She is hard at work on the second Old Maids of Mercer Island mystery, as well as the second Giorgio Salvatori mystery.

Ms. Bohart also writes a blog on the various aspects of writing and the paranormal on her website at: www.bohartink.com. She lives in the Northwest with her daughter, two miniature Dachshunds, and a cat.

Follow Ms. Bohart

Website: www.bohartink.com
Twitter: @lbohart
Facebook: Facebook @ L.Bohart/author

Made in the USA
San Bernardino, CA
07 January 2014